THE BILLIONAIRE'S
Baby

DELIZA LOKHAI

Readict Publishing

THE BILLIONAIRE'S BABY

Readict Publishing

THE BILLIONAIRE'S
Baby

DELIZA LOKHAI

Chapter 1

Amara

I paced around in the bathroom. Since it was small, I did way too many laps as I waited for the minutes to pass. By the time I heard my timer go off, I was a little dizzy, shaky, and most definitely nervous. I took a deep breath, staring at myself in the mirror as I picked up the stick.

Two lines…No, no, no. How could I have let this happen? I picked up the second stick, hoping the result would contradict the first one—only it didn't. They both had two dark lines each, telling me that I was indeed pregnant.

I couldn't be pregnant, not now. I was only 21, and I had just barely finished my two-year course at culinary school. Not to mention, the father was a one-night stand. I had to tell my mother. I unlocked the door after disposing of the tests and walked out to the living room where I saw her last. It wasn't like I could keep it a secret. I still lived with her and paid my share of the bills.

"Ma, I have to tell you something." I walked up to her and stood near the couch, arms crossed as I looked at her.

"Hmm?" she hummed, looking up from her phone.

"I'm pregnant," I announced calmly.

"What? That's wonderful! You will take Micah back at last, then!" She practically jumped up, her phone long forgotten as she reached out to hug me. I would never get why she liked Micah so much.

"No, it's not his child. I don't want that cheating piece of—"

"What do you mean it's not his?!" She unwrapped her arms from around me and glared at me. She placed her hands on her hips aggressively.

"I had sex with someone else," I mumbled, slightly ashamed I didn't know the man.

"I don't care; tell him it's his. His parents will make him marry you," Mother said with a devious smirk as if I'd follow through with her plans. Again, I didn't get her Micah obsession. Surely, money couldn't make someone that crazy.

"What the hell is wrong with you? Can't you see I don't want to be with him?" I asked, frowning and shaking my head, already walking to my room, knowing where this would lead. The last time a conversation like this happened, she kicked me out for a few days.

"I will not have you here as some sort of slut. You're ruining my reputation!" she yelled at me, pushing my door open hard. The doorknob hit the mirror behind it, cracking it. I had already pulled out my bags and started filling them up. The good thing was I had a trip already planned, so some things were packed. The bad news was I might have to cancel that trip for financial reasons.

"Your reputation is already ruined. Aren't you the army wife who slept around while Daddy was doing his tours?" I said without thinking, throwing clothes into the huge suitcase.

"That's it! You dare disrespect me in my house? I want you out!" she screamed at me, storming out and slamming the door behind her.

"You kick me out now, and I'll never come back," I warned as I stepped out of my room. I knew this was a possibility, but I had hoped she'd handle things differently. "Sorry for what I said."

"I don't care. Like I said, I don't want to be seen with some girl who opens her legs for anyone," she shouted, still stomping away on the tiled floor. I already paid more than half of the bills; I might as well move away. But I couldn't afford a place all by myself. I let out a frustrated sigh and picked up my phone to call Nicole.

"Hey, girl," she answered, luckily for me.

"Nic, hey."

"Everything okay?" she asked worriedly.

"I, uh, got kicked out," I told her, still packing up my things.

"Say no more. You can come over, or should I come get you?"

"It's fine. I'm packing up then coming to you," I answered, letting out a soft sigh.

"I'll be waiting. Hey, I love you," Nicole replied, making me smile a little. God, I loved that girl. She was the best of friends. Always had my back no matter what.

"I love you too. Thank you so much," I said hastily and ended the call.

I finished packing up and left the house. I couldn't see Mom anywhere. Not that I wanted to say goodbye, so maybe this was for the best. At least now, I wouldn't have to hear about how great Micah was daily.

***

"Wait, what? You're pregnant, and she kicked you out

again?" Nicole exclaimed, her dark brows furrowed. "Give me the full story, man!"

"Okay, okay, so I announced my pregnancy, and she got excited, saying now I'd take Micah back, but I told her no. The child isn't his, and I don't even want him back, not after what happened." I sat down on the cheap couch, the cushion barely sinking as I sat down.

"Oh, honey, no." She shook her head. Obviously, she didn't like Micah.

"I don't see why she wants me to be with him so badly. All he does is lie and cheat—constantly." I sighed, leaning back. I grabbed a fiery red pillow and played with it.

"I'm sorry for Dana's behavior. I am," she apologized for her sister's behavior.

"It's okay, Nic."

"You know, I just got a raise, and from what I've heard, you pay your mother for rent. We could rent an apartment together," Nicole suggested, taking me by surprise. I thought I'd be on her couch for a week until I found a place for myself.

"Really? I mean, you'd want to live with a child?" I asked to make sure she was really up for this.

"Do I get to be the godmother?" she asked with a cheeky smile.

"I can make that happen." I chuckled, glad this part of my life was figured out. I just hoped we could be good roommates.

"One question," she mumbled, to which I nodded, indicating for her to ask.

"Are you sure it's not Micah's?" Nicole asked, biting down on her lip.

"God, yes. We were on a break," I explained, knowing more explanation would be needed.

"How did all of this happen then?"

"Let's go back seven weeks." I smiled.

***

I got a call from Mrs. Serra saying she had a job for me. I was still working as a server, but I was sure I was working up to becoming more at the company. Either way, these people were hired for rich parties, so we all made good money. Mrs. Serra texted to let me know the dress code was silver and black. Right after I finished applying crimson nail polish, I went to take a shower and started getting ready. I picked out my little black dress along with some silver heels. I loved heels, but only for short periods of time. Unfortunately, this job required me to wear them for hours, so I had no say there. After applying some leave-in conditioner to my hair, I put it up in a high ponytail and let a few of my dark curls frame my face perfectly.

It was almost a normal workday until midway through the night when I received a Snapchat. I had one last drink to bring over, a Blue Lagoon, so I figured I could open it up. The moment I opened it, I saw Dana's video of her and Micah. I knew he had cheated before, and lied too, but he promised he'd changed, and, being the fool I was, I believed him. I should've seen this coming, yet I found myself wanting to rush to the bathroom and let it all out.

I hastily turned around, unaware there was a man behind me, and I ended up spilling the drink on him.

"Sir...I'm so, so sorry. I...let me help you clean this up." I started to panic as I put the glass on a table close by. "The bathroom's right here. Do you mind?"

He just shrugged and followed me. I was surprised he wasn't screaming his head off. This was an Armani suit. Working for these people, you learn the brands a lot faster than you'd think. He closed the bathroom door. The drink had fallen near his abdomen. Micah and Dana were long forgotten by now. I was busy trying to save my job. One complaint and I could kiss these events goodbye.

"You should watch where you're going," he spoke up while I took a cloth and wet it. I dabbed at his shirt, hoping to remove the slightly blue color from his white, overpriced dress shirt.

"I was unaware of my surroundings, sir." I looked up into his emerald eyes. I let go of the cloth, and I unconsciously ran my hand over the damp spot and felt his muscles under my fingertips. "I'll make sure to look out better next time, sir." I cleared my throat and stepped away to search for the hairdryer and plugged it in.

"Quit calling me sir," he said after I finished using the hairdryer.

"What's your name, then?" I asked as I stepped away to put the dryer back. I turned back to the man and looked up at him, watching as he took a step closer to me. My eyes were focused on the man, looking at every little detail of his face: how chiseled his jawline was with a perfect five o'clock shadow, his dark curls gelled to the back, and, not to mention, his dark eyes that stared straight into my soul.

"Zavi will do. Do you prefer being called beautiful, or do you have another name?" he answered, moving his large hand over my smaller one that was still on his abdomen.

"As much as I like being praised, Amy's the name," I answered without thinking. I was hypnotized by his beauty and eloquence but smart enough not to give him my real name.

"You like being praised?" he asked in a slightly teasing tone. I snapped out of whatever trance I was in and pulled my hand away.

"I—uh. Well, I have to go now. I'm sure I'm needed at other tables. Sorry for this again," I spoke awkwardly, realizing what I was doing.

"We're not finished yet, darling." He gently took my hand in his and pulled me back. He looked down at me, staring deep into my eyes. "Answer the question, Amy," he said, his finger smoothly tracing over my jawline.

"I-I...yes," I answered, getting lost in his eyes. Man, he was beautiful and so smooth—unlike Micah. "Everything okay?" I asked when he kept staring at me.

"Just admiring the beauty in front of me." He winked, his finger now tracing down my neck, sending shivers down my spine. I knew where this could lead, and deep down, I needed and wanted this. Part of me wanted to do this to get back at Micah. It was wrong, but I had to.

"Yeah? Is staring all you're planning on doing?" I moved my own hands up his chest, settling them on his shoulders.

"With your permission, I'll be doing more." He chuckled, lifting me effortlessly and placing me on the counter. Zavi stood between my legs, arms on my waist as he looked at me, leaning close to my neck, but he made no contact as he waited for my answer.

"Permission granted," I answered, and without a second wasted, I felt his lips on my neck, pressing soft kisses as he trailed his way to my lips. His large hands now spread warmth across my thighs as he slid his hands up. I moved my hands to the buttons of his shirt and started undoing them as we continued to kiss. He pulled me closer to him, making me moan as the kiss deepened.

***

"That's the night I hooked up with some guy named Zavi

and got pregnant. Protection slipped my mind, honestly," I mumbled, looking down at my nails as I picked at them.

"Man, was it good at least? You having a one-night stand? Never thought I'd see it!" she said, wiggling her eyebrow a little too much, which made me throw a pillow at her.

"I won't lie. He is the best I've had, and I know he's only the third person, but he made me feel things my boyfriend of two years couldn't make me feel. As for me doing it, I know it isn't me, but I wanted revenge so bad—or I just wanted to forget about Micah, and I did. Hell, I haven't even called or texted him since that night," I answered truthfully.

"If it makes you feel any better, Dana and I don't talk." She patted my shoulder.

"It's fine. The only worry I have is this little thing in me." I sighed.

"Don't you want to find the father? Maybe the Serras can give you the list of people so you can find that Zavi," Nicole suggested, but I just shook my head.

"Oh no, sweetie, the last thing I need is them firing me for sleeping with their clients, and Zavi didn't sign up for this."

Chapter 2

Amara

Three years later...

My baby was now a little over two years old. I ended up having a boy, Sebastian Silas Reid. I chose my father's name for his middle name. I always wanted to name my child after him. Raising Sebastian wasn't easy, but Nicole helped me out a little. And my sister, Amelia, ended up helping tons. Somewhere around six months, she contacted me, and we started talking again. It turned out she and her husband had bad luck trying to have their own child, so they decided to hold back and save up some money before looking into adoption. In the meantime, Amelia gladly babysat her nephew.

Nicole and I ended up finding a good apartment with two rooms and one small office that we converted into the baby's room. Her job was going well. As for me, I was head chef at a restaurant named Helene's; however, two weeks ago, the FBI busted the owner. It turned out that it was a front for his drug smuggling. I had enough money to last me a good five months, but you never know what could happen, so I'd been looking for a new job and was getting ready for an interview.

This position would be slightly different: a personal chef

for a person with a busy life. That was how it was described, and it did sound a little fishy, but I decided to still call in. A woman answered. I packed up my knives and picked up my bag and the little dinosaur bag that belonged to Sebastian too.

"Ready to go to Aunt Amy's, baby?" I asked as I watched Sebastian trying to adjust the Velcro on his shoes. It was his favorite thing to do. Every time he put on his shoes, it was like he rediscovered the Velcro.

"Yeah, Mommy," he mumbled, his olive eyes still focused on the straps of his shoe. I gave him a nod, held out my hand to him, and led the way out to the car.

After dropping him off at Amelia's, I drove straight to the address given by the woman on the phone. It was a penthouse. A fancy place meant good pay. Hopefully, these people weren't involved with any cartel members. Once I arrived, a woman led me to an office, and as I stepped in, I immediately noticed the room's theme. It was modern, black with a touch of silver. The woman introduced herself as Tessa Collins. When she sat down behind the desk, she went through a pile of folders and picked one out.

"Mrs. Reid, mother of one and 24 years old. Am I correct?" she asked, looking up from the folder. It made me nervous now that I saw how many options she had.

"Ms. Reid, and for the rest, yes," I confirmed with her.

"Your CV seems good, but you know I will be doing a taste test, yes?"

"Of course. I brought my knives," I replied, patting my bag.

"Before I show you to the kitchen, I was just wondering about your son. Will it be a problem for you to be working here?" She got up and put the folder to the side.

"Not at all. The hours will be discussed before signing the

contract, right?" I asked, getting up too. Of course, Sebastian would always be my priority, but I needed this job to make sure he could be given the best life.

"Yes, of course, along with your payment and any other rules there may be," Ms. Collins replied.

"Okay." I nodded. With that, I was led to the kitchen and given a list of things to make. I made all six dishes along with three desserts. It took a long time, but once I was finished, I set all the plates down in a row for Ms. Collins to taste.

"Oh my god, this cake! I'm supposed to start a diet, but that can wait," Ms. Collins hummed with her mouth full.

"Oh, definitely." I chuckled.

"If Mr. Fuentes didn't need a cook, I'd be hiring you for myself." She laughed, gathering some more cake on her fork.

"I'm confused; I thought I'd be working for you?" I frowned, wiping my hands on the towel. Who was this Mr. Fuentes? Why did his name seem familiar to me?

"Oh, no. I'm his assistant and best friend. He couldn't find the time to do this himself, so I decided to do it. I say we go over your contract. On my part, you're hired. Though, I do have to warn you: he's a stubborn man, and the woman whose place you'll be taking did this job for around 15 years."

"Oh, I see...I see here on national vacation days I'm expected to work?" I turned to face her. I tried keeping those days for myself and my family. Those were the one times I got to actually spoil them with my cooking.

"Oh, not all of them. Those you'd have to discuss a week before. Usually, Easter, Thanksgiving, and Christmas are spent at the family house, so you wouldn't have to cook for him. Don't worry—extra pay is guaranteed." She shrugged, getting up and walking over to wash her hands too.

"Health insurance is also covered?" I asked, surprised. At

my last job, I had to pay for half of my insurance, and it wasn't even good.

"Yes, we'll be hiring you through the company so that tax filing will be easier on both sides. This will be your salary. Do you agree with it?"

Damn, this wasn't paid per hour. This was an annual salary, and it was good—more than enough. "Yes, definitely," I replied, a little too excited.

"One more thing: you don't have to cook here; you can make the meal at home and drop it off during the given hours." Ms. Collins led the way back to the office.

"Perfect. When do I start?"

"Tomorrow, perhaps?" she asked, raising a brow at me.

"Of course." I nodded. We both heard the door open and looked over to see a man heading in—and not just any man. It was Zavi...my heart skipped several beats as my eyes landed on his emerald ones. The way he stared me down made me gulp.

"Zavi, you're back early," she said as he walked into the office.

"Yeah, the meeting got canceled. Who's this?" he asked, looking at me from top to bottom. I raised a brow at him. Did he not remember me? Part of me wanted to be offended, but the other part reminded me this was a good thing...

"Amara Reid, your new personal cook." She smiled widely while looking at him. He seemed unamused.

"Good to meet you, sir." I held my hand out to him.

"I expect you to have breakfast done by 7 a.m. every day but Sunday, lunch at 3 p.m., and dinner at 8:30 p.m.," he replied, staring at my hand.

"Understood. I read that in the contract," I replied, wanting to roll my eyes at his brusqueness.

"You make sure you remember my allergies," he warned.

"My son has the same allergies, so no need to worry," I blurted out without thinking. It seemed Sebastian got those from his dad. We continued to stare at each other. Did he remember me or not? God, I hoped not. This job would be good for me. Seeing him again reminded me just how much my boy inherited of his dad. Those big, gorgeous green eyes, the dimple he had in his right cheek and right cheek alone, and his full rosy lips. At least he had my hair, right?

"Tomorrow, then." Tessa cleared her throat after there was a long moment of silence.

"Yes. Goodbye, sir, ma'am."

"Bye." She smiled then turned to her friend. "She seems like a nice lady and makes good food. Don't be an issue again this time," she whispered, but I was still able to hear her.

***

"Amelia, Nicole, are you guys even listening?" I paced around the room.

"I know; I know. It's just not fair that you're keeping his child from him," Amelia mumbled, and I looked over at Nicole to hear what she had to say. "On the other hand, you could be accused of coming back for money."

"I swear I'm not. This job will be good for Bash and me. I just don't know if I should tell him or not. I mean, he didn't seem to recognize me." I sighed and leaned against the TV table.

"Then don't tell him," Nicole replied simply, though I could tell Amelia disagreed with her. "At least, not yet," she added.

"Wow, you scored the Zavier Fuentes," Nicole then mumbled.

"You know him?"

"Of course. The Fuentes have a big ass company. They make designer clothes and shoes and own a lot of property," she explained, and I nodded. "I did a job for them once. That's where I got enough money to pay off some of my student debt."

"I had no idea," I mumbled. I knew the people at the party would be rich, but I never imagined they could be THAT rich.

"These people and their children...they try keeping their lives secret."

"Hmm, well, it's settled. I won't tell him. What he doesn't know won't hurt him," I replied, only feeling the tiniest bit bad. Sebastian didn't need a father. He had his uncles as good role models. I wished Dad were here. He would be the only man Sebastian needed in his life.

***

I woke up early the next day and got myself and Sebastian ready for the day. I checked my phone and saw the breakfast Zavier had requested. He seemed like he was trying to give me a hard time.

"Okay, bud, you look as handsome as ever," I said as I finished combing his hair back and then kissing his forehead.

"Thank you, Mama!" He giggled and held onto me as we got up.

"Listen, baby; Mama woke up a little late. I made your breakfast, but we won't have time to eat at home, so you can eat in the car, okay?" I said, packing up the French toast I made along with some fruit in, of course, his strawberry lunch box.

"Otay!" He grinned and ran to grab his shoes, always ready to go out.

After dropping him off at his aunt's, I went to the penthouse and was led in by a maid. Amelia's car was in the shop, so I left her mine and took the bus. Once I was in, I wasted no time and headed straight to the kitchen and started preparing Zavier's food.

I cooked oatmeal in a small bowl topped with cut-up strawberries, a wholewheat pita stuffed with spinach and strips of chicken, an oddly specific coffee order, and a smoothie. A lot of things he wanted were very specific, but they weren't difficult to make.

Just as I was done setting the table, I saw Zavier coming out of his room dressed in a charcoal black suit paired with a navy dress shirt that he tucked in. His hair was swept back neatly. I greeted him and watched as he sat down and dug in immediately.

**

Zavier

I looked down at the meal in front of me. It seemed delicious. I looked up at Amara, narrowing my eyes at her for a moment. She seemed so familiar, probably because she looked similar to a model I knew. I took a bite of the pita. Damn, this was good. I was hoping it wasn't because I preferred the previous cook…sadly, I had to let her retire and be with her grandkids at some point.

"Sir?" she asked, lips pressed together. I could tell she was desperate to know what I thought.

"Hmm, not bad. Just lay off the salt a little next time, and make sure the oats aren't this hot," I replied sternly and watched as she nodded.

**

By now, a whole week had passed, and each meal she made me just kept getting better. It bugged me that I couldn't figure out who she was. Her face seemed so familiar, yet I couldn't remember her.

I finished up work late today. I had one last call to make, but it was scheduled for midnight. Mr. Wilkens was somewhere in Germany, so the time difference was the reason for the midnight call. I put no request in for dinner because I wanted to see what she could come up with herself.

I walked into the kitchen, the delicious aroma filling my nose and making my stomach grumble. I walked up behind her while she was busy behind the stove, my large hand resting on her back as I leaned over to see what she was making. Amara let out a soft gasp, and her body tensed then relaxed again when she saw it was me.

"Would you like a taste?" she asked, stirring the pot and then scooping some food onto a wooden spoon.

"Sure." I shrugged, and she held the spoon to my mouth. I let out a hum of approval, wanting more but knowing I had to wait till it was finished. "This is good."

"Thanks, I get paid to do it." She chuckled and continued making dinner.

"What made you go to culinary school?" I asked, walking to the fridge and pouring us both a glass of soda.

"Think I'm not fit enough?" Amara joked.

"No, not at all. When I saw you, I thought you were a model for the company," I replied, a slight smirk tugging on my lips as I walked back to hand her the other glass.

"I wish, but no, I'm just a cook." She blushed a little as she took the drink, her dainty fingers grazing mine.

"If you ever consider switching careers, you can try it out here." I cleared my throat, watching as she nodded and stared into her drink.

"I'll take that into consideration if my boss decides to fire me." Amara laughed and took a sip of her soda.

"You didn't answer my question from before,"

"Oh, simple—Mom's a terrible cook. Dad served in the army, so he'd teach me all these delicious recipes before going, and ever since, I preferred cooking myself," she explained, setting the glass to the side and continuing to make my dinner.

"I see. I'll be out of your hair now," I announced, setting the empty glass in the sink and walking to my room.

***

After speaking to my mother on the phone, I took a shower and got ready for dinner. I walked into the living room and could hear her on the phone with someone.

"I love you too, baby. Can't wait to get home. Tomorrow will be all about you," I heard her say into the phone. Who was this baby? I didn't know she had a man. I couldn't shake off the hint of jealousy I had over this woman I barely even knew. I walked up to her.

"I have a family gathering tomorrow, and I expect you to come along," I said to her without thinking twice and immediately regretted it.

"But, sir, I have—" Amara wanted to decline, but the way I stared down at her made her sigh, "Okay. What time?"

"You come here at 5. We'll leave at 5:30," I announced, walking to the dining table, which was already set for me.

"One more thing: I feel bad eating alone, so do join me." I pointed to the chair across from me. She stood still for a moment then walked to the kitchen, returning with a plate too, and sat down. We ate in silence. Her professionalism impressed me a lot. I had to fire many people because they kept stepping over the line, but this one seemed to want the job. Once we were both finished, Amara ended up helping Miss Elsa clean up the table, though it was not in her job description.

***

Amara

Amelia said she'd pick me up from work. Since Ivan, her husband, was out of town for business, she'd join Nicole and me. It was great being close to her again. Once I finished up with Mr. Fuentes, I was finally able to go downstairs. When I saw the car, Amelia stepped out with Sebastian, who ran up to me.

"Mama!" he shouted happily, and I welcomed him into my arms. He started kissing my cheek and telling me how much he missed me.

"I missed you too, baby." I kissed his cheek too and took in his baby scent.

"Amara?" I heard Zavier's voice, which made my eyes widen, and I looked over at him.

"Yes, Mr. Fuentes," I asked, covering Sebastian's face as I stood up and held the little boy in my arms.

"Is that your—" he asked, unlocking his car.

"My son, yes," I replied, rubbing Sebastian's back as I got nervous. Why was he stepping away from the car and walking over to me?

"What's his name?" he asked. Sebastian peeked over at him, curious to know who this man was.

"Sebastian Reid," I replied in a shaky voice. This was the closest these two had ever been to each other, and I was hoping this would be the last time.

"Nice to meet you, bud," he said in a friendly tone with a smile, but Sebastian hid his face in my chest.

"Sorry, he's a bit tired," I said awkwardly, rubbing his back.

"I can imagine how hard the life of a toddler can be," he joked, walking back to his car again. "Have a good night, Amara." He got into his car.

"Goodnight, sir." That was a close call. I got Sebastian into his car seat while Amelia stared at me.

***

The next day at 5 p.m., I walked into Zavier's penthouse and saw him coming out of his room, adjusting the buttons of his shirt and looking at me from top to bottom. He was dressed in all black as if his closet didn't have any other color. Although, I did have to admit that he was just as handsome as that night.

"You're not going dressed like that," he said, looking me up and down once again, making me shift my weight from one foot to the other.

"Excuse me?" I raised an eyebrow at him then looked down at myself. The periwinkle dress looked good enough for his family dinner.

"I can't have you going to this family meeting dressed so... pedestrian," he spoke, stopping at some point to find the right word as he motioned to my outfit. "Follow me."

"Oh. Why am I even needed at this meeting?" I asked, rolling my eyes a little as I followed him.

"Soon, I want to host a family dinner, so I'll need you to take note of their allergies and preferences. I understand that's a bit much, so let me know how much I should add to your salary for this," Zavier explained. He turned around and looked through a rack of clothing. I looked around his room. There were many pieces of clothing strewn about. It was neat but messy at the same time. I turned my gaze back to him, now noticing how tight his suit was from the back. His muscles could be seen so clearly.

"Oh, it's fine." I cleared my throat and looked over to the window.

"If you say so. Here, wear this." He walked back to me, holding a dress on a hanger, and handed it to me. I looked down at the emerald satin dress then at the tag that said, "Fuentes." He pointed to the blinds hanging from the roof, indicating for me to get behind them and change.

"Please turn around, sir," I asked him and walked over. I swapped my dress for the one he gave me. To my surprise, the dress fit me perfectly. I loved how the fabric felt against my skin. It flowed down to my ankles. However, there was a long slit leading up to the mid-thigh of my right leg. I struggled with the straps at the back. The laces were meant to crisscross! How was I supposed to do that by myself?

I walked out after strapping on my heels again. "You can turn around," I said, awkwardly staring at myself in the mirror and fixing my hair. Wow, I looked beautiful in this dress. I looked at Zavier's reflection in the mirror and could see him staring at me. The way his eyes widened for a moment was almost as if he remembered something.

"Uh, sir, could you please help me?" I asked kindly, watching as he nodded and stepped closer to me.

His finger trailed up the middle of my back, sending shivers down my spine as he did so. "This dress suits you, Amy," Zavier commented, olive eyes staring straight into mine, which widened. Amy was the name I had given him that night, and it was never to be used again…

Chapter 3

Amara

I turned around, holding my breath as I looked up at him, waiting to see what he had to say now that he recognized me.

"It bothered me why I couldn't figure out where I knew you from." Zavier chuckled, hands on his hips as he stared at me. What was I supposed to do now?

"This is a good job opportunity, and I couldn't let it pass because of something in the past," I replied truthfully, though there was more to the story. He didn't need to know it all.

"We'll continue this conversation later. Right now, we have to go," Zavier mumbled, staring at the watch on his wrist before letting the sleeves roll over it again. I nodded and grabbed my purse, following him out.

***

In the car, I took out my notepad and wrote down the questions I needed answered by his family for this dinner.

"When do you want to have this dinner, sir?" I asked, still writing down whatever questions I had along with some ideas I had. Of course, if those went against his family's tastebuds or allergies, I'd have to cross them out.

"Hmm, probably this Saturday. That's not too soon, is it?" he asked, starting the engine and letting the car warm up first before speeding out onto the street.

"No, of course not. I'll just have to check in with your people and see what they like." I shrugged. I could tell he was truly waiting till later to have the conversation, which worried me. What would he ask? What if he asked about Sebastian?

"As far as I know, one of my sisters is vegan, though she switches up her diet a lot. Three months ago, she was pescatarian," Zavier spoke, laughing at the story.

"I see. Either way, it will be done. I'll have no trouble making several dishes," I assured him and tucked away the notebook.

"Tessa will most likely be with us, but she has no allergies and loves just about anything that tastes good." He shrugged again, punctuating the last words we spoke.

***

We arrived at what I assumed was his childhood house. The place was huge with big black gates that had floral designs on the iron bars. There was a long stone path with a water fountain in the middle. He parked his car alongside all the others that showed just how rich these people were, as if the mansion didn't do that already. When I got out of the car, I noticed all the flowers that grew here and could tell they were tended to with care. Zavier led the way inside, his hand hovering over my back as we walked in together. The moment we stepped in, I could feel everyone's eyes on me.

"Amara, hey." Tessa stepped closer to me and pulled me into a hug as if we had known each other for years. I appreciated the friendly, familiar face, though.

"It's good to see you." I smiled and let go of her.

"Tessa, do you mind introducing her to the others?" Zavier asked, looking over at his friend, who nodded.

"Hmm? No." She smiled at me and motioned for me to follow her.

**

I looked over at two women who seemed like twins. They had hazel-colored eyes with brunette hair that differed in length, which seemed to be the only difference they had.

"Let's start with the twins. This is Charlotte and Carolyn." Tessa introduced me to the one with short hair first then her sister next to her. If it weren't for the hair length difference, I'd probably struggle to tell them apart.

"Hello, nice to meet you." Charlotte smiled, shaking my hand while her twin sister just stared at me.

"Who are you?" Carolyn asked, raising a sharp brow while Tessa just gave me an awkward look along with the chance to introduce myself.

"Amara Reid, Zavier's new cook. He has this dinner planned, so I'm hoping you don't mind me asking if you have any allergies?" I introduced myself then started immediately with what I needed from them.

Once we finished up with the twins, Tessa led the way to a man who looked similar to Zavier, except he had lighter hair and darker eyes—way darker.

"This is Arlo, Zav's older brother," Tessa said, unamused as the man had a smirk on his face when he saw us approaching him.

"Who might you be, cariño?" he asked, taking my hand in his and bringing it to his lips.

"Arlo, stop being a creep. This is Zav's new cook." Tessa smacked his chest, making him let go of my hand.

"A snack making a snack?" Arlo winked at me, making me chuckle nervously and look over to the side.

"So, Mr. Fuentes has this dinner planned, and I'm hoping to get you—" I tried staying professional.

"Actually, you don't have to bother with him. He eats anything edible," Tessa said and took my hand and walked away from the man.

"You're a mean woman, chiquita," he said, making her groan and roll her eyes.

"I'm not little anymore, cabron."

"Hmm," I remarked.

"What?" She raised a brow at me.

"Nothing," I teased and jabbed her. It was clear there was something between those two—maybe not romantic, but some type of one-sided hate.

"Listen, one Fuentes brother is more tolerable than the other." She winked at me.

"Which one is it then?" I joked, making her laugh.

"Your boss shouldn't hear you talking like that," she warned playfully and brought me into one of the rooms where I saw an older woman sitting with one leg over the other, her eyes focused on the book in her hand.

"Tessa! It's so good to see you. Please don't tell me that's one of Arlo or Zavier's playthings?" the woman asked, glaring me down and leaving me surprised.

"Excuse me?" I asked, raising a brow at her, watching as she was ready to tell me off, but Tessa spoke up before something could happen.

"Tia, this is his cook, Amara," she introduced me, watching as the look on the woman's face changed a little, though I was still offended.

"My apologies, dear. These boys of mine have put me

through hell." She closed the book and focused her attention on me now.

"So, you just call any woman a plaything?" I asked. Her olive eyes glared at me again as if I were in the wrong for asking something like this.

"Uh, Amara's here to get some information about any allergies and such for the dinner Zav is planning." Tessa was quick to change the subject.

***

By now, I had all the information I needed. Arlo and Tessa had no issues. Charlotte and Zavier had the same allergies: almonds, hazelnuts, peaches, and kiwi. Tiffany, Zavier's mother and the woman who called me a plaything, just mentioned hating fish. Carolyn was now on a keto diet, so I'd have to make something fitting for her. These people would have me cooking for hours.

Zavier offered me a bonus, but I declined, and now, I hoped I could instead ask for a Saturday off. That way, I could spend the whole day with my boy.

***

Zavier

I had to have a little chat with Tessa. She recruited Amara, so she might know a little more. I walked up to her and Amara.

"Hey, Tess, can I talk to you privately?" I asked, looking over at the others and then at her. Tessa hummed and followed me to one of the rooms, closing the door behind her when I signaled her to do so.

"Remember Amy?" I asked, looking over her shoulder though the doors were closed.

"Oh yeah, your party hookup?" Tessa and I had this chemistry that just worked well together. We'd always had each other's back and just understood each other in ways others couldn't. We'd been friends since high school and seen each other through phases we wished we never even went through.

"Yeah, now remember when I told you Amara had a familiar face?" I asked, resting my hands on my hips.

"No way…" Her eyes widened.

"Yes. Should've seen the look on her face when I called her Amy," I scoffed, shaking my head as I looked down at my socks for a moment.

"Wow, what a surprise, man," Tessa mumbled, still in disbelief.

"Now you know how things are with the women in my past. They always come back for something, so what will we do about this one?" I looked over her shoulder again to make sure no one was snooping around.

"Honestly, Zav, she hasn't asked for anything. Usually, they'd claim to be in love or carrying your child, but she hasn't done either of those," Tessa mumbled, walking over to the desk and leaning against it.

"She told me this job was too good to pass up because of her past," I explained, turning to face her. She'd have to know more about Amara as she was the one who interviewed her.

"It is a good job—and a very well paid one at that." She shrugged, making her thinking face.

"Are you sure she's legit? What happened at her previous job?"

"The restaurant she worked at was a front for a mob boss. She and the whole staff lost their jobs, so it's real—no lie there," Tessa responded, the sound of her long nails tapping on her phone catching my attention. I looked over the article she showed me on her phone that backed up Amara's story.

"I see...I should probably have this conversation with her later." I sighed, holding my hand out to her to help her up so we could get going.

"You should," Tessa hummed. "Has she done anything you don't like?"

"Nope, she's truly a professional. Every time I compliment something other than her cooking, she just gives me a nod," I replied honestly, stopping our movement as we continued to talk.

"She did the same thing with Arlo," Tessa mentioned, making me roll my eyes.

"Arlo's already flirting with her?" I didn't know why I felt so invested in this or why it bothered me so much.

"You know Arlo—stringing people along just to disappoint them," Tessa replied in a tone I was familiar with. Seemed like she was talking from personal experience.

"What's that's supposed to mean, hmm?" I questioned, raising a brow at her.

"Nothing," she mumbled, flashing me a quick smile followed by a nervous giggle. Funny how she still tried to lie to me even when I knew her so well.

"No, it's something. Tell me." I blocked the door so that she couldn't move. She opened her mouth but then closed it.

"Dinner's ready, sir," the butler said as he entered the room. Tessa took that as her moment to go.

Chapter 4

Amara

I ended up helping with setting the table, mostly to escape Arlo. He wasn't being creepy or making me uncomfortable, but I just hated being in that position, given my past with his brother. I was trying to ensure things wouldn't blow up in my face.

I finished setting down the key lime pie then took a seat for myself as I saw Tessa and Zavier coming out of the room they went into before. I watched as the two came over and took a seat at the table; Zavier sat next to me.

"So, Amara, why did you choose this job?" Tiffany asked. Dear God, was this some sort of interrogation?

"Yeah, it's so...basic," Carolyn commented, which made me bite my lip to keep me from being rude.

"I love cooking, and I'm good at it. Besides, it's probably the only path I could've taken where I wouldn't be in debt," I explained, twirling the pasta around with a fork.

"Oh, but there are scholarships," Carolyn commented again, and I saw Charlotte nudging her.

"I had a full ride to law school, but after a school incident, I lost it." I shrugged, staring at my food.

"Incident?" Arlo asked, getting everyone's attention.

**

A few years ago...

It was my senior year. My friends, Laura and Nicole, decided we should go out one night. We had finished up all our exams, so we were ready to celebrate. We didn't even plan to drink since we lost our fake IDs—it would just be for the dancing. We loved that, going out to dance. It was why we were all on the cheer squad.

Now, Laura—she always had poor taste in guys. She hooked up with one of the teacher's sons at that club, and the asshole recorded her. Their hookup was meant to be a one-time thing, but he wanted more and started blackmailing her.

Laura didn't tell us in the beginning, but as time passed, Nicole and I could tell something was wrong with her. When we found out, we tried bringing the issue to the principal's office, but they found there wasn't enough evidence and had no rights to his phone. I knew it was a lie; the principal was protecting the boy because his father was a board member, and if a story like this got leaked, it would ruin the school's reputation. Laura asked me to drop it, but I didn't.

I saw Wilson standing by the bleachers, smiling and flirting with some other cheerleader. Seeing him made me sick but also aggravated me at the same time. Then, I saw his phone in his hand—perfect. That was all I needed.

I walked up to him that day, and I tried being nice and gave him the option of deleting the video, but he refused to do so, so I grabbed his phone, and he didn't like that. It led to a fight. The good news was I did delete the video, but the bad news was I pushed him over, and he hit his head hard. There was only a little blood, but he suffered a bad concussion. With the video deleted, the school only found out I started a fight with a guy whose daddy had some power in our town, so the story was twisted, making me the villain and causing me to lose the scholarship. I did it for a friend. Was there a falling out between us? Yes, but she did say she'd always be thankful for what I did for her. For me, what mattered was that I did something good.

***

I snapped back to reality and looked over at them. "That's not important right now. What's important is that Mr. Fuentes's food is always taken care of," I answered, changing the subject.

"How are things going for you, Tess?" Tiffany asked, making Tessa cough as she was caught off guard.

"Normal, tia. Just hoping that I can build my apartments this year," she answered, smiling.

"That's great, mija." Tiffany smiled at her then glared at me, making me frown at first. Oh, well. Someone didn't like what I said before.

"I can imagine being Zavi's assistant is a drag, though," Arlo commented, reaching over for his wine.

"With good pay, any miserable boss is tolerable," Tessa joked, nudging Zavier's side.

"Hey! I have feelings, you know." Zavier pouted while the others laughed. I felt my purse vibrate and checked my phone to see it was Amelia. I stepped away from the table to pick up the phone. She wouldn't call me unnecessarily, so this had to be important.

"Everything okay there?" I asked, walking farther away from the others, not wanting them to hear my conversation.

"Not really. The little guy isn't feeling too well," she

replied. I could hear Sebastian rambling about something in the background.

"Should I come over?" I asked, knowing he always preferred me when he got sick.

"No, no, not yet. I just wanted to let you know," she answered, the sound of Sebastian becoming less loud as she probably moved away from him.

"Please call me if you need me to come get him," I told her. I knew she'd think this dinner was more important, but trust me—I'd do anything for Sebastian.

"I will. I just wanted to give you a little heads up for now. I'll try putting him down for a nap," she replied.

"Okay, take care," I replied. I walked back to the table. Everyone's eyes were on me again as I sat down.

"Everything okay?" Tessa asked, setting down the wine glass. Her question, of course, made everyone stare at me again.

"Yeah, Sebastian is just feeling a bit unwell," I answered, forgetting they didn't know who that was.

"Is Sebastian your boyfriend?" Carolyn asked.

I chuckled and quickly answered, "No, my son."

"I see his father didn't put a ring on it, then." Arlo smiled as he looked over at me, making me roll my eyes.

"I'm a single mother, sir. If things worsen, can we leave early? Or can I take a cab and leave?" I answered, wanting to change the subject, and looked over at Zavier about my request.

"Of course," he said after swallowing the bit he was chewing on.

Not long after, my phone rang again, and I excused myself to pick it up. Once again, it was Amelia. I was hoping it would be good news, but it turned out things had worsened, and the boy was crying for me.

"Sir, my son's situation has worsened. I need to go," I informed Zavier, already collecting my stuff.

"It's my fault you're here, so I'll give you a ride." He got up too, leaning over to kiss his mother on her cheek.

"I can take a taxi," I assured him, hating that I interrupted their family dinner.

"Do you know how long it takes for a taxi to get here?" he insisted, following me to the front door and taking his jacket off the hanger. "30 minutes." He answered his own question since I was clueless.

"Fine. A ride would be appreciated," I replied, giving up on finding my way back by myself.

"Good. We still have to continue our conversation from before," he mumbled, walking out the door after one of the staff members opened it up for us. He led the way to his car and waited until we both had our seatbelts on before driving. It was silent for the first five minutes. All that could be heard was the music playing at a low volume, mostly muffled by the wind blowing through the trees. You could say the mansion was in a deserted area. The only thing surrounding it was nature.

***

Zavier

"So, Amara—or is it Amy?" I finally spoke up, looking over at the woman and watching how she adjusted herself in the seat.

"Amara is my legal name," she answered, eyes focused on the road as if she were the one driving.

"Why didn't you tell me before who you were?" I looked

over at the GPS to see the location she had put in for me to drive to.

"Sir—" She sighed, but I cut her off.

"Zavier. I think you earned yourself the privilege of calling me that." I looked over at her, and her brown eyes focused on mine as she gave me a nod.

"Okay, Zavier. I thought Tessa would be my boss. When I saw it was you, I thought you'd recognize me, so when you didn't, I figured I'd shut up and enjoy my job," she answered, not exhibiting a single drop of sweat or stutter or even change in tone. She seemed to be telling the truth.

"So, this isn't you inserting yourself into my life?" I asked to be sure.

"All due respect, but I think you're full of yourself," Amara answered, making me chuckle. I chose to ignore her words.

"Our past won't be an issue, will it?" I asked now that some things had been uncovered.

"Has it been an issue till now?"

"No. Let's keep it like that, okay?" I slowed down and looked over at her, earning a nod from the brunette.

"Wasn't planning on changing the situation."

***

We arrived at her sister's place, and I waited patiently in the car as she went to get her son. She returned with her son in less than five minutes. She sat down with the boy lying on her chest. He had dozed off, but I could tell by his tired face and the tearstains on his cheeks that he had been crying a lot.

"Do you know what's wrong with him?" I asked, leaning over to turn the AC up a little.

"Maybe some sort of flu? It's difficult to figure these things out by yourself," she answered, all her attention on her son as she gently rubbed his head.

"You should probably take him to the doctor," I suggested, finally driving again, going a bit slower and more carefully than before now that there was a child in the car without a car seat.

"If things don't get better by tomorrow, I will take him to go see the doctor," Amara replied, adjusting the blanket over Sebastian's body.

I hummed and nodded. I stayed quiet so Sebastian could get his rest and not be interrupted by our talking. Finally, we arrived at her place, which wasn't too far away from her sister's. It was already dark, and I could see a few people, mostly men, hanging out outside, so I decided to be kind enough to help her up and carry her son's bag.

The moment we stepped foot into her apartment, the little boy woke up and started crying loudly. Now with the lights on, his face was in clear sight, and I saw him clearly for the first time. Amara sat him on the counter and took off his shirt as he kept tugging on it.

I set down the bag on the couch and looked over at her son. Then, I saw it—that mark on his shoulder...I inherited it from my father. We both had it in the same spot, and now, the same mark was on Sebastian, though his was smaller. I also knew the night I met Amy was the first time I didn't use protection.

"Who's the father, Amara?"

Chapter 5

Amara

There it was—that question I never wished to hear. For a moment, I thought if I ignored him, he'd drop it. I mean, Sebastian was still crying, and on top of that, the phone started ringing, and Nicole wasn't home to answer it. I walked over to get the thermometer and check Sebastian's temperature, all while he was still crying and the phone was still ringing nonstop.

"You know, I have that same mark on my shoulder. So do my father and my grandmother," Zavier said, clearly not dropping the subject. Did he know? I mean, Sebastian looked a lot like him, and I thought his birthmark was just his unique thing. How was I supposed to know it was hereditary? Zavier and I happened years ago, and it was a one-time thing.

"Zavier, please drop it," I asked of him, checking the thermometer. The temperature was high. I picked up Sebastian, rubbing his back as I walked to the medicine cabinet.

"If Sebastian's mine, I deserve to know, don't you think?" Zavier asked, still applying pressure that was made worse by the loud crying of our son and the stupid phone going off.

"Yes! Dammit, he's yours. There, happy?" I shouted at

him. Just at that moment, the phone stopped ringing, and my answer made him shut up.

I took out some ibuprofen for children and gave Sebastian the amount he was allowed to swallow. Luckily, he downed it without hesitation. Thank the bubblegum flavor for that.

"Why haven't you—" I heard Zavier's voice ask, but right now, I was not having it. Sebastian was starting to calm down.

"Let me put him to sleep, and we'll talk if you want after that," I offered, not even giving him a chance to answer me before I carried Sebastian to his room and helped him into bed.

"Goodnight, my angel," I whispered, kissing his forehead and then handing him the teddy bears he loved and making sure to tuck them in too. I took my sweet time getting up from his side. He was out the moment I flicked off the lights. I made sure to turn on his nightlight then finally exited his room. I looked down the hall and saw Zavier had made himself right at home, sitting comfortably on the couch with his legs slightly spread apart and his arms on the armrest.

"He's asleep?" Zavier asked, looking at me as I walked into the kitchen.

"He fell asleep the moment his head hit the pillow," I answered, filling the kettle with water and then putting it on the stove before finally facing Zavier.

"So, he's mine?"

"I've answered your question before. Yes," I replied, adding some honey to the tea I was making for myself, forgetting to offer him some. But then again, he was more of a cold brew guy.

"How come you never came to find me to let me know, huh?" he asked, using an inquisitive tone I didn't appreciate. "You are here for money, aren't you? He probably isn't even mine," he accused me, standing up with his finger pointed at me. I set the mug down and stepped up to him.

"How fucking dare you!" I slapped his pointing finger away. "We had our encounter three years ago! Don't you think if I wanted money, I'd come to you the moment I found out about my pregnancy?" I lashed out at him. His accusation was pissing me off. I didn't deserve to be treated like this. "I never even asked for money. The only reason we met again was because I saw a job listing, and on top of that, you are the one who asked me who the father of my child was." I sighed, walking away to go pick up my tea again.

"Then why didn't you tell me? I demand a DNA test."

"You know what?" I shouted at him and walked to the bathroom to grab Sebastian's toothbrush. I shoved it into Zavier's chest and then opened the door for him. "Get out of my house. Now." The neighbors could see and hear me, but I didn't care. They were not the ones who had to deal with this bullshit.

***

Zavier

Was she serious right now? I opened my mouth to say something then checked my surroundings. People were watching. This would have to continue some other day. We were both clearly too angry to pursue this conversation. I took my leave, calling Tessa the moment I got into the car. I had to go over to her place; I really needed to talk to someone.

***

"So, how do you feel about that?" she asked, crossing one leg over the other as she lay back on that indigo couch of hers.

"Me being a father and just finding out about it?" I asked, sipping the coffee she made for us.

"Duh." She rolled her eyes.

"It sucks. I feel like I should've been there, but also, at the same time, I wasn't ready to become a father," I openly admitted. Tessa was always someone I could be open with.

"You know the consequences of not using protection," she mumbled into the mug then loudly sipped her coffee.

"Yeah, but when she never called, I figured we got lucky, or she was on the pill." I sighed, rubbing my temples as I sank into the matching one-person seater.

"How did she handle you finding out?"

"She was pissed when I asked. Then, I asked her if she came for money—" I replied awkwardly.

"You fucking asshole," Tessa said, resting the mug on the coffee table.

"What?"

"You don't just do that. Jeez. It's clear she doesn't need your money. She picked up this job without even knowing you'd be the boss, and you go and accuse her of something like that—and on top of that, you also accused her of lying?" She smacked my shoulder, making me whine.

"How was I supposed to know?" I groaned, rubbing the spot where she hit me.

"The boy looks a lot like you when you were little." Tessa shrugged.

"How do you know what he looks like?" I frowned, looking at the lady.

"I may or may not have stalked her online," she mumbled, picking up her phone and going through it.

"What...let me see." I peeked over her shoulder, wanting to see more of the little boy. The best and closest I'd seen of him was today, and it was only for five minutes—less, even.

"See the green eyes, the lips, maybe even the nose. The photo where he's wearing the red polo shirt reminds me of the one your mother hung up in her office." She pointed at her screen, and my eyes went over every little detail of the little boy.

"He does look like me…" I said softly, slightly smiling before remembering what situation I found myself in. "What do I do now? I have a child, Tess!"

"For starters, you'll have to apologize for your behavior," she advised me, and I nodded.

"Okay. That can be done easily."

"Now, as for your son, do you wish to be in his life?" She raised her dark brow at me.

"I have to, right?" I asked, brows still furrowed as I tried to figure this mess out.

"But only be there if you're serious about being there," Tessa replied, looking down at her hands. I understood right away what she meant: her mother had only been there for financial support.

"Maybe I should ask her if I could get to know him then?" I suggested. Sebastian deserved to have his father or at least know about him.

"Try that. He does seem like a sweet boy." Tessa smiled, putting away her phone and leaning back into her seat.

"Tess, my mother will kill me. A child out of wedlock?" I mumbled, just now realizing how bad this was. I didn't care about the public's perception—only my family's.

"Yeah, no kidding. Not to mention, she doesn't like Amara." She laughed, making me glare at her, which only made her laugh more.

"Fuck," I groaned, covering my face with my hands and

slowly running them up to my hair.

"Hey, you'll get through this. Maybe he'll end up being the best thing to ever happen to you," Tessa assured me, rubbing my back to comfort me. I remained silent for a few moments, trying to collect my thoughts.

"I hope so...I know you've got meetings tomorrow, so I'll get out of your hair." I stood up; it was also getting late.

"I should start charging therapy money," Tessa joked, getting up too and slowly leading the way to the front door.

"Name your price." I winked at her, making her smile and shake her head.

"Good night, Zavi."

"Night, Tess." I waved at her. "Good luck with those meetings."

***

The next morning, I got up early and got ready for the day. Finally, it was a day where I could dress casually. I picked out my black jeans and paired them with a maroon Henley shirt. I put on my watch, picked up the keys, and was out of the house. The first stop was to get donuts and coffee. I even picked up some cake pops for toddlers. They were supposed to have less sugar. I didn't know—I was so new to this.

Now that I had everything I needed, I made my way to Amara's apartment and knocked on the door, hoping that today would go much better than last night.

Chapter 6

Amara

After I kicked out Zavier last night, I ended up calling Amelia and Nicole. Nicole was staying at Enzo's, her boyfriend's, place, and she even offered to come back home, but I didn't need or want that. I just wanted someone to talk to, and they were both there for me as I was for them when needed. At some point, I managed to get some sleep, but Amelia did mention she wanted to talk to me in the morning.

When I woke up, I checked up on Sebastian, and when I saw he was still sleeping, I decided to get myself ready for the day. While I was putting on my clothes, I saw my phone ringing. It was my sister.

"Hey, Ames," I answered the phone.

"Good morning! How are you and Bash?" she asked, some pots clinking in the background.

"Little guy is still asleep, and I, uh, I'm good," I said, mouth gaping a little as I applied mascara. I was not so sure what the plan was for today, but I did plan on being ready for anything.

"Can we talk?" she asked, using a tone I feared a little.

"Of course," I mumbled.

"Will you allow Zavier to be in his son's life?"

"I'm not sure yet..." I sighed, picking up the phone and walking out to the kitchen to start my breakfast.

"What do you mean?" Amelia asked.

"He came into my house and disrespected me like that," I replied.

"As much as I agree with you on that, I still think he deserves to get to know his son,"

"He never even knew about him, so what harm will it do?" I tried to avoid this conversation and hoped she would too.

"Amara—" She sighed but was still determined.

"Whose side are you on, Amelia?" I asked angrily, clenching my fists as I stared at the phone.

"Sebastian's," she answered confidently. "Right now, he's a happy little boy, but at some point, the boy will grow curious about his father," Amelia spoke calmly, trying to argue her point. I knew deep down she was right. Sebastian deserved to know his father, and Zavier had the right to get to know his son. "I have to go. There's someone at the door," I mumbled, ending the call as fast as I could.

I hung up and went to see who it was. Was it Nicole? Perhaps she forgot her keys again. Or maybe it was the old man above us. His cat always escaped and would sit out on our fire escape, but Ginger wasn't here, so it couldn't be him.

"Yes? What are you doing here?" I glared at him, holding the door open a crack.

"I'm here to apologize...donuts and tea?" Zavier said sweetly, holding a box in one hand and a cup in his other.

"What tea is it?" I asked, looking down at the drink he had brought me.

"Mango," he answered, squinting his eyes a little. He probably guessed it because his own tea was almost done.

"Fine, come in," I mumbled, opening the door for him.

"Thank you," Zavier grinned, coming in immediately.

"I know I crossed the line yesterday as you're still my boss, but—" I started to say, knowing I still wanted this job, so in a way, I'd have to apologize for my behavior.

"I know. And you don't have to explain yourself. I was out of line and shouldn't have accused you of those things," he said, sitting down on the couch.

"Mm-hmm. I understand how it may look to you, but I'm really not here for your money," I replied, surprised at how calmly we were both handling this.

"I think I was just too surprised and acted in the wrong manner. I'm just shocked you never searched for me," Zavier said, leaning forward from where he was sitting and inching closer to me.

"I could've, honestly, but I didn't. It was a mistake, and I didn't want you dragged into it." I shrugged, sipping at the tea he had just brought me.

"Amara, this isn't something casual. I have a son I never knew about." Zavier frowned at me. I bit down on my lip, feeling slightly guilty now.

"Fine. Let's go back three years. Were you ready to be a father then? Are you even ready now?" I asked, raising a brow at him. I knew I wasn't ready back then. I was pro-choice, but I didn't feel comfortable with abortion myself, which was why I had Sebastian.

"Back then? No, but I would've stepped up to my fatherly duties," he mumbled, looking down at the lid of his cup.

"Just like you will now? Only because it's your duty?" I asked. I didn't want Sebastian to be a burden to others. That was why I never told Zavier.

"I just have to get to know him. Yeah, I'm mostly doing it because it's what's right, but I'm also hoping I do indeed start loving him," Zavier admitted, setting his cup on the coffee table.

"I see…" I sighed. It made sense. He didn't even know Sebastian yet.

"Will you allow me to meet him?" Zavier asked nervously, and I slowly nodded.

"Yes, under one condition. I decide when your family can know about him, and please keep him out of the public eye," I requested. Before, I didn't even know he was this famous, and although I barely saw him in the news after doing my research, I could tell the media would be thirsty for some gossip, and I refused to let that be Sebastian.

"You don't have to worry about the public. Tessa already knows about him, but as for the others, they don't. Though, I hope you don't make me keep this from them for too long. Sebastian is the first grandchild."

"I know…" I mumbled, leaning back into the couch now that the air was cleared, and it seemed we were both on the same page.

"Can you tell me about him?" he asked curiously, and I smiled and nodded.

"Uh, he was born on the third of December. He shares the same allergies as you, and he likes the color red. He will throw hands for a good cake pop and loves the little pizzas I make for him."

"I see. I, uh, got these too." Zavier chuckled, showing me a little brown bag that had three cake pops inside.

"Oh man, he'll love those. Oh, and he loves vintage cars." I laughed and remembered Sebastian's latest obsession, which seemed to confuse Zavier.

"Huh?"

"His uncle got him a set of vintage car toys, and he likes

them a lot," I answered, taking a raspberry powdered donut from the box.

"He seems quite interesting. What's his full name?" he asked, taking a Boston creme donut for himself and then placing the donut box on the coffee table.

"Sebastian Silas Reid. Silas was also my father's middle name," I answered, looking over at him as he nodded.

"I see."

We stared at each other for a moment. I saw him reaching closer and could feel my heartbeat picking up as I stared into his olive eyes. I felt the pad of his thumb swiping over the corner of my mouth and saw some raspberry jelly on his thumb.

"Oh. Thank you." I smiled awkwardly, wiping my mouth with a napkin as he licked his thumb.

"Morning, Mama!" Sebastian came running to me. He seemed a lot better today.

"Good morning, baby. Had a good nap?" I asked, picking him up and placing him on my hip as I leaned over to kiss his forehead.

"Mm-hmm. Who that?" he asked, pointing at his father and tilting his head as he looked at the man.

"Hey, Sebastian. I'm Zavier, but feel free to call me Zavi," he introduced himself, holding his hand out to Sebastian.

He looked up at me first, and I gave him a subtle nod, and he then shook Zavi's hand. "Okay!"

"I got you and your mother a little something." Zavier handed him the bag of cake pops, which he took eagerly.

"Thank you!" He smiled widely and dug in, looking at me again for permission to eat the cake pop.

"Go ahead, Bash." I ruffled his hair and watched as he bit in immediately, wasting no time.

"Thank you for these," I said, looking over at Zavier.

"You're welcome," he mumbled, eyes focused on his son as he smiled, watching him eat his cake pop.

Chapter 7

Amara

"I heard you like your vintage car toys," Zavier said, trying to make conversation with his son.

"Yeah! Come, come," Sebastian said excitedly and jumped off of me, taking Zavier's hand in his. Zavier looked over at me, probably checking to see if I was okay with this.

"You can go—just know that you brought this on yourself," I joked, and Zavier laughed nervously in response. I knew my boy; he'd end up showing Zavier all his toys one by one, and if he were lucky, he'd get to touch Sebastian's favorite one.

"Okay, buddy." Zavier followed along with the little boy.

I watched as the two played together in Sebastian's room. It started with Sebastian showing his father all his car toys. Sebastian seemed quite fond of him because he even let him play with his 1969 Chevrolet Camaro, his favorite! I left the two and went ahead to start my chores. There wasn't much— just some clothes I had to wash and fold along with the dishes from last night. When I finished up, I went and checked on the two and saw Sebastian had managed to get Zavier to read to him. The little boy leaned on his father's chest, two pairs of green eyes on a book about a tiger and his family. I quietly closed the door and went to the living room, deciding to watch a bit of my favorite TV show for now.

***

I heard the door open, and when I saw Nicole step in, I walked up to her after pausing the show.

"Who is Bash talking to?" Nicole asked, putting down her bag by the door and walking closer to me, frowning as she looked towards the boy's room.

"His father..." I answered, giving her an awkward look.

"Excuse me?" My friend frowned.

"Shh, let's go out on the balcony and talk." I tucked away my phone and got up, leading the way to the balcony.

"Yeah, we definitely need to talk," she said, eyes opened wide. I took a seat on the chair across from her and started telling her all that had happened. She seemed confused at first but then a lot more relieved.

"I'm glad things are working out, then. College will be expensive in a few years," Nicole joked, looking through the glass door and then back at me.

"I don't want Zavier to be in his life just for financial support, jeez." I shook my head and sank into the chair.

"I know; I'm just teasing. The fact that he's been here for so long proves he's enjoying the time spent with his son," she assured me, patting my shoulder. She was right. Zavier was spending quite a lot of time here, and I could hear waves of laughter and giggles coming from Sebastian's room whenever I got close to the door.

"Hey, sorry to interrupt." Zavier walked through the doorway, his eyes focused on me before he realized someone else was present too. "Oh, I'm Zavier—"

Nicole cut him off. "Fuentes, I know. I'm Nicole. Nice to

meet the father of my godson." She shook his hand, a broad smile on her lips as she then looked over at me with a brow raised. My God, she was going to embarrass me, huh.

"Oh, uh, nice to meet you too," he replied before almost being pushed over by Sebastian, who ran over to me.

"Bath time, Mama!" I looked at Sebastian. He was full of color with lots of paint all over his arms, face, and even his chest.

"Yeah, uh, we started painting, and he must've mistaken himself for the paper." Zavier laughed awkwardly while Sebastian just smiled, proud of himself. Nicole just giggled and offered the little one a high five.

"It's okay. Come on, baby." I got up and picked up Sebastian, resting him on one side of my hip.

I took Sebastian, who was giggling, to the bathtub, and got him ready for a bath. Once I finished up, I was a little wet and wrapped Sebastian in his towel. I took my eyes off him for a second, but in that second, he ran off to Zavier, hugging the man.

"Let's get you some clothes, bud." Zavier walked to his drawer and opened the first one.

"Blue shirt, please," Sebastian asked sweetly, holding onto the towel. His head was tipped up, so he could see his father.

"Um," Zavier mumbled, looking at the drawer he just opened, which had his pants.

I opened the one next to it and took out the blue shirt. "Here you go."

I helped Zavier put on Sebastian's clothes and get him ready. I was honestly quite surprised he was still awake. Usually by now, Sebastian would go down for a nap, but the boy seemed to be having quite some fun, so I let it pass for today.

"Come read, please?" Sebastian ran to Zavier, his little

legs moving as fast as they could as he clutched a book in his right hand.

"Again?" Zavier asked, pouting. Sebastian was definitely making use of this opportunity to get in lots of fun with the man he had just met.

"Yes, please," he asked, climbing onto his father's lap and handing him the book.

"Oh, okay," Zavier mumbled and opened up the book. I watched the two for a moment as Zavier read the story to him and patiently answered all the little questions Sebastian had. A slight smile formed on my lips, and Zavier looked over at me for a moment before Sebastian asked him what happened to the dinosaurs.

***

By now, more time had passed, so I decided I'd check in on the two. They both seemed to be enjoying the time spent together a lot, so I let them be, but at some point, I grew curious. Didn't Zavier have work? I heard his phone ringing many times until it was switched to silent.

"I don't mean to interrupt, but don't you have work today?" I asked, leaning against the doorframe.

"Sundays are my days off. If I'm intruding, do tell me. I didn't mean to stay this long," Zavier said, looking at the time on his watch and then at me.

"No, no. It's okay. Will you be staying for dinner?" I was quick to say.

"Is Nicole okay with that?" he asked softly, looking over my shoulder as he held the car toy Sebastian had just handed him.

"She's going out for dinner." I shrugged.

"Then I hope you don't mind," he replied, placing the car

on the track as Sebastian did the same with his car.

"We're racing, Mama! I'm winning," the little boy said happily, green eyes glued on the track as his red car remained in the lead.

"Really? That's amazing, baby." I winked at Zavier.

"Yeah, Mama!"

"I'm going to make pizza. What toppings would you like on yours?" I asked, looking over at my son's father.

"Cheese and sausage!" Sebastian answered the moment he heard pizza. His attention was now all mine.

"I was talking to Zavi, but okay." I chuckled, as did Zavier.

"Anything but pork." He shrugged and reset the track, picking out another car.

"Yeah, yeah, allergies," I mumbled and walked off. I couldn't believe I invited him for dinner. Just yesterday, I was screaming at him and kicking him out.

***

Zavier

I never expected to have so much fun with a two-year-old. He was full of so much energy and life. The picture he painted was a gift to me. It wasn't the prettiest, but I sure would treasure it. Perhaps knowing about him before now wouldn't have been bad. While reading, Sebastian fell asleep on me, and I carefully put him on his bed and let him rest until dinner. I pulled out my phone and saw several missed calls from Tessa and my sisters and a lot from my mother.

"Hey, Mama." I called her back, which resulted in her scolding me in Spanish. "Lo siento. I was just a bit busy and wanted some time for myself. I'll come by tomorrow, maybe," I replied and waited till she said her goodbyes before ending the call and then texting my sisters. Now, time for Tessa.

"Tess, I'm sorry I ignored your calls. I was busy spending time with Sebastian…I swear he's the coolest little boy I know," I said, full of excitement; I couldn't contain it.

"I'm glad you two got to bond," she said happily, and I hummed in response before remembering she had her meetings.

"How'd your meetings go, Tess?"

"Somewhat good, but they want me to get a different architect," Tessa answered, almost squealing.

"That's fine. I'll help you search for good ones. I'm proud of you, but, uh, I've got to go. Dinner time," I said, looking through the glass door and watching as Sebastian ran around his mother and giggled, looking up at her. She picked him up and planted a kiss on his forehead before letting him down again.

"Mm-hmm, me too, and thanks! Enjoy dinner," she said then ended the call.

I walked back inside and saw the pizzas lying on the table. The smaller one belonged to Sebastian, and I assumed the large one topped with mushrooms, chicken, cheese, and bell peppers was for Amara and me.

"This looks delicious," I said, helping Sebastian up to his chair.

"Yeah! Mommy always makes good food!"

"I know, bud." I smiled, sitting down too, and watched as Amara smiled at us and sat across from me.

"Well, thank you both so much." She placed a slice on Sebastian's plate and cut it up into smaller pieces for him.

Once dinner was over, Amara got Sebastian ready for bed. I helped by reading him yet another story. Luckily, he passed out after three minutes of reading. I turned off the lights and walked to the kitchen, where I saw Amara cleaning up the table, and I joined her so I could ask her a question. "So, I was wondering if maybe, from time to time, you can bring him over? Maybe for dinners?"

"That would be easier for me, so it would be possible, yeah. What about the staff at your house? Won't they see?" Amara asked, placing Sebastian's pizza in a container along with the last slice of the one we ate.

"There are only two, but I guess I'll send them away earlier if that will be better for you," I offered, hoping she would say yes. Dinner with Sebastian would give me the chance to see him daily.

"It would. Thank you."

Chapter 8

Amara

A week had passed since we started having dinner together, and Sebastian loved every moment of it. Zavier even bought him some toys he could play with at his place. Usually, Zavier would be home 15 minutes after I prepared dinner, but ever since we started eating together, he came home an hour earlier and would play with Sebastian. Last night, we told Sebastian who Zavier was. He had many questions, mostly wondering where Zavier was before, but luckily, he was only two, so the subject was brushed over quickly.

"Bash, are you ready, bud?" I asked, walking out of my bedroom and trying to tie up my hair.

"Yeah, Mommy!" he answered, looking up from the straps of his shoes and running to me, holding onto my hand.

"Okay, come on then, baby." I squeezed his hand and winked at him. I helped him to the car and handed him a toy and book after strapping him in his car seat. When I got into the car, I heard a notification from my phone and went to check it.

"Do you mind if Tessa comes over for dinner?" Zavier texted as I put on my seatbelt. I thought about it for a moment.

"Uh, I suppose not?" I replied and started the ignition.

"She says it's for a little business advice, but she was dying to get to know Bash, so I think it's a cover," he texted back. Of course, she'd want to meet him. She heard about him and even asked me little things about him whenever we saw each other in the morning.

"It's okay. I guess it's about time she meets him. She keeps asking about him whenever we see each other," I replied.

"I see. Well, till later, then," he texted back.

"Yeah, till later," I replied, then put away the phone and started driving.

I won't lie—we recently got very close. Nicole warned me to be careful, whereas Amelia was happy. She was always a bit more optimistic. I just tried being friendly. He was the father of my son, and he was genuinely good to him. Once we arrived at Zavier's penthouse, we made our way up, and Sebastian ran off to jump onto the couch.

"Do you want to watch some cartoons while I cook, bud?" I asked, kicking the door shut gently with my heel.

"No, wanna help!" he replied as I sighed. He wanted to help cook.

"Oh, okay then. Come on." I led the way to the kitchen, little Sebastian happily walking behind me.

I set him down on the counter and handed him a wooden spoon to hold onto, letting him feel like he was truly doing something. I decided to make chicken alfredo pasta. Tessa once mentioned that she liked my pasta. I let Sebastian add the pasta to the boiling water and stir it around for a moment before taking him away from the stove. He always wanted to be included in cooking, but I always feared he'd get burned, so I tried letting him do very little.

"I'm home," Zavier said as he walked through the door.

"Daddy!" Sebastian said excitedly, running over to his father and hugging his leg.

"Hey, bud, Amara." He smiled, looking down at his son and ruffling his hair. Zavier then looked over at me.

"Hello, Zavier," I said, drying off my hands and then joining the two. I sat with them for a few moments before deciding it was about time to start the pie for dessert. I walked back to the kitchen, pulled out all the ingredients, and saw the two were still in the kitchen. "Yes? Can I help you two?"

"Wanna help," Sebastian said, looking up at me and then at his father, who shrugged.

"Oh, dear. Come on, then." I smiled. I decided to cut the apples and let the two start on the crust. I instructed them on what had to be done, which wasn't much. It was just taking the dough out of the fridge and rolling it out. Zavier had a decent-sized kitchen big enough for all of us, yet they insisted on being so close to me. I pushed Zavier to the side with my hip.

"Snow!" Sebastian squealed, throwing some flour in the air and letting it fall on his father.

"Hey—" Zavier groaned, glaring at me as I chuckled. "Bash, why don't you throw some at your momma?" He smiled mischievously.

Before I could say anything, Sebastian said, "Okay!" and threw some at me.

"Sebastian," I groaned and wiped my face.

"Sorry." He pouted and reached over to help dust me off.

"It's okay—it's your daddy's fault." I smirked and threw an apple at Zavier, who raised a brow at me and grabbed a handful of flour.

"No, no." I laughed and ran away. I kept running from him, Sebastian laughing and giggling at us. I managed to stay away from Zavier, but once we got to the living room, he got a hold of my hand and pulled me to his chest, his other hand moving to my waist. I looked up into his olive eyes, slowly getting lost in them, and he did the same with my eyes, which trailed down to his lips as he licked them and opened his mouth. Then, just as he was about to speak, we heard a knock on the door.

I cleared my throat and stepped away from him. "That's probably Tessa," I said and then quickly put the pie in the oven. Zavier dusted himself off before opening up the door, Sebastian at his leg.

"Zavier—oh my! Is this Sebastian?" Tessa walked in and looked at us, a little surprised, but was then awed by Sebastian.

"Mm-hmm. Who that, Daddy?" the little boy answered and looked up at his father, slightly tugging at his pants.

"Um, this is my best friend, Tess." He picked up Sebastian and brought him closer to Tessa, who held her hand out to him.

"Hey, buddy, I've heard so much about you." She shook his hand, offering him a warm smile I was familiar with.

"Oh...wanna play?" he asked, reaching out to Tessa, and, with her permission, Zavier handed Sebastian over.

"Now?" she asked, a little confused.

"Please?" He gave her his pouty face.

"Hey, Tessa," I finally greeted her once I came closer.

"Uh, can we?" Tessa asked, looking at both Zavier and me.

Before I could answer, Zavier did. "Um, yeah, sure. We need to clean up."

She looked at our outfits again and chuckled. "I'm assuming there's dinner, right?" she asked, setting Sebastian down, who was already dragging her to the living room.

"Yeah, don't worry. This, uh, pie-making went wrong." I

laughed and shook my head. Zavier led me to a bathroom and handed me some towels to clean up the flour, though it would take more than that.

"I'll just bring you some clothes," he said after watching me struggle to clean up for a few minutes.

"It's not necessary," I mumbled, wiping the wet towel against my shirt harder, but it just made matters worse.

"Are you sure?" Zavier raised a brow at me. I bit down on my lip, sighed, and gave in.

"No..."

"I'll get you some." He chuckled and walked out. He came back with a sundress. It was quite chic, but then again, what else could be expected from a Fuentes? Their line of clothes was stunningly beautiful. I put on the dress, folded my previous outfit and put it in a bag, and walked to the dining table to set it for dinner.

"Can I help?" Tessa asked, joining me while Zavier was busy with our son.

"Oh, yeah, sure. Here." I handed her glasses to place on the table.

"I'm glad you let me meet Sebastian. He's a great kid, and Zavier wouldn't stop talking about him," she told me, eyes focused on me for a moment.

"You're welcome...really?" I frowned a little and looked over to see the two boys laughing about something. I guess I never truly viewed it like that, nor did I even imagine he'd love Sebastian as much as I did.

"Yeah, and to think he wasn't too sure about being a father." Tessa laughed softly and helped arrange the plates as I placed the food in the middle.

"Sebastian is quite a charmer."

"A true Fuentes, then." She chuckled, making me laugh

softly. There was no lie there. They were all the same.

"How'd the business thing go with Zavier?" I asked, taking interest in her.

"Oh, I forgot...it's just some architect problem. The person I hired bailed on me," she replied casually, though I could tell it was bothering her. God knows long she had planned this already.

"That sucks. You know, my friend's an architect." I shrugged and sat down.

"Do you mind sending me her work number? Maybe she'd be interested in working with us," she asked, sitting down too.

"Of course." I smiled and sent it immediately. Who knew—this could be good for Nicole. "Boys, dinner's ready."

We all ate our dinner and, of course, dessert. Tessa and Sebastian were both big fans of the pasta. Sebastian wanted more, but I knew if he had any more, there wouldn't be room for some pie. Tessa stayed afterward to help clean up and then went to talk to Zavier about business stuff, I assumed.

"Come here, bud," I called Sebastian over and started to pack up his things. I could tell he wanted to stay a bit longer, but we had to go home. It would be his bedtime soon. He sat down on the couch as I checked to see if I had forgotten anything.

"Hey, I can drop you two off," Zavier said, peeking through the door of his office. I looked at him and bit down on my lip as I thought about it for a moment.

"It's not necessary."

"Are you sure?" he asked, raising his dark brow at me.

"What about my car? It's still here." I sighed. Deep down, I did want to be driven home. I was a little too tired to head back by myself.

"I can send a driver to come to get you," he offered,

shrugging.

"Um, it's late and dark, so yeah, I guess I'd appreciate a ride," I replied. Now that there was a solution to our problem, it didn't seem too bad.

"Okay, give me five minutes so I can finish the conversation with Tess." He grinned then disappeared back into the room.

"Okay, sure," I mumbled. Once the five minutes passed, Tessa said her goodbyes, and Zavier helped me bring Sebastian to the car. The poor guy was knocked out on the couch. Zavier drove us back home, and our conversation was better. I didn't know he was such a great guy. I had written him off as an asshole, but really, when you got to know him, he was very nice.

"I'll help with Bash," he said, unlocking the doors and stepping out. He carefully picked up Sebastian, who was still asleep, and I took my bag and pulled the keys out. When we stopped at my floor, I noticed a guy standing in the hallway. At first, I assumed it was my neighbor's friend since he always had many people over, but as we got closer, the person turned around, and it was Micah.

"Who's that?" Zavier asked, stopping by my door as he did.

"Micah, the little man's father." Micah grinned, looking at Sebastian and then at Zavier and me.

Chapter 9

Amara

I stared at Micah, eyes wide open and mouth slightly hanging open. I couldn't believe it! The audacity of this man to come back around after almost four years! Nicole did mention her sister, Dana, had gotten into a relationship with some rich corporate man. I assumed that meant she dumped Micah, so was that why he was back? Did he see me as his second chance, thinking that I'd actually take him back after he cheated on me with my best friend's sister?

Zavier's whole mood had changed. The friendly energy he was radiating had dimmed completely, and instead, he was now pissed and confused. This other man was now claiming to be Sebastian's father, which was probably making him question me.

"You have some nerve showing up here, Micah," I fumed, glaring at him. How dare he stand in front of me so proudly?

"Come on, Amara, you know you still love me. I do, too—it just took me a bit longer to realize how much you meant to me," Micah concluded, lips turning up into a smile. That look once made me turn to putty, but now, it just raised my blood pressure. Zavier remained silent and just held onto the sleeping boy as he looked back and forth between the two of us, following the conversation slowly.

"No, it took the lady you cheated on me with leaving you for a rich man to come crawling back here," I corrected him and motioned for him to step away from the door, which he did. Once he stepped back, I opened it and let only Zavier into the apartment.

"Amara, give me a second chance. I'll be good and an even better father to our son," he pleaded, wanting to come in too, but the stern look on my face made him back away.

"Fourth. It would be your fourth chance, and I'd be an idiot to give you that. Sebastian is not your child," I corrected him, looking over at Zavier to see him walking to Bash's room.

"Who is he, Amara?" Zavier then asked when he had returned to Micah and me.

"Nobody important," I said coldly and moved to shut the door, but Micah stopped me.

"Her ex, who she was dating when she got pregnant," he said with a smug look. "Around two or three years ago, right?"

"Amara—" Zavier was about to speak when I interrupted him.

"Micah, get the fuck out of here and never show up again. Next time you come around, I will call the cops. I bet they'll love the little farm you and your father have," I threatened, mimicking his proud look from before.

"You're making a mistake. At least let me be in his life." He glared at me.

"You're a stranger to him." I laughed in his face.

"Plea—" He tried to speak, but I shut the door.

"Leave. Now," I shouted at him and could hear his footsteps receding.

"Did you date him when you got pregnant?" Zavier asked not a moment after I turned around.

"Yes and no," I sighed, rubbing my temples.

"Is he my child, Amara? Have you been lying to me?" he asked me, raising his voice slightly. It was shaking a bit like he was panicking, scared of what the truth might be, yet angry at the same time.

"No, dammit. What do you see me as?" I snapped back at him, once again getting sick of his accusations.

"What do you expect from me? To just take your word after Micah shows up?" He raised a brow at me, and I turned around to face him, shaking my head in disappointment.

"Micah cheated on me, and I found out. He begged for another chance, which I gave him, but I told him he'd have to wait before we'd have sex again. When I worked that party, a woman sent me proof of the two of them having sex. After that, you and I happened," I started to explain, taking a step closer to him with each sentence and poking his chest with my index finger. "And don't forget: you're the one who forced yourself into Bash's life. I never wanted you in it," I added, shaking my head in disappointment.

"Don't pretend it hasn't made your life easier," Zavier replied, skipping over many facts and his accusations. "And you can't blame me." He shrugged, once again using the same reasoning for his behavior.

"Seriously? Not even an apology? Get out and stay out of our lives." I raised a brow at him and didn't give him a chance to answer. Instead, I just walked to the front door and opened it wide.

Zavier opened his mouth to say something, then closed it again and stormed out.

***

Zavier

After leaving Amara's apartment, I headed to my car and made my way back home. The first thing I did when I arrived was head to my office. I always had very little trust in people who weren't family, and I always tried being careful with situations that included pregnancies and children. Therefore, I was questioning Amara's integrity.

Pulling a brown envelope out from under a pile of unopened mail, I looked at it. This envelope held the truth. I had submitted a DNA test when I first confronted Amara but had never read it since I had previously taken Amara's words as the truth. I ripped it open and pulled out the paper.

It was a match...I was indeed the father of Sebastian, and I felt relieved. I had grown to love the child a lot. However, I now realized how much I had screwed things up with Amara, but I assumed she'd understand. I'd go over tomorrow with donuts, coffee, and cake pops to make it up to her.

***

I took the day off from work because I needed to meet with Amara. We had to smooth things over. It was all just a misunderstanding, and I assumed she'd get it. But, of course, she had every right to be angry with me right now. When I got to her apartment, I knocked on the door and waited patiently for her to open up, but instead, I saw a very irritated Nicole at the door.

"Oh, good morning. I'm here for Amara," I said, looking over her shoulder and instead finding that the apartment was too quiet for one where a toddler lived.

"Amara's not here right now," she informed me in an

annoyed tone. I assumed this meant Amara told her about what happened last night.

"Nicole, I'm serious. Let me in. I need to apologize to her," I demanded kindly.

"Oh, so now you believe her?" She raised a brow at me, leaning against the doorframe.

"The test confirmed so," I answered quietly.

"You're a funny man, Zavier. I just never thought you'd be such an asshole." Nicole shook her head, and man, it did not feel good being judged in person. With things like tabloids, it was different because they didn't actually know me.

"Nicole, I just want to speak with her and see my son," I requested kindly once again.

She stared at me and then sighed. "They left."

"Where to?" I raised a brow at her, slightly panicking. What if she left for good?

"I won't tell you that," Nicole replied.

"Did she say when she'd be back?"

"She said when she felt like it. Also, I assume that means she quit her job?" Nicole mumbled. I could tell she wasn't lying. If Amara and Sebastian were home, the little boy would've been running around already by now.

"Just tell me where she went, please," I begged, but it was no use. Nicole made up her mind, and I couldn't blame her for looking out for a friend.

"No. Now, good day, Zavier." She shut the door in my face, making me blink, my mouth hanging open before I collected myself.

I stood there staring at the door and took a deep breath. Where did Amara go? Did she run away with my son? She better not have. I had no idea where she might be—not to mention, she didn't have her car either. I got into my car and hesitated about whether to call Tessa or not. I knew she'd scold me, but I could really use her advice, so I rang her up, and to my luck, she was available. As predicted, I got scolded, but she did mention Amara might be at her sister's place. It was worth a try, so I started the ignition and drove there. I saw another man standing there. His eyes were locked on mine as I walked up to the house.

"This is private property," said the man, who I assumed was Amelia's husband.

"I just want to know if Amara's here," I replied, looking around and trying to see if she was here. It was a lot harder now that she didn't travel in her own car.

"You're Zavier?" he asked, blonde brow in an arch.

"Yes, I am," I answered and watched as his expression changed to a disappointed one.

"She doesn't want to see you right now. Leave," he said, walking past me to the front door.

"Just let me apologize to her, man," I begged, letting out a sigh.

"After you humiliated her so many times and questioned her integrity?" he asked, getting angrier with each word that left his lips.

"I made a mistake; let me fix this. She can't keep me from our son," I said, my eyes going to Amara, who just opened the door.

"Amara, I'm handling it," the man said, looking over his shoulder.

"It's okay, Ivan. Let me finish this up quickly," she replied and stepped out, waiting for Ivan to leave first before turning to me. She didn't say a word. She just stood there, eyes glaring into mine with her arms crossed.

"Amara, I'm so sorry—" I began to apologize but was

interrupted.

"What made you come back? I don't want to see you. Don't you get that?" she said rudely, shaking her head in disappointment.

"I came to apologize," I said calmly.

"So you can accuse me of being a liar and gold digger again? No, thank you," Amara replied, coming down the steps to be closer to me and making me back away slowly. I hoped my chest wouldn't get poked this time.

"Ama—"

"Are those donuts, coffee, and cake pops?"

"Yes, I—"

"You can take them with you. We don't want them. Now, leave." She pointed away from where she stood.

"Are you really going to be like this?" I sighed, shoulders slumping. I didn't come here to fight; I just wanted to make things right.

"Like what, huh?" Amara raised a brow at me, never giving me a chance to answer. "Did you expect I'd just accept your apology like that?"

"What can I do to make it up to you?" I truly wanted to fix things. I had to fix things. She didn't deserve to be treated this way.

"Nothing. What do you want?"

"To be in Bash's life. I took the day off. Can I take him to the park?" I replied, letting out a sigh again at how difficult she was being.

"Oh, so now he's your son?" she asked, laughing to herself.

"The DNA test says so." I shrugged.

"Of course..." she muttered to herself.

"Let me take you out. I swear I'll make it up to you," I promised. All I wanted was one more chance, and this time,

I wouldn't mess it up.

"No. What you'll do is take our son to the park, and I'll accompany him because I don't trust you to be with him by yourself," she answered. She seemed to have made up her mind and was unwilling to change it.

"Seriously?"

"You're my son's father and my boss. Nothing more," she snapped, making sure I knew where we stood. This was my fault. I hadn't trusted her, and it ruined things between us.

"Fine. When can we head to the park?" I asked. Taking baby steps might work.

"After he's done with breakfast," she answered.

Chapter 10

Amara

It had been a week since Zavier's so-called apology. Though he seemed sincerely sorry, I still couldn't let us become as close as he wanted. He seemed interested in me romantically, and before the whole accusation, I did consider it. Sebastian would have a somewhat normal childhood with both parents. However, after he questioned my integrity, I realized that things would not work out between us. There was supposed to be trust in a relationship, and he couldn't give me that.

Nicole and Amelia didn't like that I went back to work for him, but in the end, they let it be. I needed to work, and this was by far the "simplest" job I had that allowed me to have so much time with my son. I noticed Zavier buying Sebastian more and more gifts, almost as if he were trying to make up for doubting he was his child.

We were all currently at the park. This wasn't a regular park. Most people here seemed to be famous, and the park was quite private. It had to be for the sake of Sebastian's privacy. The media didn't know about Zavier's son, and we wanted to keep it that way for as long as possible. I didn't want him dragged into the press at such a young age.

I licked my cherry-strawberry ice cream, my eyes mainly focused on Sebastian as he ran around with his father. I looked down at the ice cream. It tasted heavenly, but I was still unsure if it was worth three times the normal amount I'd pay at a regular park. I shrugged to myself and looked up to see Zavier returning to me.

"He has officially abandoned me for another child," he sighed dramatically as he sat down next to me.

"Poor Zavier," I said sarcastically, looking over to see a mother holding onto her large sun hat as she rushed over to make her daughter spit out the sand she had just put in her mouth. Kids. Sebastian did that once and ended up crying. He hated sand for a short period of his life.

"Is the ice cream good?" Zavier then asked, turning to face me, making me inch away from him. I wouldn't be able to focus if we sat so close to each other. I could smell his black amber-scented perfume from here. And it wasn't just his intoxicating scent that made it difficult for me—it was also the way he smiled at me, flashing not only his perfectly pearly teeth but also his dimple on one cheek. The way his dark brow slightly arched and the way his intense green eyes were focused on me made me feel like I was the center of his world, but I was over that. At least, I tried to be. I had to be for the sake of my heart and Sebastian. I knew if anything else were to happen, I wouldn't be able to forgive him, which would lead to destroying Sebastian's bond with his father. I didn't want that to happen.

I snapped back to reality and saw he was still staring at me with the same smile as before. I cleared my throat and looked over at Sebastian to see him chasing after a girl and a little boy. They were playing catch.

"Amara, I truly want to take you out on a date. I was

thinking—" Zavier started to speak even though he heard my sigh, but that wasn't what stopped him. He was stopped by my phone receiving notifications constantly and his phone starting to ring. Odd. I looked over at him, mirroring the frown on his face.

I looked down to see a bunch of texts from Amelia and Nicole. I opened up Nicole's and stared at the top to see an article with a horrendous headline: "One of the country's most eligible bachelors, Zavier Fuentes, has been keeping his adorable son a secret from us, but the real question is: who's the lucky lady?"

I skimmed through the article and saw they used a photo of my son. All my accounts had been switched to private, so where did they even find this? I scrolled down and saw they had made a potential list of who the mother might be.

"Where did they get all of this? We were as careful as possible," I texted Nicole and Amelia back and could hear Zavier was on the phone with someone.

"It's just us, Tessa, Ivan, and Zavier who knew about all of this, and I don't think any of us did it," Nicole responded.

"Micah—he knew too, right? Do you think he did this?" Amelia texted back, making me sigh. Of course, it would be him. I threatened him, so he fired back.

***

Zavier

I looked down at my phone and saw several messages from my family. The latest one was from Tessa saying they knew about Seb. With shaking hands, I answered the phone.

"Mama."

"Zavier Alejandro Fuentes, tell me it's a lie," she demanded.

I could tell she was panicking. Her voice was shaky like it was that one time I forgot to tell her I wouldn't come home straight after school.

"What, Mama?" I asked, letting out a sigh, already knowing where this was headed.

"No eres un idiota. You know what I'm talking about. El niño," she scolded, making me want to laugh. Her voice turned so high-pitched whenever she did that.

"No, it's not a lie. I have a son, Mama," I said truthfully and could feel Amara's gaze on me.

"How did this happen? Are you even sure?" she then began to ask, and I sighed.

"It's a long story, Mama."

"Venido and explain it," she replied. I could tell she was freaking out by the amount of Spanish she was speaking.

"I'm currently at the park with him and his mother," I muttered, looking to see Sebastian going down the slide with his new friends.

"Good. Bring them too," she said coldly, making me end the call and turn to Amara.

"Amara, my mother wants to meet you two," I said, watching as she bit down on her lower lip and got lost in her head for a moment.

"I-I thought I'd decide when that would happen," she mumbled, bringing her palms to cover her face.

"I know, but now the secret's out," I replied softly, understanding her point but also hoping she understood where I was standing right now. "If he becomes overwhelmed, I'll bring you two home immediately," I promised.

***

Amara

I didn't want Zavier's family to meet Sebastian yet. I was scared of their judgments, but now, I couldn't avoid it anymore. They already knew about him. I gave Zavier a nod and then got up. There was still a bit of my ice cream left, but I didn't want it anymore. I felt full and sick at the same time. I went to get Sebastian. Of course, he wasn't happy, but I explained how he had some other family members to meet.

Zavier helped me bring Sebastian to his car seat. When we got into the car ourselves, I noticed he put his phone on silent, probably because it kept getting notifications. Once we started to drive, I finally looked over at him to talk.

"Do you happen to know how this happened?" I asked, though I already had a clue.

"No clue. It's only Tess who knew from my side. You?" He looked over at me for a moment then focused back on the road.

"Micah. He must've done this." I sighed and leaned back into my seat.

"That asshole," I heard him mutter under his breath. "Well, it goes without saying you'll have to move to a secure location," he stated, making me frown.

"What's wrong with my apartment?" Was he questioning my ability to keep Sebastian safe?

"Micah knows the address, and I fear you'll have paparazzi there," he explained, and I nodded and calmed down. He had an excellent point, though I felt guilty about leaving Nicole like that with rent and all.

"I can't just leave Nicole there. I'm responsible for half the rent." I sighed.

"You can keep paying that." He shrugged, almost as if it

were no big deal for me to pay rent for two places. He saw things differently.

"I know you pay me a lot, but I don't want to spend my paycheck on rent alone," I reminded him.

"You'll stay at my penthouse with Bash," he replied in an oblivious tone, almost as if I should've known that already.

"I don't feel comfortable moving in with you, Zavier." I glared at him. Was this yet another move of his to get us together?

"No worries. Just take the penthouse. You'll only be responsible for your groceries. I'll move into my house." He stopped at the red light and looked over at me.

"You have a house?" I asked, surprised.

"Mm-hmm. It's a little further from work and big and empty, which is why I favored the penthouse more, but it's fine," he explained, and I just nodded. I always assumed his house was just the penthouse, and the other real estate he owned were just assets.

"Are you sure?" I asked to make sure I wasn't overstepping or anything.

"Of course. The safety of you and Bash matters to me," he said in a serious tone, green eyes focused on me. I nodded and turned back to look out the window. We kept passing many luscious, deep green trees as we went up the hill, slowly arriving at his parents' mansion. This now made me curious about what happened with his father.

"Feel free not to answer, but I'm wondering if your father is still around," I then asked, making me think back to my dad. He was such a sweet man. Sebastian would've loved him a lot.

"No. He passed away a few years ago," he replied coldly.

"Sorry for your loss," I mumbled.

"What about you? Where are your parents?" Zavier asked,

looking over at me.

"You already know my dad passed away during one of his tours, and my mom, well, she kicked me out when she found out I was pregnant. So, I cut all ties with her, and Amelia did so as well years before me, so I truly have no idea if she's even alive."

"Oh..." he muttered, probably trying to wrap his head around it all. After the conversation ended, it remained like that for the rest of the ride.

When we arrived, I picked up Sebastian, held him at my hip, and followed Zavier inside. The butler by the door took Zavier's coat and my scarf. By now, Sebastian was already awake and looking around at the unfamiliar scene. I assured him things were okay. I heard footsteps coming down and saw it was Charlotte and Arlo. Tessa was in front of us and greeted Sebastian, who laughed and waved at her.

"Is this him?" Arlo asked, looking at Sebastian. He hid in my chest as he looked at the two. I gave him a nod and rubbed his back to assure him he was safe.

"Yes. Meet my son, Sebastian Reid," I said and kissed his forehead.

"He's adorable," Charlotte said, awed, taking his little hand in hers and kissing it.

"Thank you." Sebastian grinned and finally reached out to her.

"How old is he?" Arlo asked, his attention split between my son and me.

"He'll be three in a few months," I answered and turned to Sebastian, who was distracted by the teddy in Zavier's other hand.

"So, uh, are you his chef, or was that just a lie?" he then asked, frowning.

"No, I'm still his chef," I replied awkwardly. The explanation for this was just as awkward and confusing.

"It's a long story," Zavier butted in and took Sebastian from Charlotte, making her pout.

"The short version will do for us." Charlotte shrugged.

"We met three years ago and spent a night together, and three years later, she sees a job opportunity and takes it. We meet again, and I find out about Seb, and here we are," he told them while playing with Sebastian, handing him his stuffy.

"So, you never knew about him?" Arlo raised a brow at him.

"He didn't. He found out about Sebastian himself," I replied, and the two nodded.

"What a coincidence you two crossed paths again," Tiffany said as she came down the stairs with Carolyn.

"Couldn't be much of a coincidence," the other twin sister said, looking at me from top to bottom. I was once again getting judged by these women.

"She must've set this up," Tiffany concluded. All of us just stared at the two. I could tell by Tessa's behavior that she, too, didn't like their tones. The others were harder to read, probably because they were all family.

"How much money has she demanded already?" Carolyn asked, glaring at me, which made me roll my eyes. I had to keep in mind I didn't want to act out in front of Sebastian. That wouldn't be me.

"Mother—" Zavier was about to say, but the two weren't done villainizing me yet.

"Was she the one who leaked it to the press?" his sister asked, finally at the bottom of the stairs and standing right in front of us.

"Is that thing even yours, Zavier?" Tiffany glared at my

son, making Sebastian hide in his father's chest.

I had enough of their disrespect and was about to open my mouth when Zavier beat me to the punch. "I will not have you disrespect them like that." He looked at them both sternly. That look carried so much power. You could tell he wasn't playing around.

"I'll go outside with him." Tessa reached over for Sebastian. She knew how this conversation could go and wanted to make sure the little boy wouldn't have to deal with it. "Let's go see some trees, Bash."

"Zavier—" Charlotte began to say, but her brother shut her up.

"No. You listen to me. If you plan on staying in my life, I expect you to treat them both with respect. Sebastian is my son," he said as he looked at them all. I felt bad for having put his family in this situation. I knew it was not my fault, but perhaps things could've been handled differently. "And I will not have you two be the reason I can't be in his life." He made it clear to his mother and sister.

"How is any of this a coincidence?" Carolyn asked calmly.

"When I applied for the job, his name wasn't on the job listing. In fact, even after I found out who he was, I never asked him for a cent. The only money he gives me is what he owes me for being his chef," I explained simply. There was nothing I could do about that; it was almost as if fate brought him into his son's life.

"So what? He's now supposed to take care of your son?" Carolyn raised her brow at me, arms crossed with the same bratty look as before. I could tell Carolyn and Charlotte apart easily now. One was a total bitch, and the other was a sweetheart.

"Their son, Carolyn. And yes, I'm quite curious about

that. I never pictured you being a dad before all of us," Arlo corrected.

"Sebastian's my son and a wonderful one at that. I love him and do plan on being in his life. We were still figuring out how I could be in his life a bit more while avoiding the media, but I suppose that won't be necessary anymore," Zavier said. God, I loved the way he spoke about our son. It assured me he wasn't just a burden to him.

"My bad for assuming the worst of you. I guess I always try to protect my children too much," Tiffany mumbled. "I'd love to meet Sebastian."

"I hate to ruin this nice moment, but what will be done about Mr. Fischer and the deal you two had?" Arlo asked awkwardly.

Chapter 11

Amara

"Uh, who's Mr. Fischer?" I asked, looking at the people in the room. They all seemed to really care about this Mr. Fischer guy. I wasn't exactly from their world, so I didn't know all the businesspeople they dealt with and such.

"How does she not know these things?" Carolyn said, letting out a stressed sigh, her shoulders dropping down as she did so.

"Maybe because her interests are different from yours," Charlotte replied, frowning as she looked at her twin sister, who then rolled her eyes at her.

"Mr. Fischer is exactly what the company needs. We can hopefully strike a deal with him and do other better things," Arlo then told me, leading the way to the couch for us all to sit down. I could tell this would be an interesting conversation.

"And how does this involve me?" I asked, taking a seat on the cream-colored couch. It was much more comfortable than it looked.

"Oh, dear. How do we explain this without upsetting you..." Charlotte mumbled, looking over at me. She bit down on her lip as she got lost in her trail of thoughts. These people were acting like I was in a hospital and waiting to see whether a loved one would survive.

"Mr. Fischer is a family guy. I'm talking about a happy family man. He's extremely rich, and his collaborations are all successful. However, he's very picky about who he works with," Zavier blurted out, luckily killing the awkward silence.

"The last time there was a solid collaboration happening, it was with Whitly's; however, things fell through the moment two ladies came forth who were pregnant with Whitly's children. He had abandoned one and was still with the other," Arlo explained, and I slowly nodded in response. I was still a little confused as to why this would involve me.

"And this involves me how, exactly?" I asked, raising a brow at Zavier, wanting an answer from him.

"He doesn't do business with 'broken' families," Carolyn replied, making me look in her direction.

"And with the news release, he'll probably think I abandoned you or something like that," Zavier said. I nodded, already understanding where this would be heading. Mr. Fischer would probably wonder why Sebastian hadn't been heard of before.

"Why does he care so much?" I asked curiously.

"His father was a cheater and, at some point, left him, his mother, and siblings with nothing. He built everything up from the very bottom," Tiffany explained. I could tell everything she felt towards me was eating her from the inside. She was still speaking with such spite.

"Amara, I know you won't like this, but could you lie for me?" Zavier asked quietly, giving me a sincere look.

"Excuse me? Why?" I frowned. There was no way I'd do this for them.

"This deal would allow us to give our employees a raise,

open several new stores, and accomplish several more good things for the company," Charlotte explained, surprisingly okay with this.

"So, I have to lie because you billionaires aren't happy with the money you have?" I shook my head, finding it unbelievable.

"Amara, this isn't just about me." Zavier sighed and got up.

"One little lie is all we're asking for. We'll give you whatever you want," Tiffany said, trying to look less annoyed with me as she spoke.

"What do you want me to lie about?"

"The situation between us. If he sees things are actually good, he won't pull out of the deal," Zavier said, resting his hands on his hips. I hesitated. The answer would obviously be no. However, before I could tell him that, he spoke.

"Can we go talk in private?" he asked, and I sighed and nodded, getting up to follow him. He opened the big dark oak door to one of the offices. He closed the door behind me and walked to the desk, pointing to the comfortable seat in front of it as he sat on the end of the desk.

"You really want this, don't you?" I raised a brow at him. Now that we were all alone, I felt I could better ask him things. His family made things a little...intense.

"If it were just about me, I wouldn't be trying this hard. But this is mostly for my family's advantage." Zavier leaned back a little, resting his weight on the palms of his hands as he looked down at me.

"How so?" I frowned, leaning back into my chair, wanting to get comfortable too.

I could tell he was hesitant to tell his story at first, but he gave in.

"Years ago, I got kicked out of the company's board by my father after we had a disagreement. That's when I started my own company using the real estate my grandmother left me," Zavier started to explain.

"So, the shoe company—you built it up yourself?" I asked, surprised. I always thought he was given everything by his parents and worked it up further.

"Very much so, yes. All I used from my father were his contacts, you could say." Zavier looked at the blank notepad on the desk and fidgeted with it.

"I see...so why do you want to do so much for the company you have no shares in?" I raised a brow at him. I wasn't the smartest person, but I knew there surely must be something in it for him.

"After my father passed away, we merged under my mother's request, and she changed the shares to be equally split between her and her kids." He shrugged.

"I see," I hummed, looking around the room. There were a ton of bookshelves and plants but not a single framed photo or painting. It was a dull office to me.

"Amara, the real reason I want this is so he can consider starting a business with just me in the future." Zavier took my hand in his and looked into my eyes as he spoke. "I know it's a lot of me to ask you to lie, but I think I have a deal you won't be able to reject."

"Zavier—" I pulled away and let out a sigh. I didn't like being bought like that.

"Just listen. The profit made on my side from this deal I'll put into a bank account for Sebastian. Every single penny earned," he offered, already writing down the offer on the notepad.

I had to admit; he convinced me he truly wasn't in for it for his own profit. It all seemed like he wanted that private deal. The offer seemed promising and had me intrigued, though I wasn't sure I wanted to be bought like that. "What would be the condition?"

"I'm thinking we twist the truth with a little lie. We've been together since the night we had sex, and you then found out you were pregnant. Neither of us wanted our life to be in the media, so we kept it all a secret, along with our child." He got up and paced around the room as he spoke, my eyes following him until he stopped to face me.

"Won't he wonder why we're not 'together together'?" I wondered, wanting to be clear about the rules.

"Hmm, we're taking things slow. We don't want to rush into marriage?" Zavier asked, raising a brow, just as unsure as I was.

"Um, okay. What about our living situation?" I then asked, watching as he froze for a moment and squinted his eyes, something he often did when he got lost in thought.

"We could move to my house where the dinner for Mr. and Mrs. Fischer will be hosted," was the solution he came up with, making me laugh before I realized he was being serious.

"How long do I have to think about this?" I asked, pressing my lips together. If I did this, it would be for my boy.

"Less than a day? He'll most likely call the moment he sees the news," Zavier said, letting out a sigh too as he walked to the desk again.

"Oh—" I frowned and got cut off by his phone ringing. Zavier looked down at the contact's name then back up at me before answering.

"Good evening, Mr. Fischer. I mean, not really, but I hope you're doing better than I am," he answered, letting out a nervous chuckle. "I knew you'd see it. The situation between the mother and I?" he mumbled, trailing off, and Zavier looked over at me, seeking an answer to give the man.

I could tell how badly he wanted this, and I, too, wanted this. Sebastian's college funds would probably be taken care of if I accepted his deal. I gave Zavier a nod, letting him know I was going along with his plan. He then put the phone on speaker so that I could hear.

"The situation between the mother and me? Why don't you ask her yourself?" Zavier said confidently, looking over at me.

"Good evening, Mr. Fischer," I greeted a little nervously.

"Oh—hello there, Miss?" he replied, surprised.

"You can call me Amara, please," I replied, trying to be as friendly as possible.

"Well, it's nice to meet you, Amara," he replied in a kind tone.

"Likewise, sir," I mumbled.

"How are things between you and Zavier? How is your child? We never heard anything about the two of you," he asked, reminding me of the nosy people who would always keep asking private questions with no shame.

"Sebastian is happy. Zavier and I were hoping to keep this hidden for as long as possible, but that didn't last long," I answered, looking up at Zavier, who just gave me a slight nod and smile.

"I'm sorry to hear the media caught up to you," Mr. Fischer said, making me sigh.

"We are too."

"Listen, that dinner we were talking about—I'll have my assistant send you a list of possible nights I'm free. I'm sure we'd like to get to know each other better before going into business," Mr. Fischer offered, and Zavier's face lit up immediately.

"Of course, Mr. Fischer. We shall stay in contact, then," he replied with a grin and ended the call.

Chapter 12

Amara

"That went good?" I asked, a little unsure as I looked up at Zavier and straight into his beautiful jade eyes. I watched as his lips curled into a smile as he looked at me.

"Yes, thank you so much," he said sincerely, resting his hand on my shoulder and rubbing it. I got lost in his eyes for a moment, my thoughts wandering before I came back to my senses, remembering I was still a little angry at him.

"I'm doing this for Sebastian's future. You better not screw me over," I told him after clearing my throat and looking away from him.

"I'm a man of my word, Amara," he said, getting up and tucking his phone in his pocket. "Shall we go tell the others? They should be aware, so they can keep up with their part," Zavier then asked, already walking to the door.

"Mm-hmm," I hummed and followed him out the door to see his family still sitting in the living room, waiting for us to see what the final decision would be.

"We decided to come up with a story to let him believe things are going good between us," Zavier told them, pointing to one of the seats for me to sit on and sitting down next to me.

"And she's okay with that?" his mother asked, pointing to me as if she couldn't just ask me herself.

"We came to an agreement," I answered for Zavier, pulling one of the pillows onto my lap.

"Well, what's the 'truth,' then?" Arlo asked, raising a brow at this as he leaned back into his seat. His body was less tense than before. Everybody was less tense. They were all relieved that their contract wouldn't be lost.

"We met, and she got pregnant early, but we didn't want the media involved, so we hid it until now when things got exposed to the media," Zavier explained, looking at me and speaking slowly to make sure I could correct him whenever I didn't like what he said.

"That's it? What if he asks why you're living separately?" Carolyn asked, taking much more interest in this than her mother. I could tell she didn't like this but wanted the deal.

"We'll just say we recently moved in together for safety reasons. In the past, we just met up a lot in private, and as for us not being married or engaged, we figured it would be too early to jump into things." Zavier leaned a little closer to me, his strong-smelling cologne filling my nose and making me sigh.

"Seems like you have it all figured out then." Charlotte looked at us as we just nodded.

Zavier said, "We hope so. I got the dinner invite."

"Really? Oh my," Tiffany asked loudly, mouth hanging open as she was shocked by this. Just a week ago, everything was pending, and now, dinner was spoken of.

"What deal did you have to cut with her?" she then asked, narrowing her eyes a little at me. Zavier looked over at me, seeking permission first, but I didn't react at all. I didn't know if I wanted them to know about that.

"That's none of your business. However, if she finds she wants to tell you, that's totally up to her," Zavier said, looking at his family.

"Wow," Carolyn scoffed and shook her head in disappointment.

"One more thing," Zavier said, clearing his throat and standing up to walk closer to his family. "I expect you two to treat Amara and our son with respect. I expect you to be on your best behavior, understood?"

"Yes..." Carolyn mumbled softly as he looked at her and their mother. I felt guilty to have put them in such a situation, but I did deserve respect. I was nothing but kind towards them.

"When will you move in together?" Arlo then asked, looking over at the window where Tessa could be seen running after Sebastian.

"Hopefully today," Zavier said while I just nodded.

"We'll have to talk to Nicole and my sister."

"Of course," Zavier muttered.

"Can we come to visit tomorrow?" Charlotte then asked.

Zavier answered by saying, "Yes. For now, we'll be going."

I said my goodbyes to them and got up, following Zavier outside to take Sebastian. I picked him up and cuddled him close to me. I held him by my hip as I walked to the car while Zavier chatted with Tessa.

Once Zavier was done talking to Tessa, he joined Sebastian and me in the car. While Zavier drove, Sebastian looked around before starting to ask what most of the trees were. Zavier managed to tell him the names of most of them.

"Should we stop for lunch or anything?" he asked me, looking at Sebastian through the rearview mirror.

"Yeah, sure," I replied, knowing I wouldn't have time to

make us lunch, and Sebastian must be hungry right now.

"What should we get?" he asked, checking the streets before driving again.

"Anywhere with fries and dino-shaped nuggets," I shrugged, picking Sebastian's favorite. It was still sinking in—what we planned on faking...

"Okay," he mumbled and put in a different address in the GPS.

"I texted Amelia and Ivan. They will wait at my apartment to discuss everything," I informed him as I tucked away my phone for now.

"Perfect. I'll pick up some boxes and tape," he replied and slowed down as we got to a parking lot.

"If you don't mind me asking—what did you and Tessa talk about?" I asked curiously. They always talked a lot in private. She did say they were childhood best friends, but I felt I had the right to know if it were something more.

"She said we'd need to take some photos tomorrow, so the story looks more real," Zavier answered, turning off the engine and looking over at Sebastian to see him asleep again.

"Oh, okay. But I had long hair back then." I looked over at our son.

"That's fine. We'll get you some hair extensions." He smiled and tapped my shoulder.

"We're really going all out, huh?" I chuckled, imagining myself with such long hair again.

"Pretty much. We'll only need a few photos other than a few family photos as well to decorate the house," he answered, opening the door and looking at me as he finished the conversation. Then, he went in and bought us lunch.

***

When he came back with our lunch, I joined Sebastian in the back to feed him while Zavier drove to the apartment. When we got there, Nicole, Ivan, and Amelia were all waiting for us on the couch, so we started explaining everything to them.

"What about rent? It's a little too much for one person," Nicole said, scratching the back of her head as she looked at me, making me feel guilty. We got a bigger place because of me since I needed more space for my son.

"You won't have to worry about that. I'll pay for it," Zavier told her, making her let out a relieved sigh.

"How long will she have to put up with your lies?" Ivan asked bluntly as he held the toy that Sebastian handed him.

"Even after I get the deal, we'll still have to go on a little longer," Zavier answered, picking his words carefully with Ivan.

"We can gradually break up," I told them and looked down at Sebastian as he took the car from my hand and gave it to Nicole.

"Zavier, how do we know you won't hurt her?" Amelia finally spoke up. I knew this bothered her a lot, but it had to be done.

"Listen, I know I made mistakes in the past, but I will never doubt her again," Zavier said in an honest tone, almost fooling me completely, but I knew I had to be a lot more careful with him.

"What about dating? I mean, it will take a while before the deal gets finalized. What if you find a lady?" Nicole asked, not giving him a chance to answer before asking him another question. "Will you abandon her then?"

"No, of course not. During the deal, I shall remain single or, to the public's eye, Amara's boyfriend." Zavier was quick to answer, not liking Nicole's question by the tone he used, almost as if he were disgusted by her words.

"And Amara, then?" Amelia looked over at me.

"I was hoping she'd be okay with waiting till the deal was over before seeing anyone romantically," Zavier mumbled and also looked at me.

I nodded and said, "That would make sense." The last thing I'd need was to be exposed to the media as a cheater or something.

"Let's get to packing, then," Nicole sighed and looked around.

"Oh, for Sebastian, just grab his favorites. I had his room decorated, and he now has everything a child needs at my—our house," Zavier informed me. He was making plans without telling me, but then again, he didn't get much time to tell me all of these things. "The rest of the things, I will send someone to get and put in the penthouse," he then added, making me nod.

"Oh, okay."

"Wait, so by the end of this, she will own the penthouse?" Amelia asked, getting up and taking one of the boxes in her hands.

"Mm-hmm. As a little bonus, yeah." He shrugged as he handed her the tape too. His words left me a little shocked. I thought the penthouse idea was over, but by the looks of it, I'd be getting it in the end.

"You rich people have a different idea of little," Nicole mumbled under her breath, making me nudge her.

* * *

After we packed our things, we went to "our" home. The first thing Zavier did was lead Sebastian to his new room.

The little boy fell in love with his room. Zavier had painted the walls white, and one wall was a soft hue of red. The bed was car-shaped. The whole theme was based on cars—vintage ones, to be exact. Sebastian ran around the room out of happiness and pointed out everything that excited him, which was the whole room. At some point, I managed to get him down for a nap, and Zavier and I quietly stepped out of the room. I then looked around and noticed the decor inside matched a modern bungalow house. It was decorated with the same modern touch the penthouse had. There was a lot more artwork around, but I assumed a few would be replaced by our photos to add a homey touch to it.

"I'll show you to your room. It's across from mine." Sebastian rested his hand on the small of my back as he led me to where the room was. The feeling of his hand on me sent shivers down my spine.

"Okay," I said and looked around the room. It was kept simple with warm earth tones. It needed a bit of green, maybe some fake succulents, and then it would be perfect and just to my liking.

"If you don't like this room, there's also another one," he said, watching me for my reaction.

"Oh, no, this is perfectly fine." I smiled and walked over to the curtains to pull them closed just a bit.

"Oh, okay. Do you need help unpacking?" he asked as he looked over at the pile of boxes I had.

"Um, no, I'll do it myself," I mumbled, not knowing which boxes my clothes were in, and I did not want him to go through those, so it was best if I did it myself.

"For dinner, should I order something?" he asked, leaning against the doorway as he looked at me. I bit down on my lip as I thought of what he asked. We already had junk food for today, so I figured I could cook us something.

"Do you have fresh ingredients?" I asked.

"A few things, yeah," Zavier answered, frowning for a moment.

"I'll cook us something," I replied, sitting down by the edge of the bed and watched as he nodded.

"Okay, I'll be in the office downstairs, then." Things were still slightly awkward between us.

I watched as he left the room and closed the door behind him. I went through the boxes and searched for the ones containing my clothes. I opened the closet and saw it had a few clothes inside, all of which happened to be my size. I frowned a little and made a mental note to ask about that later. Meanwhile, I unloaded my stuff in there. Once I finished with my clothes, I did the rest of my things, which weren't that much—just my room decor. I liked to keep things a little simple. After I placed the photo of Sebastian and me on the desk, I sat down on an undeniably comfortable chair.

After resting for a few minutes, I finally headed down and went straight to the kitchen to start dinner. I wanted to finish it before Sebastian got up. I cut up the vegetables and seasoned the chicken. While that was marinating, I went ahead and put the rice on to cook, walked to where I assumed Zavier's office was, and knocked on the door.

"Yes?" he said, and I stepped in, standing by the doorway as I looked at him.

"Hey, I have a question," I said and watched as he shut his laptop and gave me all of his attention.

"Go ahead." Zavier got up, walked to the front of the desk, and sat down on the end.

"I found some clothes in the closet. Should they stay there or…?" I asked and watched as he tilted his head a little.

"Oh, those are yours. Are they not the right size?" he asked with a frown.

"They are my size. I just didn't know they were mine," I replied with a slight smile.

"Yeah, I had some put in for when I'd invite you and Sebastian to the house, which was apparently sooner rather than later," he answered and took out his notepad and pen.

"Oh, okay." I nodded and looked around, trying to avoid eye contact.

"Those are from Fuentes. You wore a dress once. Do you have any feedback on it?" he asked, making me frown a little. Why did he want my feedback? I thought back to the dress, which was now hung in my closet.

"The dress was quite comfortable, and the design was nice. The ones in the closet look incredible too. I just don't know if I, an average person, would be able to afford those," I told him truthfully. I did love their clothes. They offered comfort and were pretty. However, I wouldn't normally be able to afford one.

"We were thinking of starting another line that's a little cheaper, so we have clothes for everyone," Zavier told me as he wrote something down in his notepad.

"That would be a good idea," I replied, giving a timid smile. I knew Nicole would love that, and I would as well. We went to their online shop once and found really nice outfits, though the price was a little more than we could afford. "Oh, I have to go now. I'm cooking." I remembered the chicken and left the room.

I started making kimchi fried rice on one side and some crispy chicken on the other side. I pulled out plates and put the rice on them, along with the chicken. The fried rice looked delicious. I finished by frying the eggs that would top the rice and finally called the two boys down for dinner.

It felt so normal being in a house with just the three of us and eating at the dining table together. I didn't often get to do this with my family growing up. It was only when Dad was in town. Sebastian was truly happy and most definitely loved his food, as did his father.

After dinner, Zavier helped clean up and then went to play a bit outside with our son. After an hour, I called them both in. I had to get Sebastian ready for bed and then go to bed myself too.

Chapter 13

Amara

I could hear the birds chirping, and a thin streak of sunlight peeped through the curtains and shone on my face, sharing its warmth with me. I let out a loud sigh and went to check the time. I had to get up and make breakfast for the two boys. I got out of bed and walked to the bathroom to wash my face, brush my teeth, and put my hair up in a bun.

Once I was half-ready for the day, I checked on Sebastian and saw he was already up. He was sitting on the ground and playing with a few of his car toys.

"Good morning, baby," I said sweetly, walking towards him and bending down to his level.

"Morning, Momma." He smiled at me, handing me one of his trucks. He always did that. I suspected that was his toddler love language.

"How was your sleep?" I asked, pulling him into my lap and placing my head on top of his.

"Good," he answered, rolling the wheels of the green car toy on the rug then looking up at me.

"Are you hungry?" I asked, brushing his dark hair out of his eyes.

"Yeah!" he exclaimed and threw his little hands in the air.

"Let's go down, then." I tickled his stomach and got up. I picked him up and carried him downstairs, all while he used me as his racetrack for his red car toy. When we got downstairs, I set him down and turned on some cartoons on the TV before going to the kitchen to make us all breakfast.

At some point, I heard Zavier coming down the stairs. I quickly poured his smoothie into a glass cup, added a metal straw for him, and placed it on the counter. I still followed his schedule from when I was just his personal chef. I liked it better that way because I knew exactly what he wanted for his meals.

"Good morning, Bash," I heard Zavier say to our son.

"Morning, Daddy," Sebastian replied.

"What are you watching?" he asked.

"Cartoons!" he answered with a giggle. Clearly, someone woke up on the right side of the bed.

"Oh, wow. Are they good?" I heard Zavier ask him.

Sebastian answered, "Yeah!"

"Okay, I'll join you in a moment, okay?" Zavier ruffled Sebastian's hair and walked off. I heard the footsteps coming my way.

"Okay," Sebastian mumbled softly.

"Hey, good morning," Zavier said as he stepped into the kitchen, and I turned around to look at him.

"Morn—oh, hey." I cleared my throat, my eyes focused on his bare torso as I tried to form a proper sentence but couldn't. He wasn't the most muscular man, but he also didn't lack muscle at all. He had just the right amount that fit his frame.

"Shoot, I'm sorry. Should I put on a shirt? Usually, I don't wear one until I leave, and I figured Bash would want to run around. I'll go put one on," Zavier rambled as he looked down at himself, then back up at me, and stood there a little awkwardly.

"No, no. It's fine; it's your house, after all. I was just surprised," I muttered and turned around to focus on the scrambled eggs that were making a sizzling sound.

"Thank you. Is breakfast ready?" Zavier asked, picking up his smoothie.

"Yes, could you get him?" I asked, looking over my shoulder and seeing him give me a nod as he sipped the smoothie and walked off.

I pulled out three plates, placed them on the table where we would sit, and then returned with the scrambled eggs, toast, chicken bacon, and a bowl of cut-up fruit. Zavier helped Sebastian sit on his chair and then got the apple juice, water, and cups for us to drink out of.

"Will you be leaving for work?" I asked, picking up a piece of the bacon and bringing it to my lips.

"Yes, I have a meeting to attend," Zavier answered, taking another sip of his smoothie.

"Okay." I nodded.

"What do you have planned?" he asked me. I thought for a moment before finally answering him.

"I'm not sure yet. I might play outside with Sebastian a little," I answered and looked over at the glass door that led to the backyard. We never had a backyard before, so this would be fun. At Amelia's, there was a backyard, but it was pretty tiny.

"When I come home for lunch, I think we'll be doing the photoshoot. Are you okay with that?" Zavier continued to talk, setting down the fork as he waited for my answer.

"Okay, sure." I just shrugged, knowing we had to do it to make matters much more believable.

"Alright." He hummed and continued finishing off what was left of his breakfast. "Maybe we can also go out at some point?" he added slowly, looking at me.

"As a family, right?" I asked. There was no way I'd go out on a date with him. I knew that in the public eye, we'd have to fake things, but that was where it ended. The last time we got close, he accused me of many bad things, and it really hurt me.

"I was thinking the—or yes, as a family." He sighed.

We continued to have breakfast together. When we finished up, Zavier went upstairs to continue getting ready for work while I cleaned up. By the time he came downstairs again, I had finished up, so I walked him to the door with Sebastian, who was pouting as he waved at his father. We watched as he drove away then got back inside. I got Sebastian ready for the day and then got ready myself with a short shower. I didn't like leaving Sebastian alone for too long.

I ended up doing a bit of writing. Finally, my muse came back, and Sebastian was playing in my room while I wrote. At some point, we went outside and ran around a little. There was a single swing set that I placed him on and gently pushed him. He was the happiest he could be for now.

When lunch hour came closer, I put Sebastian down for a nap and started making lunch, deciding to make extra as Zavier had mentioned that Tessa would come and help with the photos. His family also asked to come over today. They hadn't said anything yet, but I assumed they'd come, and I would like to be prepared if they did.

Just as I sat down to take a breather, I heard the gate rolling open. I went to look and saw many cars coming in. Zavier's family did come after all. I watched as they all stepped out of their cars, and I quickly opened the front door for them.

"Hey, Mara," Tessa greeted me as she walked up the three

steps to the door.

"Tessa, hey. How are you?" I smiled, opening the door wider for her.

"I'm really good. You?" she asked, stepping in and leaving her shoes by the door, already knowing the rules that the Fuentes family had set.

"I'm doing fine," I answered and saw Charlotte coming in too.

"Hello, Amara. Where's Sebastian?" she asked excitedly and looked around for the little guy.

"Hey, Charlotte. Oh, he's taking a nap, which he should wake up from any minute now," I said and checked the time on the clock hanging on the wall.

"Can I go get him?" Tessa asked, looking up the stairs.

"Of course. First door to your left," I told her.

"Okay."

I watched as Tessa and Charlotte rushed upstairs to get Sebastian. Then, I turned to the others and greeted them too as they walked into the house.

"Where's Tessa?" Zavier frowned and looked around for her.

"She went to get Bash," I answered, stepping aside so he could come in.

"Ugh, come on. Help me get the things from her car." Zavier dragged Arlo back outside.

"Why do I have to go?" Arlo whined and looked at me with puppy eyes as if I could help him.

"Because Carolyn will complain that her nails may break." Zavier shrugged.

"I'm right here!" Carolyn reminded them, and they just shrugged.

"And I'm correct, aren't I?" Zavier looked over at her.

She opened her mouth, wanting to deny it, but she couldn't and just muttered, "Yeah."

"Come on in, Mrs. Fuentes," I said, looking over at her. That woman still scared me a little. "How have you been?" I decided to ask and be polite.

"I've been better," she mumbled, walking to the living room and sitting down on the one-seat couch.

"Okay…" I said to myself and shook my head.

I heard giggles coming from the stairs and looked over to see Charlotte, Tessa, and Sebastian making their way down together. The little boy was truly loved by the two. He had many aunties who adored him, and it made me proud to know that he was loved by others too. Zavier and Arlo walked in with three suitcases. I wondered what was in them.

"Be careful with those. My camera is in there," Tessa warned Arlo, who just nodded and carefully put down the bag. For billionaires—well, Zavier was the billionaire, and the others were multi-millionaires—it still surprised me how much they did by themselves.

"You'll be taking the pictures?" I asked Tessa. I thought they'd hire a photographer, but perhaps for privacy reasons, this was the best option.

"Yes, I will! I think we should do your and Zav's first," she answered, letting go of Sebastian.

"Okay." I looked over at Zav, who stared at me.

"Arlo, can you help with the set-up?" Tessa asked, walking to him.

"Um, sure. Caro, come help out." He sighed and called his little sister over.

"We'll do three shots. A casual summer vibe one, a fancy family dinner one, and a semi-formal one," Tessa informed us, staring at the notes she made on her phone. Professional Tessa terrified me a little. "Zavier, your clothes. I'll help Amara. Also, for the family picture, we'll add Sebastian in the last one, and then we'll take another with just Sebastian and Zavier."

"Um, okay." Zavier frowned a little, probably doing his best to remember it all.

"Come on, then." Tessa linked her arm with mine, taking one of the suitcases in the other and leading the way to a room downstairs.

"Let's get you all dolled up." She sat me down on one of the chairs and turned to her suitcase, already opening it up to let a pile of clothes flow out.

"What's the first outfit?" I asked, looking at the many outfits she had.

"I was thinking you could wear this," Tessa suggested. She held up a red floral maxi dress. It was one of those wrap dresses that tied at the waist and looked exceptionally stunning.

"Do you like it? Or maybe something else?" she asked, a little unsure as she looked at me.

"No, this is perfect!" I jumped up from the seat and walked over to take the dress.

"Okay, we'll do your hair longer. We can pretend this is when you two found out about your pregnancy," Tessa said, handing me the dress and pulling out a pair of brown sandals.

"Okay, should I put this on first?" I raised a brow at her and looked around to see where I could change.

"Yes, go ahead. I'll get the makeup and such ready," she said and looked around for something in the suitcase.

I went behind the blinds to change out of my current outfit and put on the dress. It was yet another Fuentes dress, so it went without saying that it was comfortable. Once I was done, I walked out to face Tessa.

"You look stunning. Wow." Tessa smiled, looking at me

from top to bottom with a proud look on her face.

"Thank you." I blushed a little and walked to the seat she patted for me to sit on.

"You know, you can always come model for us." She adjusted the mirror in front of me and picked up a few bottles of foundation.

"Now you're just lying," I laughed, watching as she mixed her foundation on the back of her hand.

"I'm serious." She narrowed her eyes at me for a moment and lifted a purple sponge.

I just smiled at her and remained still as she began applying my makeup, luckily keeping it natural. She added in the hair extensions and curled them to the front. Once I was ready, I stepped outside, where I saw Arlo and Carolyn setting up everything for the photoshoot. I looked over and saw Zavier. He was dressed in form-fitting black jeans that were ripped and paired with a green dress shirt that brought out his eyes. His hair was styled a little differently. It was exactly how it was years ago when we first met.

"Amara, you look so lovely," Zavier said, eyes a little wide as he kept staring at me from head to toe, making me a little nervous as I shifted my weight from one leg to the other.

"Thank you. You don't look too bad yourself." I smiled, trying to look away so he wouldn't see me blush.

"Okay, come on, people." Tessa clapped her hands, making us all jerk a little.

Zavier and I walked to where Tessa pointed. For this photo, Zavier stood behind me and rested a hand on my shoulder while we looked into the camera with a slight smile on our faces.

"Guys, this isn't good. You look like you just met each other. Zavier, try wrapping your arms around her and holding her to your chest," Tessa whined and pointed out to us how we should stand and where.

"Oh, okay," Zavier mumbled awkwardly, looking at me. I gave him a nod, and Zavier did as he was told. I felt his large arms wrap around my waist, pulling me into his chest. All I could feel was his muscles underneath me. I remained a little stiff, trying not to breathe in his intoxicating smell.

"Amara, can you look up at him with adoring eyes? Rest your hands over his and stop holding your breath, please." Tessa sighed.

I mumbled a soft "sorry" and did as she told. I looked up at Zavier, letting out a loving sigh, and tried to look at him like he was the last piece of cake I desperately wanted. Tessa took a few more shots while we were in this outfit and then sent us to go change.

***

Zavier

I went back to my room and searched for the perfect suit to wear. Perhaps this navy one would suffice? I put it on and looked at myself. It was a perfect fit. I neatly styled my hair to the back to match the occasion and swapped my watch for another one. I walked to the backyard, knowing I shouldn't waste time. The last thing I needed was Tessa flipping out on me.

I saw Amara walking towards me, dressed in a rosewood silk dress. It had the thinnest straps and hung quite low, exposing her skin. Her hair was up in a bun, and her makeup was still kept natural, though her lipstick was much brighter. Her diamond earrings matched the necklace she wore.

For this photo, we were both facing each other, my hands

wrapped around her waist while hers were over my shoulders as she looked at me.

"This dress was made for you," I whispered in her ear, making her smile a little, and right at that moment, Tessa took several photos.

"Okay, give each other the most romantic look you can muster," Tessa then ordered. I looked down at Amara and cupped her chin, looking into her brown eyes and smiling a little. Then, I leaned in a bit closer. I could feel her gaze on my lips, and mine was also on hers.

"Good! Now go change for the last one!" Tessa shouted to us, making us take a step back.

We went ahead and changed for the last photo and met up again. This time, Tessa had us sit down on a bench and went for a slightly more serious look. Amara was not wearing hair extensions as this was supposed to be a recent photo.

**

Amara

Now that I was done taking photos, I went back inside, changed back into my casual wear, and went to find Sebastian. He had a picture to take with Zavier. I looked around and couldn't find him till I walked into the living room.

I saw him all cuddled up on his grandmother's chest, fast asleep, his lips slightly parted as he clutched the blanket she used to cover him.

"Oh, he's asleep," she said softly, looking up at me with a—wait, was that a smile on her lips?

"He looks so peaceful," I said quietly, watching as he took deep breaths in his sleep.

"I know, right?" Tiffany said, rubbing his back gently. "He

reminds me of Zavier a lot," she added, making me frown a little. I never knew what he was like as a child since Tiffany and I barely spoke. Amelia was able to tell me little things she remembered from when I was born.

"Really?" I asked, sitting down next to her.

"Mm-hmm. He wouldn't sleep when he was so full of energy, but the moment I picked him up and cuddled him, he'd drift off to sleep," she told me with the brightest smile on her face.

"Aw," I said, imagining a little Zavier. Sebastian already looked so much like him.

"Is it his turn for the photos?" she asked.

I nodded in response and said, "Yeah…"

Luckily, she woke him up gently and even helped get him ready for the photo. And to think that I was worried she'd hate him—she was already wrapped around his tiny finger. Sebastian was a pro at taking photos with his father. When it was all done, he ran to Arlo and pointed to the swing.

Zavier went inside to pick up a call, and not five minutes later, he walked up to us. "We have dinner with Mr. Fischer next Saturday," he announced.

Chapter 14

Amara

"Really?" Arlo asked happily, setting down the camera carefully and leaning on the tripod as he looked at his younger brother.

"Yeah, man," Zavier grinned, looking over at me and giving me a nod.

"That's so good!" Carolyn said excitedly, already smiling, and went inside to tell her mother, I assumed.

"When will you get these printed?" Charlotte asked Tessa, referring to the pictures we had just shot.

"I will send them to the editors as a high priority, so you might have them by tomorrow?" Tessa explained as she put the camera in its case and then in the suitcase she came with.

"Sounds good," Zavier said and tucked away his phone into his pocket. Once again, he was dressed in the suit he wore to work this morning.

"One little problem, though," Charlotte pointed out, catching everyone's attention. What could we have done wrong this time?

"What might that be?" I asked, sighing as this had barely started and was already becoming too much, but it was too late to back out now.

"You two are as close as strangers," she pointed out. I frowned a little and looked over at Zavier. His green eyes were focused on me. We did know some things about each other. When things were good, we talked somewhat...That had to count for something, right?

"We know stuff about each other," Zavier scoffed, almost as if he were offended by what Charlotte said.

"Let me rephrase that: you two act like strangers," Charlotte said and walked closer to Tessa. Tessa made a thinking face for a moment as she looked at us.

"You know, I think Fischer might ask personal questions, and if you choke during that, he might get suspicious," Tessa said, biting on her lower lip.

"Perhaps you two should go out for dinner and talk things out," Charlotte pointed out, making me choke a little. A date? Was she out of her mind? I was scared of the thought, knowing I wouldn't be able to stop myself from falling for him, which would only end up with me hurting.

"What things?" I asked, hoping we could just forget about this horrific idea.

"Um, you know—basic first date stuff where you get to know the person," Tessa said, shrugging.

"I'm not too sure about that," Zavier mumbled awkwardly as he looked over in my direction.

"Well, you should get to know each other before Saturday night." Charlotte shrugged and went on her phone.

"I'm free tomorrow night," Zavier said, looking over at me.

"I can babysit for you two," Charlotte offered, looking at me since the final answer lay with me now. There was no escaping this; they were right. We had to go out, just the two of us, and get to know each other better.

"Fine. Dinner it is," I said.

"By the end, you should know each other's dreams, deepest fears, and pet peeves." Tessa narrowed her eyes at us, once again switching to professional Tessa, the one that scared us all.

"Yeah, yeah," Zavier grumbled, shaking his head.

"Let's go and have lunch, which you deprived us of," I said, glaring playfully at Tessa, who rolled her eyes and smiled.

"Well, if you two knew how to stand in front of the camera, this would've gone a lot faster." She smirked, and we all laughed.

I helped Tessa pack up the suitcases, and the men helped her load them into her car. We all then sat at the dining table and started eating the lunch I had made before. Sebastian was seated on his grandmother's lap, neither of them letting go of each other. We all had a good time together. There was little to no tension between us all. Once lunch was over, they all went back to work. Charlotte was the only one who ended up helping with the clean-up, and she left afterward. Zavier hadn't left yet; he was showing Sebastian some card trick.

"Don't cook anything for dinner," Zavier said, standing up from where he sat and walking over to me, little Sebastian following right behind him.

"Why?" I raised a brow at him as I put the dressing back in the fridge.

"We'll go out as a family, remember?" he replied, shrugging. I had almost forgotten about that.

"Oh, okay. Where to?" I asked and looked down at Sebastian, who had his arms wrapped around my leg.

"Whatever you want. Message me. I'll shower at work then come and pick you two up." He smiled and waved at Sebastian as he stood by the door now, ready to leave too.

"Okay, sure. Drive safe." I waved at him, watching as he stepped out, and could see the pout forming on Sebastian's lips.

"I will. Bye, Amara. Goodbye, buddy." He waved at us and smiled before heading off to his car.

After Zavier left, Sebastian and I went back to the living room, and we called Amelia, so he could chat with her. After a good fifteen minutes, I took Sebastian upstairs and put him down for a quick nap before we'd have to start getting ready. I finally made my mind up; I wanted burgers from Rifa's. They were the best, in my opinion. I texted Zavier the location, and he replied with an "okay" and sent me the time he'd be picking us up.

I got myself ready for the outing, picking out a pair of black skinny jeans and sliding into them. As for a shirt, I looked through all my options and settled on a satin lilac tank top. I put on a gold necklace and a belt. I then went to wake up Sebastian and start getting him ready. I put him in some black pants with a bright yellow shirt that had a duck on it and paired it with his sandals, the ones he couldn't take off himself. Just as we walked downstairs, we heard the car.

Zavier opened the door and saw us both standing there. He smiled as he looked at us. "You two look adorable." He took Sebastian from my arms and held him, kissing his cheek.

"Are you okay with the place?" I asked Zavier, stepping out of the house and locking up.

"Yeah, of course. It's been a while since I had burgers. I do have one question: is there food for him? I can imagine a burger being a bit too much for a two-year-old," he rambled on, leading the way to a different car, opening the door for me, and strapping Sebastian into his car seat.

"Oh, no worries, they have some sort of kid's meal. He loves it; it comes with mango juice," I assured him, knowing how much Sebastian loved the food from there.

"Yeah!" our son cheered and grinned, understanding where we were going—or maybe it was the mango juice that got him all amped up.

"Well, let's get going, then," Zavier said.

When we arrived, we noticed it was quite crowded, so we decided to have our meal in the car. It would be a lot better that way. Plus, that was actually how I usually did it with Sebastian. I went in and placed our order for two chicken cheeseburgers with extra sauce and a side of fries and chicken strips. For Sebastian, I got fries, dino-shaped nuggets, and, of course, the mango juice. When I got our order, I walked back to the car and found Zavier had already taken Sebastian from his seat and placed him on his lap.

I dealt out the food, giving each person what belonged to them. We started to eat, with Zavier helping Sebastian out a little so that he wouldn't make a mess.

"Is it good, bud?" Zavier asked, looking down at our child as he ate his dino nugget.

"Yeah." He smiled and looked up at his father.

"Do you like it?" I then asked Zavier, not too sure whether this was truly his thing or not.

"Yes, it tastes so good. I never even knew about this place," he replied, taking the last bite of his chicken tender.

"Nicole and I found it when I was pregnant and starving one night," I told him, smiling as I thought back to the night we came across this place. Nicole and I were both impressed by how good the food and service were.

"Ah, I see. Do you eat out often?" he asked, wiping the corners of his lips.

"Not very often. I always preferred my own cooking, but certain places have some dishes I like," I replied truthfully. "You?"

"Not as much. It's one of the reasons why I had a cook." He shrugged, putting everything in one bag so we could dispose of it easier.

"I see…" I sipped on my soda then popped the drink back in its holder.

"All done, bud?" Zavier asked, checking his paper bag to see if there was still something left.

"Yeah, Daddy," he answered, clapping his hands.

"Come on, let's get those hands cleaned." I took a wet wipe from my bag and leaned over to clean up Sebastian's hands and mouth. Once we disposed of our trash, we decided to head back home after a bit of chatting, of course. Sebastian didn't talk too much before we met Zavier, but ever since his dad had come back into our lives, he had started talking more and more.

After we got home, we got Sebastian ready for bed and tucked him in. I watched as Zavier read him a story. It was quite adorable to see him interact with our son. I pressed a kiss to Sebastian's forehead before getting up soundlessly and walking out of his room, closing the door. I went to my room and got ready for the night myself. As tired as I was, I couldn't fall asleep yet, so I decided to go downstairs, where I saw Zavier sitting on the couch and watching a movie.

He had changed into his nightwear which consisted of just a grey pair of jogging pants. Just that and nothing else.

"Can't sleep?" He looked over at me, his hair a mess like he just left it as it was after he stepped out of the shower, and honestly, I found it quite adorable.

"Nope, not yet." I snapped out of my thoughts. "Do you

mind if I join you?" I looked at the TV to see what was playing right now.

"Sure, the movie just started." He moved aside and patted the seat next to him.

I nodded and sat down next to him, keeping a safe distance between us, but the longer we watched the movie, the closer we got to each other. At some point, I fell asleep and unknowingly found myself on his chest with his arm wrapped around me, holding me close to him. We slept through the night like that. It wasn't until morning that I woke up and jerked out of his hold. Luckily, he was a deep sleeper. I rushed to my room and went to shower.

I kept thinking about how warm his skin was and how his firm hold made me feel safe. His scent was still on me, even though all we did was cuddle. I washed off the soap from my skin and then changed into a pair of shorts and a shirt before heading downstairs to start on breakfast.

When I got down, I saw Zavier wasn't there anymore. He must've gotten up already.

I shrugged it off and went to start making us all breakfast. While doing so, I started chatting with Amelia briefly. She just wanted to check on me and see how things were going. By the time I finished up breakfast, I had ended the call and saw Zavier rushing down with Sebastian on his back, both of them giggling.

"Good morning, baby," I said, smiling at Sebastian.

"Good—my bad," Zavier mumbled and laughed it off.

"Uh, good morning, Zavier." I laughed awkwardly.

"Morning, Amara." He smiled and set Sebastian down, who finally got a chance to greet and hug me.

"Come on. Breakfast awaits us." I smiled and patted their shoulders, leading the way to the table.

"You're incredible, you know that?" Zavier said without thinking after he saw the way the table was set out. Amelia was right—the way to a man's heart sure was food.

"I do have such an idea." I smiled and sat down.

"Charlotte asked for your number, so I gave it to her. She mentioned picking out a time for her to come to pick up Bash, so we can go on that 'date' later," he told me, pulling the chair for Sebastian.

"Oh, okay. I wonder how he'll do with her," I said out loud, not meaning anything towards Charlotte. I just never left Sebastian with anyone besides Amelia, Ivan, and Nicole.

"I only know she's good with kids, and she seems to love him, so I think he's in good hands," he assured me. Everything went the same as yesterday. Once we were done with breakfast, Zavier went upstairs to put on the rest of his suit then rushed back downstairs, played with Sebastian for a good 10 minutes, and left for work.

Charlotte started texting me around 9 a.m. and asked if she could come to pick Sebastian up at 2 p.m. I figured that'd be fine since it would be after I dropped off Zavier's lunch. It was a little early, but she mentioned having the perfect day planned for them. I got myself and Sebastian ready and, of course, Zavier's lunch. When I stepped into the office, there were many eyes on me, but luckily, Zavier was standing right in the middle of the floor, so I was out of the room the moment I handed over the bag.

I was now on my way to meet with Nicole for lunch. I still had to tell her about the little "date," which I was not looking forward to. I arrived at the cafe and took a seat outside. It seemed like I had gotten there first. I pulled out my phone and went through my social media, finding articles about Sebastian, his father, and Zavier's mystery woman all over the place. There was a reason I stopped going on social media, and this just reminded me why. I tucked away my phone and looked up to see Nicole arriving.

"Hey." I smiled and looked up at her as she took a seat.

"Hello. Man, I miss you," she said, reaching for the menu.

"Me or my food?" I raised a brow at her teasingly.

"Your food and little Bash," Nicole smirked and winked at me, making me roll my eyes.

"I see how it is." I sighed dramatically and threw my head back a little.

"Tell me all about living there," she then demanded and leaned forward towards me, so our conversation wouldn't be too loud.

"It's so peaceful; there's so much space and privacy. I truly missed living in a house," I explained with a smile on my lips. I was already loving it, and that was bad.

"Is he a good dad to Bash?" Nicole asked curiously.

"Yeah, he really is. Even his mother warmed up to Sebastian," I answered truthfully. There was no denying what a good father Zavier was to Sebastian. He seemed to love the kid and wanted to be in his life.

"What about you? How's your life?" I then asked Nicole, nudging her.

"I might have a big project with Tessa coming up; I'm so excited," she said, grinning. I could tell just how excited she was about it.

"I can imagine. You totally deserve it." I winked at her. "I also have a date with Zavier..." I muttered softly, looking down at the menu.

"A what?" she asked loudly.

"It's to get to know each other and make an appearance for the public," I explained, hoping she'd understand.

"Hmm," she hummed, seeming like she wanted to say something else.

"Hello, can I take your order?" a young waiter came up and asked with a friendly smile.

We placed our order. We ate, chatted, and hung out a little longer before each going our separate ways. Once I got home, I did some laundry and cleaned up a little before taking a well-deserved nap.

When my alarm went off, I got up and took a long shower that included washing my hair, scrubbing my body, doing my skincare routine, and shaving—the whole package. I stepped out, wrapped a towel around my body and hair, and went in front of the mirror to continue my skincare routine. I let my hair down and used the blow dryer.

Since we'd be going out in public, I figured I should wear something pretty, so I went through the dresses in my closet and stumbled across a Fuentes dress. It was a gorgeous red bodycon dress; I had to wear it. This wasn't even up for debate. I'd wear it with my nude heels, which reminded me to quickly put some red nail polish on my toes. After putting on the nail polish, I slid on the dress and started doing my hair. I planned on leaving it loose, but it had to be styled a little. I put on my jewelry and checked the time— Zavier would arrive any moment now.

Chapter 15

Amara

I sat down on the couch, legs crossed, as I replied to a text from Amelia. I saw an unknown number had texted me, but I left it alone since I didn't know who it was. I received several more messages, so I finally blocked the number. It was probably a scammer. If it were someone important, I knew they'd identify themselves.

"Guess what we're up to," Charlotte texted me. I immediately replied with question marks, curious to know what my little guy was up to. She sent me a picture of her and Sebastian both dressed in aprons and making little pizzas. Sebastian's hands were covered in red sauce, as was his mouth.

"Oh wow, seems like you're both enjoying making a mess," I texted with laughing emojis after the sentence.

"Good thing we wore aprons," she replied.

"It's very much needed when cooking with Chef Sebastian." I smiled as I replied to her text. They were, indeed, needed. I knew that from the number of times Sebastian "helped" make something.

"I can see that. Enjoy your date," she replied, to which I responded, "Enjoy your pizzas."

I heard the motor of the gate working and Zavier's car driving over the gravel, coming closer and closer. I didn't realize I had become nervous; it wasn't an official date, yet I felt this way.

I got up, fixed the dress, then walked to the mirror by the door and checked my makeup. I heard footsteps coming up the steps and the door opening.

"Oh, wow—" Zavier's green eyes widened, slowly going down my body and then back up to my face.

"Hey." I smiled, looking straight into his gorgeous eyes. I couldn't help but get lost in them.

"You look beautiful," Zavier added, making me smile. I walked to the seat we had outside and sat down to put on my heels. "Is that a Fuentes dress?"

"Yeah," I answered, looking up at him as I pulled on my right shoe.

"You know, all these clothes from the line you've been wearing have never been released because we found they didn't fit right, but now, I see they just never had the right model wearing them," he said, eyes focused on me as I put on my other shoe. His words made my cheeks heat up a little.

"I'm no model—just a chef." I laughed awkwardly, looking up at him.

"Your energy is friendly and warm, and your smile radiates the same energy. That's all it takes for us," Zavier said calmly, giving me his hand to help me stand up.

"I'm ready," I told him, changing the subject, which worked.

"Let's go, then." He led the way to the car and opened the door for me.

On the drive to our destination, we barely spoke since he was getting constant calls regarding his business. He apologized for them, but I understood. He mentioned the influx was because he had been a little disorganized the last few days. I knew that the news about our son going public and us making this plan to deceive Mr. Fischer only gave him more tasks to do and increased his workload.

When we arrived, the place looked like some ordinary hotel, which confused me. What was his idea of dinner? I looked over at Zavier, waiting for him to finish up his calls.

"Sorry about that," he said and tucked away his phone.

"It's okay; I understand," I replied, watching as he fixed his hair in the mirror and then got out of the car.

"Thank you for understanding." He looked over at me as I stepped out, reaching out for my hand and holding onto it as he led the way.

"Um, is this your idea of dinner?" I asked, raising a brow at him.

"Do you even know where we are?" Zavier asked.

"Uh, Hotel Sunrise?" I laughed a little as I read the name of the place.

"Well, yeah, but the top floor of this place is actually a restaurant called The Private Grill," Zavier informed me with a smile, moving his hand to my waist and walking a little faster now.

"No way." I looked up at him, my mouth hanging open a little. The Private Grill was somewhere only celebrities could go. It was just for them, and the locations were difficult to find out. Even when you knew the location, the security was impossible to get through.

"Mm-hmm, one of the three." He smiled and opened the door for me.

"Wow," I said, surprised.

"Sorry for holding you so close. I think people were taking

photos," he whispered in my ear, and his breath on my skin sent shivers down my spine. I frowned when he mentioned that people were already taking photos. I knew this would happen and was prepared for it, but it still felt so weird.

"Already?" I frowned and looked over at him.

"It seems so..." He sighed.

He walked us to the elevator. When it stopped at the top floor, there were many guards in the lobby. Once they saw Zavier and confirmed he had reserved a table, we were free to walk in, and a hostess immediately showed up and led the way to a table. It was near the edge of the room, giving the best view of the city—not to mention the nice breeze we had up here. It was also very well-lit. There was a vase with a single pink rose and little tealights surrounding it on the table.

"I'll return with the menus in a moment. Let me know if the table is to your liking, Mr. Fuentes," the waitress said kindly after showing us to our table.

"We will," Zavier said, pulling out the chair for me and then sitting down across from me.

"So, what do you think?" he asked.

"I love the place; it looks amazing," I said, looking around in awe. I noticed a well-known artist was sitting not too far away from us.

"I'm glad you like it." He smiled and looked over at the waitress, who laid the menus down on the table for us.

"Here you go. I'll come back in five minutes to check if you're ready to order."

"Thank you." I smiled and opened up the menu. Most of these dishes sounded so fancy. The place I worked at had fine dining dishes too, but not like these.

"Any idea what you want?" Zavier asked, looking up from his menu and leaning back a little.

"The braised leeks with mozzarella and fried eggs sound good," I replied in a slightly unsure tone.

"Oh yeah, I tried that once. I'll try the pappardelle with chicken and cauliflower," he replied and looked up at me.

"Sounds good. Please order the drinks for us. These names are confusing me." I laughed awkwardly. Sure, I drank wine, but Nicole was usually the one who picked it out.

"You got it." Zavier laughed too and checked the drink section.

When the woman returned, he placed our orders and then looked back at me. We stared at each other for a moment, slightly smiling before breaking the ice.

"So, what would you like to ask?" he broke the silence. I thought about it for a moment. This was what we were here for, so we should get to know each other in case Mr. Fischer started asking questions.

"Um, why don't you have any staff at the house? Or drivers? I thought rich people had people to help make things easier," I asked, accidentally letting more come out than intended.

"I like my privacy. My family does have maids and butlers and all of that, but I personally don't like them. Some can be nosy, and I want my privacy to be respected. I do have maids coming every Tuesday and Thursday between 2 p.m. and 4 p.m. to clean the house, which I forgot to tell you about," he answered. I made mental notes of the days the maids would come, which relieved me a little. The house was a lot bigger than the apartment, so the upkeep would be much more difficult.

"That's okay. So...what's your question?" I then asked, giving him the chance to do the same as me.

"Do you truly want this?" he asked, catching me a little by surprise.

"What part?" I asked curiously, unsure if he meant my job, living situation, or something else.

"Being stuck with this job and having a child so young?" he asked bluntly.

"Honestly, I am truly happy with my job. Same with Sebastian. He is incredible, though I sometimes wish I would've waited till I found a partner so that Sebastian could have a normal family," I answered truthfully, tracing little figures onto the clear vase.

"I see. Makes sense. I honestly didn't think I'd find myself being a father in such a situation, but it's incredible getting to know Sebastian every day," Zavier replied, playing with the folded napkin.

"What do you do for fun?" I asked, wondering what he did besides working and playing with Sebastian.

"I like to watch movies, read, or go out somewhere. You?"

"Writing. I always loved doing that." I smiled, thinking of the many projects I had going on. I'd never completed one, though. "What else should we know about each other?" I then asked, unsure of what would come next.

"I don't know... Oh, do you have any allergies?" Zavier frowned a little as he asked his question.

"Nope, none..." I answered, pressing my lips in a thin line. "Uh, what's something you hate? Anything?" I asked, hoping to know what I should avoid so that we could live under one roof without any issues.

"Citrus fragrances," he replied without hesitation.

"Let me guess—it reminds you of cleaning supplies?" I asked, relating to that hatred so much. I always bought cleaning supplies with a different scent.

"Yep, you hate it too?" He chuckled.

"Yeah, it irritates me." I laughed and then asked after a few moments, "What was high school Zavier like?"

"Oh, uh, he was something else. In public, he was the perfect child, but behind the scenes, he'd rebel a bit." Zavier shrugged. Of course, he'd rebel a bit. "What was high school Amara like?" He wiggled his eyebrow a little.

"Oh, she just tried passing her classes and enjoying the time she had with her friends." I shrugged, thinking back to high school. It was around that time that I lost my dad, so I was pretty numb for a while. "I think we know enough now, right?" I asked, clearing my throat.

"For now, yeah. Let's enjoy our meal," he said as he spotted the waitress coming back with our food.

We ate our dinner then ordered some lava cake as dessert. We still had the whole bottle of wine to go through, but given that Zavier would be driving back home, we decided to finish it off at home. Delicious was an understatement if I had to describe the food. Before leaving, we took a picture together for the media's sake and then finally drove back home. Charlotte texted me saying Sebastian was asleep, and she didn't like driving out late, so she asked if he could sleep over. The answer was yes, as I'd hate for her to drive back late too.

Once we got inside, I kicked my shoes off and looked over to see Zavier right behind me. He loosened his tie and put his jacket to the side, leaving him in just his dress shirt. He pointed to the wine we still had left. We were both a little tipsy and only halfway through. I said we'd only have one glass, but instead, we drank it all and a little more from another bottle before finally calling it a night.

I stood in front of my mirror, trying to unzip my dress. It went perfectly fine putting it on, but it was now giving me a hard time, maybe because I was drunk. I had even forgotten to close the door.

"Need help there, Amara?" Zavier asked, his deep voice startling me a little.

"Please." I giggled, looking at his reflection in the mirror as he got closer and closer to me.

"Did I tell you how beautiful you look?" he asked, his fingers going down to the middle of my back as he pulled my zipper, exposing my bare back to him. He lowered his lips down to my shoulder blade and pressed soft kisses to it. I tipped my head back and pushed up against him.

"You mentioned it before," I said, biting down on my lip. I moved a hand to the side of his face and caressed him.

"I should probably stop," Zavier mumbled, pulling away from me and leaving my skin cold. I turned around to face him, looking up into his emerald eyes and slowly trailing my eyes down to his perfect lips.

"Yeah, we should," I agreed, looking back up into his eyes. I couldn't help it; I rested my hands on his shoulders, slowly stepping closer to him. I pulled him down, my lips ghosting over his before he finally kissed me.

His lips were warm over mine, and we moved perfectly in sync. I could still taste the wine on him, which made me deepen the kiss, wanting—no, needing—more. It had been way too long since I had done this, and the alcohol sure loosened me up.

I felt his hands moving down my waist as mine traveled to the buttons of his shirt and began undoing them. He pulled away from the kiss, leaving my lips swollen. He started kissing down my jawline and my neck, and he sucked on my skin, making me moan loudly, my hands grasping his hair as I pulled him closer. I traveled down his skin, feeling his muscles under my touch, and then I finally took off his shirt. His large, warm hands pushed down my dress, letting it pool by my ankles. He picked me up and brought me to the bed, setting me down gently.

"Give me your hands," Zavier said in a low tone, removing his tie from around his neck.

Chapter 16

Amara

I felt the sun's rays spreading their warmth across my skin, as I had forgotten to close the blinds last night. I felt another body next to me moving. I opened my eyes immediately and saw it was Zavier. My eyes widened as I saw that he was shirtless, which made me look under the covers. I was naked too.

Memories from last night flooded my mind, and I realized what we had done. I should never have drunk that much. I saw Zavier moving, rolling onto his back before he faced me, his eyes wide too.

"Fuck," he groaned, covering his face with his hand and letting out a sigh. "This shouldn't have—" Zavier began to say, sitting up but keeping the blanket on his lower body so he wouldn't expose himself, but instead, he put his abs on display.

"No, it shouldn't have," I said, clearing my throat and looking towards the other side of the room in case he wanted to get up and change into something.

"I'm sorry. The wine must have gotten to me," he apologized. I could hear him stepping out of bed and moving around the room.

"Yeah, me too...we shouldn't have drunk that much." I sighed, rubbing my temples. I had a slight headache, but now, I wasn't sure if it was from all the alcohol we had last night or because of this situation. I heard the movement of his zipper and finally turned over to look at him, holding the blanket close to my body.

"It was good, though," Zavier said, slightly smiling for a moment before he frowned, realizing how it sounded. He quickly added, "The wine, I mean."

"Yeah, it was..." I replied, thinking back to last night. I sure wasn't talking about the wine... "Shit, did we, uh, use protection?" I panicked, sitting up and clutching onto the blanket as I looked at him. I knew exactly how this went; Sebastian was the outcome of the last time.

"I—" he stuttered and walked to the bin, seeing what I assumed was a used condom. I felt the wrapper under my body, which confirmed it. "Yes, luckily." Zavier sighed, his hands on his hips. He stared at me, and I stared back, biting down on my lip, unsure what to do next.

"Um, Sebastian and Charlotte will be here in an hour. I have to get ready," I told him, looking around the room for a moment.

"Yeah, I have to leave for work soon. Uh, see you later?" Zavier replied with a frown on his face for a moment, but then he just went with it and held onto my door handle.

"See you later." I gave him a quick smile and watched as he finally left the room. Once the door was shut, I got up, locked the door, and closed the blinds. I let out a loud sigh as I leaned back and thought of everything that had just happened. I knew this wouldn't affect our agreement, but we hadn't said anything about us. It was a mistake, so we'd keep it at that.

Hopefully, he'd forget about it. I removed the bedsheet and went to shower, trying to scrub away his strong scent.

When I went downstairs, I heard his car drive off. I checked the time and saw he left right on time for work. I then checked my phone.

"Hey, are you up?" Charlotte had texted me over an hour ago.

"Hey! Yeah, how are you? How's Bash?" I replied, setting the phone down on the countertop and walking to the fridge to grab the ingredients for pancakes.

"We're both good. Can I bring him over? I have some things to do for the company later," she replied.

"Of course. Should I make you pancakes to go? Or will you join us for breakfast?" I replied, and she just responded with a thumbs up.

Forty-five minutes later, Charlotte and Sebastian arrived. We all ate our breakfast together, and she helped clean up the table afterward before leaving to finish up her business. I then cuddled up to Sebastian. I missed his cute, chubby cheeks. Once I put him down for a nap, I called Nicole and told her everything and made her promise not to tell Amelia. If Amelia knew, she might force me to stop this whole deal immediately, but I couldn't pull out of it now.

***

Tessa

The next day...

I watched as Arlo spoke with a model, and I couldn't help but feel jealous of the way he was flirting with her. He didn't owe me anything, yet it sure felt like it. After all these years, it still affected me somehow. Maybe he was the reason

I had commitment issues. I had to try to keep things cool and pretend like everything was okay, like I had been doing around him for years now.

"Arlo, I need you to sign these." I cleared my throat, holding the piece of paper out in front of him. He read the header then frowned, took the paper, and told the model to give him a moment.

"What's this about?" Arlo asked, making me roll my eyes. Couldn't he read?

"The agreement with the new photographer?" I informed him, resting the palm of my hand on the surface of his desk.

"Shouldn't Zavier be signing these?" Arlo asked, reading through the first page and then looking back up at me.

"Yes, but he's not here right now. He went with Sebastian to get some sort of shots," I explained, sliding the pen over to him so he could sign it.

"Shots? Isn't he too young for alcohol?" Arlo frowned, looking up at me. I looked at him for a moment, wondering whether he was serious or not, and he seemed to be deadly serious.

"Vaccine shots, you cabron." I sighed and shook my head.

"Oh! Oh, okay, okay." He laughed awkwardly.

I watched as he read through the agreement for a minute, signed the papers, and handed them over to me. While I checked if he signed correctly, I heard him call the model over and began chatting with her again.

"Hey, there's also a meeting you'll have to attend on his behalf," I reminded him when I realized Zavier would never make it back on time. I did have to say—since his date, he had been acting somewhat different.

"Why can't you do it?" Arlo groaned.

"Because this has to do with the clothing line, which I

am only a secretary for, but for the shoe line, I am the right woman." I shrugged, turning on my feet to walk away after checking everything.

"So, I have to attend?" he asked, raising a brow at me.

"Yes," I mumbled.

"Okay, I'll see you tonight, okay?" I heard him say to the lady, and I couldn't help but roll my eyes. Luckily, I wasn't facing them. I started walking towards the room where the meeting would be held and heard Arlo coming up behind me. "Will you be attending the meeting too?"

"Yes, for the shoe line, as Zav will not be present," I explained.

We both went to the meeting; this was the first time I was in a meeting with Arlo there. I couldn't help but stare at him at certain moments, at the way his lips parted whenever he got serious and how he would let that strand of hair dangle in front of his gorgeous eyes. I took a deep breath, looked down at my notepad, and listened to the proposals being made, trying to focus solely on that.

Luckily, after the meeting, we all went our separate ways, and I finished up the work I had at the office before taking care of my things with Nicole. She seemed to be a good architect, and we were both excited to be working together. Just when I thought I was done with work, Zavier called me back in for one last request.

***

That night...

Once I got home, I kicked off my heels, threw my bag to the side, and walked straight to the kitchen to get a cold glass of apple juice. I pulled my phone out of my pocket and saw my phone had a notification. I opened it up and saw my photo gallery showing me a prom photo from years ago. Wow...

Zavier was two years older than me. I switched schools when I entered middle school and was placed two grades higher. I happened to be a little more advanced, and my parents made sure I'd be in the right grade, mostly to brag about it, but it turned out to be a good thing for me. I met Zavier, who was the first person to be kind towards the new girl. We immediately became best friends. Our families became close to each other too. They'd joke around about Zavier and me, but what they didn't know was that I had my eyes on his older brother, Arlo. I never acted on my feelings, given that he was five years older than me.

At a Fuentes dinner party, Arlo and I started chatting because Zavier was out that night. Arlo confessed he had always liked me but knew I was too young for him. I was surprised and ended up confessing to him, telling him I liked him too. It was then that we pursued a secret relationship. I kept asking when we'd tell the others, and he told me one day. We decided that day to be prom, almost two months into our relationship. He said he'd be my date, which would be the right time to tell the others.

Zavier was excited for me, knowing that I never had an official date with Arlo. He even designed my dress, saying I'd blow his brother's mind. Back then, I didn't like to dress too extravagantly. Even now, I preferred simple outfits. Zavier's dress, however, was stunning. It was a blush pink dress with thin straps and a V-neck, and the back hung quite low. My waist was covered with sheer pink fabric with stones all over, down to the tulle skirt. I looked like an absolute princess that night, and I was excited too. I wouldn't have to keep things a secret anymore. Only—Arlo never showed up. In fact, he didn't even respond to any of the texts I sent and pretended nothing had ever happened between us when we met at family dinners and parties.

Even after all these years, I still felt something towards him, and I knew it wasn't right. This was the only secret I'd kept from Zavier, and I planned on taking it to the grave. I swiped out from the app and saw that my neighbor had texted me. She was a sweet old lady with a young dog. She asked if I wanted to take Fluffy out on a walk, as she was a little too old to do that herself, and the dog was a gift from her grandchildren. She said Fluffy made her feel less lonely, but she worried she wasn't a good owner, which was why I offered to walk Fluffy in my free time to make sure he got in his exercise.

I grabbed my keys, water, and phone and went over to take Fluffy for a walk. When I returned her to Mrs. Hellena, she gave me some cookies, which tasted just like my grandmother's. I checked the time and bit down on my lip. I was craving some fun, some sort of adventure. I decided I wanted to go to a club, so I went to the bathroom and took a long shower, shaved, and washed my hair too. Who knew—some guy might just get lucky tonight.

I blow-dried my hair and added the hair products I liked to use for my hair to go back to its natural, moisturized curls. I then walked to the closet and searched for a specific red dress that clung to my skin like a glove and had a crisscross design on the back. Once I found it, I slipped it on and put on a pair of black heels with it. Next, I put on some jewelry, filled my clutch with necessary items, and then stopped at the full-length mirror to take a picture before heading out. Hopefully, I could make these boy problems go away.

When I arrived at the club, I walked in and headed straight for the bar to order a virgin bloody Caesar. I patiently waited for my drink and looked around. I saw a blonde man looking at me with a smirk and making his way over to me.

"Care for a dance?" he asked confidently, his voice loud enough to be heard over the booming music.

"Yes, when I finish my drink," I replied in the same tone as his, with a smile playing on my red-tinted lips.

"I'll have what she's having," the stranger told the bartender, earning a nod in response. "So, are you here by yourself, or will some guy come knock me out when we start dancing?" he asked, leaning closer to me.

"I'm very much single." I laughed, still not telling him that I was here by myself.

"I'm Owen, and you are?" he finally introduced himself, smiling and showing his dimples.

"Tessa," I replied and looked over at the bartender, who just gave us our drinks. Owen ended up paying for them, and I thanked him.

"What are these? Virgin drinks? Really?" He frowned after taking a sip of his drink and looked at me, almost disappointed.

"Hey, don't look at me like that. I'm a responsible driver." I shrugged, throwing my hands up and then going back to sipping my delicious drink.

"Fair enough." He chuckled and drank the bloody Caesar.

Once we finished up our drinks, we hit the dance floor, and wow, it had been so long since I felt this way. Owen really made me laugh. The man had some moves, and he was handsome. Score! I bumped into someone and turned around to apologize, which was when I saw him—Arlo.

Chapter 17

Tessa

Was he here too? Dammit, I was trying to escape and forget about him, yet here he was again.

"Tessa?" Arlo frowned, looking at me. The model he was with slowed down her dancing and clung to him as she looked at us.

"You know him?" Owen asked, resting his hands on my shoulders as he stood behind me.

"Eh, come on, let's go back to dancing." I shrugged then turned back to Owen, wanting to ignore Arlo. I always found it weird to be at the club with co-workers, let alone one who was so close to my family. Even with Zavier, it could get a little weird sometimes. He'd judge the men I chose, but I never blamed him too much because I did the same with the women he picked up. In the end, we just wanted what was best for each other, and funnily enough, we sought it in nightclubs like a couple of idiots.

"Eh? I've known you since you were 11." Arlo frowned even more, taking offense at the way I ignored our connection.

"Go back to your lady, Arlo. We'll make sure not to bump into you," Owen told him and twirled me around so that I could face him. I then realized he called Arlo by his first name without anyone having mentioned his name.

"Wait, you two know each other?" I asked, looking at Owen, who continued to dance, but my hips were not moving.

"Something like that. Come on." He shrugged and tugged on my hand, pulling me farther, so we could dance somewhere away from Arlo. We continued to dance and laugh our asses off some more before we finally took a step back when the volume lowered.

"Care to take this somewhere a little more private? I don't live too far from here," Owen whispered in my ear.

"I'll go for a drink first, and then I'll join you back here, okay?" I winked at him and walked back to the bar through the busy and drunk crowd.

I called the bartender over and ordered a virgin pineapple mojito, leaning on the counter as I waited. I felt someone coming up behind me, brushing against me before squeezing in next to me.

"Hey—oh, it's you." I rolled my eyes when I saw it was Arlo.

"Tessa, I think it's best you find someone else." He leaned over to me to speak loudly and clearly into my ear.

"What do you mean?" I raised a brow at him, wondering what he was up to this time.

"Owen isn't exactly good news," Arlo explained, though I didn't appreciate it.

"Seriously, Arlo? Not this shit again." I rolled my eyes once more.

A little over a year ago, Arlo and I met at a fundraising event, which was expected. Considering our work, we met up a lot at social events. I came across a man named Taylor and was planning on getting to know him and probably do more with him. However, Arlo butted in and kept saying Taylor had some allegations against him about being abusive towards his exes, but he had covered them up. I wasn't planning on listening to Arlo, but he must've gotten to Zavier somehow because he asked me to be careful.

"What shit? I'm just looking out for you." Arlo frowned, turning completely towards me as we began to engage more in the conversation.

"You know what? Forget the virgin. Just make it a pineapple mojito." I waved at the bartender, who gave me a nod in response and took out the rum. "For what, hmm? Keeping me from getting my heart broken?" I raised a brow at him.

"Of course. I wouldn't want you to get hurt," Arlo said, almost making me laugh out loud.

"Funny coming from you," I said in an annoyed tone, handing my card to the bartender and beginning to sip my mojito.

"What's that supposed to mean?" He frowned, watching as I sipped my drink.

"Forget it," I mumbled, not wanting to get into it right now, and just walked away after getting my card back.

"Where are you going?" he shouted through the busy crowd.

"To Owen," I answered, but then I felt his hand on my elbow, pulling me back to him.

"Dammit, Tessa, why don't you listen to me?" Arlo's dark eyes glared down at me.

"Why should I, huh?" I asked, bringing the straw to my lips and sucking the liquid through it.

"Last time, he took home one of our models. He filmed them having sex and posted it online. We had to sue to get it taken down, and even after that, her reputation was still ruined," he said in a harsh tone, leaving me speechless. I rested my half-full glass on the counter.

"I—" I stuttered, not knowing Owen was that type of guy.

"Go ahead. Go to Owen now." He let go of my elbow, slightly nudging me away.

"God, I fucking hate you, Arlo," I groaned in frustration.

"Great. Now you'll go cry to Zavier, and he'll lecture me." He sighed, resting his hands on his hips as he shook his head at me.

"I really wish I'd never met you." I poked him in the chest.

"Right, 'cause having you in my life is such a blessing." He laughed in my face. I stared at him for a moment, shocked, then collected myself.

I stormed out of the club, leaving Owen, and went straight to my car. I started the car, turned up the AC, and just sat there, staring. I heard a knock on the window and looked over to see it was Arlo. I stared at him, raising a brow. What did he want now? He pointed to the door for me to unlock. I hesitated for a moment but still unlocked the door.

"What do you want now?" I glared at him, looking at him from top to bottom.

"I'm not here to fight, Tessa." Arlo held his hands up.

"What do you want, Arlo?" I asked, locking the doors again.

"I didn't mean to be so...mean towards you. You were just so stubborn." He sighed, speaking in a calmer tone than before.

"Hmph," I grunted and stared at the view in front of me. It wasn't much—just the back of some red car.

"You are a blessing, and not just to the company. It's pleasant to be around you, knowing you'll always be there whenever we need you," he then said, smiling and showing his laugh lines.

"Apology accepted, Arlo. You can go back to your lady friend," I replied, tapping his shoulder and then pointing to the door of the club.

"I already ditched her politely." He shrugged.

"Now, why would you do that, Arlo?" I shook my head.

"In case you were gone already, I planned on showing up at your place with some salted caramel ice cream," he explained innocently.

"My favorite. Why would you go through so much trouble? You could've left things as they were." I frowned, looking at him. It was always weird when people other than my family and best friend remembered stuff about me.

"In case you did indeed tell Zavier. I just didn't want to be told I was an asshole, so I came to apologize immediately," Arlo explained himself. The proud little smile on his face made me shake my head.

"Of course. Well, like I said, apology accepted. You can go now," I replied, trying not to sound pissed at him. Today wasn't the day for him to try me. I still harbored all this hate towards him, which I hoped to let go of or forget about someday.

"Is there any chance you could drop me off?" he asked, scratching the back of his head, slightly messing up his man bun.

"Are you kidding me?" I raised a brow at him, only to find he was dead serious.

"I could call a taxi, but you know, just wondering if you could," he offered, already pulling out his phone.

"Fine. It's on the way anyway." I sighed and checked the mirrors before pulling out of the parking spot. I began to drive us to his house. The whole ride there he didn't say a thing. We just listened to the radio, which had quite a mix of songs, but we just went with it.

"Want to come in for a drink? I'm sure I can make a better mojito, and one you'll get the chance to finish," he offered, taking off his seatbelt.

"I don't know," I mumbled, a little unsure whether I wanted to engage more with this Fuentes brother or not.

"Come on." He looked at me, dark green eyes focused on me and only me. I tried to say no but then decided, why not? He did make good drinks. I gave him a nod as I silently cursed myself for not being able to say no. At his place, we started drinking and enjoying our time together, rather than fighting, and just kept chatting and chatting until he asked a specific question.

"So, what did you mean when you said, 'Funny coming from you'?" Arlo asked, taking a seat on the couch right next to me.

"It's nothing, really," I mumbled, hoping he'd move on.

"Come on, I feel like it was something," Arlo pressed, looking at me with pleading eyes. Deep down, it bothered me that he didn't know what I was referring to.

"Do you seriously not know?" I raised a brow at him, watching as he thought for a moment.

"Know what?" Arlo asked, making me sigh.

"What I mean by it?"

He shook his head, looking at me awkwardly.

"Arlo, we dated, remember?" I reminded him, watching as his face changed, realization hitting him. "Things were going good. We had actual chemistry." I began to talk, and it all just poured out. I had wanted to say this for so long. "Heck, we even planned on telling our families so that we wouldn't have to go out in secret anymore," I continued. "You asked to be my prom date. You said we'd tell them all that night. I got all dolled up for no fucking reason. You never showed up, picked up my calls, or even read my messages. In fact, you spoke so normally to me in public afterward, as if nothing had ever happened between us." As I spoke, I got much angrier with each sentence that left my mouth.

"Tessa—" he tried to say, but I cut him off.

"No, wait. I've wanted to get this off my chest for a while," I said, still never giving him a chance to speak to try to defend himself. "What was your fucking reason, Arlo? Do you know how long I waited for you that night? Screw that—every other guy I tried being with just didn't work out because, in the back of my mind, I kept thinking, 'What if he ghosts me too?' I never got to go in fully with them." I poked him in the chest twice as I stared at my finger and then looked up into his eyes. "Had I known you were like that back then, I would've never wasted my time," I replied coldly.

"Like what?" he asked. Was that all he could say after that whole rant?

"Switching girls every month. That's what it was, no?" I asked, raising a brow at him and then standing up and walking to the sink to fill a glass with water. "Which was I? The spring edition?"

"Tessa, I swear it was never like that." Arlo stood by the kitchen island and looked at me. "Can I have the opportunity to explain?" I remained silent at his request but then slightly nodded, permitting him to do so.

"I honestly thought you were over it. That you forgot about it. I never knew it affected you and that you still thought about it." He walked over to the couch, patting the seat next to him. I silently followed him and sat down.

"How could you think that? You know, back then, boys barely even looked at me, but you, a handsome guy—you did, and as much as I hate to admit it, it made me feel special," I said, frowning. Was he really just all looks and no brain?

"You are special, Tessa. Please, let me explain. You're so fucking beautiful, smart, and funny, but you were barely even eighteen, and I was twenty-three. Tessa, you know our lives are constantly being shared in the media, and I didn't want to be seen as a groomer or anything like that. But, most importantly, your friendship with Zavier—" he began to speak, some words sticking with me and other parts just raising many more questions.

"What about our friendship?" I asked. I knew Zavier was my best friend, but it wasn't like we said we couldn't date each other's siblings.

"One time, I mentioned you looked nice in front of him, and he scolded me, saying I shouldn't ever try to hit on you," Arlo explained, carefully picking his words. This was a story I had never heard from Zavier.

"You should've said something. You just pretended like nothing ever happened. If our age truly was so bothersome, then why did you still kiss me that night? Why did you ask to pursue a relationship?" I asked two of the many questions I still had.

"Tessa—" Arlo sighed. He took a moment to figure out what to say next. "I don't know. I should've waited, but instead, I messed up and confessed that night," he said in a genuine tone. I could tell he was earnest by the look in his eyes. "I'm sorry. I did enjoy those two months, and trust me, if you weren't so young, I would've done my best to be the best person for you." He took my hands in his, staring into my eyes as he apologized. "I'm sorry I hurt you, Tessa. Trust

me, if I could go back in time, I'd wait for the right moment."
I sighed and pulled away from him.

"Thanks for the apology and explanation, I guess," I mumbled, looking over at the TV.

"Are we good?"

"Yes, Arlo," I replied, looking back at him. We stared at each other for a moment before he ruined the moment.

"Now, if I recall, you called me handsome?" he teased, nudging me to the side.

"And you called me beautiful, funny, and smart." I listed off each adjective with a smirk and rolled my eyes at him.

"And I meant every single word of it," he said, catching me by surprise. "Let me walk you to the car," he offered, getting up and walking me out to my car. "Have a good night, Tessa," he said in a sweet tone. I looked up at him for a moment, my eyes traveling down to his lips. Out of nowhere came the sudden urge to pull him into a kiss, which I did briefly before letting go of him.

"Tessa—" he then said. Reality hit me like a train, and I realized I'd just fucked shit up.

"Arlo, I'm so—" I opened my mouth to apologize, but instead, my lips were merged with his again, moving much better than before. He tasted like cranberries from the drinks we had. I felt his hands resting on my hips, pushing me against the car as his body was pressed to mine.

Chapter 18

Amara

It had been a few days since that morning, and I had to admit that I thought things would be weird between us. Instead, it seemed like we were getting along better, even though we were acting like we had forgotten about that night—like it had never even happened. Of course, for me, things were a little different. Every time he'd touch me with innocent intentions, my mind would go back to that night.

I looked over at Sebastian and Zavier. Sebastian was sipping on some leftover smoothie. In the past, he never liked smoothies. It must have been the texture, but ever since he saw Zavier drinking his in the morning, he kept asking for some, so at some point, I started giving him his own little cup, and he seemed to be liking it. I watched as Zavier did some card trick, blowing Sebastian's little mind, and I knew I would be hearing all about it later.

Tomorrow, we'd be having dinner with the Fischers, and I still hadn't figured out what I'd prepare for them. I did have a few ideas, but I needed to run them past Zavier first.

"Hey, Bash, can I borrow Daddy for a moment?" I asked, looking over at the little boy.

"Otay," he answered, shrugging and running off to the basket that held some of his toys.

"What's wrong?" Zavier asked, walking over to me into the kitchen. There was a slight frown on his face as he looked at me.

"I just needed to talk to you about the dinner tomorrow," I replied, sitting down on one of the barstools.

"Yes, of course. What do you want to talk about?" He also sat down and leaned towards me a little.

"The actual dinner. I have a few ideas of what I can make; I just need your confirmation to do the grocery shopping," I said, pulling out my phone and opening up the notepad app, hoping he'd pick out something from there.

"Oh, I thought we'd be ordering food." Zavier frowned, confusing me as well.

"Won't they wonder why your so-called girlfriend who has a degree in culinary arts isn't the one making the meal?" I asked, nudging him playfully with a slight smile on my lips.

"Uh, no, because her so-called boyfriend is a billionaire?" he replied in the same playful tone and smirked at me, making me sigh.

"Fair enough, but I think I still want to be the one to prepare the meal. A homemade meal just makes it feel a lot more special, you know?" I tried explaining, hoping he'd understand where I was coming from.

"That is true, but won't a five-course meal be too much for you?" Zavier asked, playing with the cuffs of his dress shirt and struggling a little with the buttons.

"Not at all. It's not like I have to prepare for a whole party." I shrugged. The restaurant I used to work at had many different dishes that I had to prepare daily, and even with help, it could be a little much sometimes.

"Okay, then. Sure." Zavier shrugged.

"One question: can my sister come over tomorrow? She'll be able to look after Seb while I prepare the meals," I asked, turning so we could face each other and taking his hand. I held it in front of me and started doing the buttons he was struggling with.

"Of course. Uh, one question: what will we do with Sebastian tomorrow? Should we call someone to babysit him?" Zavier asked, his olive eyes focused on me and what I was doing. Once I finished one side, he gave me his other arm to do as well.

"My sister already offered. She and Ivan will take him out and bring him back after dinner," I replied, finishing up the buttons and looking up into his green eyes. He thanked me softly, and I just smiled and nodded.

"Oh, that works perfectly. They must really love him," Zavier mumbled and seemed lost in thought.

"They do. They always talk about adoption but get scared to do it. I've told them many times they'll be great parents." I shrugged, getting lost in my trail of thought too. Amelia was so happy when I was pregnant. It was slightly weird, but I understood why. She'd always loved babies.

"With the way they look after their nephew, I can believe that." Zavier smiled. I got lost in his eyes for a moment then looked over at the clock.

"Oh my god. We're running out of time for the menu." I sighed and unlocked my phone again.

"Yes, yes," he mumbled.

"Okay, for appetizers I have in mind: cheese-stuffed mushrooms, shrimp tartlets, smoked salmon, deviled eggs, or ginger-tuna kabob," I offered. Only two of these things were food I truly liked.

"Oh, his wife really loves cheese-stuffed mushrooms and, um, the shrimp tartlets too, if possible," Zavier answered, picking the two I wanted. I smiled at his choice.

"Of course," I muttered, writing them down and then offering the next dish. "Now, for soups, we could either do French onion soup or cream cheese chicken soup."

"I'll say French onion soup." Zavier got up and stood straight, fighting with his red tie.

"Okay, now for the salads: summer Asian slaw or cherry tomato couscous salad?" I then asked, crossing off what had been eliminated.

"What would you like?" he asked, making me think for a moment. What would fit better and, of course, taste the best?

"Cherry tomato couscous salad," I picked.

"Okay. What will the main course be? Can I make a recommendation?" Zavier asked, pulling out his phone and starting to type something.

"Yes, of course." I wondered what he'd pick.

"Beef enchiladas, but it's a specific recipe. I can send you the link," he then said, looking at me.

"Um, yeah, sure." I shrugged. I was sure if there was a recipe, I could follow it and not screw it up. That was how I managed to make all my father's dishes perfectly. He wrote down every little step for me.

"Thanks. You can pick the dessert," he answered, sending me the link.

"What do you think of cinnamon apple pie with vanilla bean ice cream?" I bit down on my lip, already looking forward to tomorrow's dessert.

"Sounds delicious to me." He smiled.

"Okay, perfect." I checked the last box.

"Goodbye, now. I'll see you later." He waved and winked

at me.

"Yes, bye." I watched as Zavier walked to Sebastian and hugged him, kissing his forehead before waving at him and walking to the door slowly. A very upset Sebastian walked up to me, pouting.

"He left," Sebastian pouted, looking at me with his arms crossed.

"He has to work, baby." I ran my fingers through his brown strands. "Tell you what—do you want to play with Aunty Charlotte?" I asked, knowing that would cheer him up. Charlotte had asked if she could take him out. After confirming with Zavier first, we had settled for today.

"Yeah!" Sebastian cheered.

"Great. She'll pick you up in an hour. Let's get you ready, hmm?" I patted his head and got up from my chair.

"Otay, come." He took my hand and started leading the way.

I followed Sebastian up to his room and started getting him ready, making sure to pack his bag with some of his favorite toys and an extra pair of clothes too. By the time I was done getting him ready, I had around fifteen minutes left and decided to finally do my hair and make-up and change into something else. Today, I woke up earlier, so I had a shower before going downstairs. Now, I just had to finish getting ready.

"Okay, baby, a red sundress or yellow sundress?" I asked, holding the dresses to my body.

"Red!" Sebastian pointed to the red one.

"Okay, then. Red it is." I smiled and put the yellow dress back into the closet.

I put on the dress and did my hair and make-up while reading to Sebastian. It was a very short story about a turtle, and he seemed to like it. Then, I heard my phone ringing; it was Charlotte. She had arrived.

"Come on, Bash." I picked him up and carried him and his dino backpack downstairs. I opened up the door and set him down, letting him run and hug her legs.

"Hey, buddy. Missed me?" Charlotte asked, barely balancing on her heels as she bent down to pick him up.

"Yeah!" He grinned, holding onto his aunt.

"Hello, Amara." Charlotte then looked at me, smiling. I really liked her; she was sweet.

"Hello, Charlotte. Everything good?" I asked, leaning on the archway.

"Yes, I'm glad I'll get to hang out with my little buddy. How are you?" she answered, tickling Sebastian's neck before looking over at me.

"I'm good. Do you want to come in?" I asked, stepping aside. Deep down, however, I hoped her answer was no because I had some plans.

"No, no, we're just leaving." She smiled and waved at me.

"Be careful," I told them, waving back to her and Sebastian.

"We will," Sebastian grinned, making me smile.

I had plans to go out with Amelia. It would just be a simple brunch. Maybe we would even buy groceries together...boring stuff, I know, but we liked doing that together. I took the keys, locked up the house, and got in the car. Before driving, I checked social media under Zavier's hashtags to figure out what news about us was out. When I scrolled down, I saw there were pictures of him and me from our date night. Luckily, the quality was a little bad, and you couldn't really make out my face. My identity was somewhat safe, but I knew sooner or later, it wouldn't be. I could find all of the Fuentes' exes and even flings on here if I searched. It was clear strangers really loved these people and their personal lives.

I decided to wear some sunglasses. It wouldn't cover much, but who knew—it might help. I drove to Terry's Terrace, where Amelia and I planned on going for brunch. I arrived right on time and could see her walking to a table. I followed behind her.

"Hey." I smiled, taking a seat across from her.

"Mara, hey. Right on time," she replied, handing the second menu over to me. "So, how's everything been so far?" she then asked as I looked through the menu to see what I'd order today.

"Good, actually. I really love living in a house," I answered truthfully. I crossed my arms on the table as I looked at her.

"That's good. I'm assuming Seb is happy too," Amelia said, flipping through pages.

"Very much. He does miss you and Ivan from time to time," I said, thinking of the times he asked about them.

"Yeah, we miss him too," Amelia said, sighing. I bit down on my lip. Should I just tell her now? It was best that she heard it from me.

"I have to tell you something, though. The night of the date, Zavier and I were drunk and ended up sleeping together," I whispered to her in case someone was listening in on our conversation.

"You what?" she whispered-yelled, making me glare at her.

"I know, I know. We both agreed it was a mistake—" I was quick to say, but her face was already judging me.

"So, you're telling me you both swept it under the rug?" she asked sarcastically with a brow raised at me.

"Yes..." I answered, her look making me slightly unsure now. I didn't like that look; it intimidated me. It always had, ever since we were little and she was babysitting me.

"See, this is why I knew this was a bad idea." Amelia sighed hopelessly.

"It won't happen again; trust me," I assured her, knowing how bad it sounded. It was a mistake. One that wouldn't happen again.

"Let's just order food," Amelia said a little coldly.

We did just that and started talking about other things. I asked if she was sure about babysitting Sebastian tomorrow, which she and Ivan were. We chatted more about her and Ivan. They'd planned on moving, but it seemed like they'd put that on hold. Once they moved, they would be a lot closer to us. Sebastian and I would love that. After brunch, we went to do our grocery shopping. Amelia was surprised by the number of items I needed, but I needed to make a five-course meal the next day!

After grocery shopping, I had to go home again to make Zavier's lunch. This time, he sent a driver to get it, so I was all alone again. I decided to go for a jog and do a little workout.

I felt a little safer jogging in this neighborhood because of all the security and privacy. It was clear that rich and famous people lived here. I fixed my baseball cap, slid up my sunglasses so they wouldn't fall, and jogged back home. When I got home, the first thing I did was shower, followed by a nap.

Whenever Sebastian wasn't around, I liked to sleep and get the rest I deserved but sadly didn't always get. Around noon, my alarm went off, waking me. Knowing I had to prepare dinner, I went downstairs and started prepping. I made a broccoli and chicken salad for starters and then pizza too. I popped it into the oven but didn't turn it on yet because I wanted it to be fresh when we ate.

I made a mini pizza and packed it up nicely with some of the salad for Charlotte. When she dropped Sebastian off, I gave it to her, and her face lit up.

"Oh my, thank you!" She grinned.

"You're welcome. Enjoy, and thank you for taking the little man out." I smiled, holding onto Sebastian, who hugged my leg.

"Of course, have a good night." She smiled and took her to leave.

After she left, Zavier came home and went upstairs to refresh himself. After he finished up showering, we all had dinner like a family. Then, of course, it was Sebastian's bedtime, so we both gave him cuddles and then read him to sleep. I then got myself ready for bed and went down for a glass of water when I saw Zavier sitting on the couch in the living room, watching some movie.

"Hey, could you come over here?" he asked, and I nodded, going over to him.

"Everything okay?" I asked, looking at him and then at the screen. I noticed he was now wearing shirts at night.

"Yeah, I just think we should discuss a few things, so we know for sure we won't get stuck tomorrow." He patted the seat next to him...the last time we had this conversation, things ended differently.

"Okay, yeah, sure," I mumbled and sat down.

"Let's start with our full names. Mine's Zavier Alejandro Fuentes. I'm 32, and my birthday is on the first of November," he said, lowering the volume of the TV and turning to face me. I had no idea he was so much older...and I couldn't believe I was learning this just now.

"Okay. I'm Amara Iris Reid. My middle name is the same as my mother's name. I'm 24, and my birthday is on the first of October," I then replied, pulling my leg up to sit with them crossed.

"Oh, you're only 24?" Zavier asked, surprised, looking a little like he was in disbelief.

"Mm-hmm..." I hummed awkwardly. I supposed he thought I was a little older.

"Okay, so if they ask about our parents, you already know I wasn't too fond of my father, but I love my mother. With you, it's the other way around. You refuse to talk about your mother, and your father taught you to cook." He changed the subject, luckily. It seemed like he was paying attention when I spoke to him.

"Yes, yes, sounds good." I nodded. Everything he said was correct.

"Okay, I remember the schools you went to from your portfolio, so that's good. I went to River High and then to Spain for two years to finish a business course. Then, I stopped and focused on my business," Zavier continued. I found it fascinating how he had built himself up—of course, his parent's foundation helped too, but he did do a lot himself.

"Yes, your shoe line took off that year, and you also started doing real estate, right?" I asked curiously, sipping my water as if it were wine.

"Mm-hmm. What's your goal in life? Surely, it can't end at just wanting to be someone's cook," he then asked me, taking me by surprise a little.

"I've always wanted my own restaurant, but I don't know if that will still happen." I shrugged, playing with the sleeve of my shirt.

"How so?"

"Sebastian. Having a child was a blessing to me, but with my loans and such, I'm not too sure if I'll be able to save enough for myself. But, I know I'll have enough for his college," I answered. My parents didn't have enough to send me to the best colleges, but I wanted to make sure Sebastian could go wherever he wanted without going into debt, even if it meant I'd never get to achieve my dreams from when I was a little girl.

"You won't ever have to worry about Sebastian as long as I live. I plan on paying for everything he needs, Amara," Zavier said in a serious tone, hand resting on my shoulder as he made me look up into his mesmerizing eyes.

"You know you don't have to," I whispered, never wanting my son to be someone's burden.

"I'm his father. It's my duty to take care of him too," he replied, frowning a little, almost as if I had offended him.

"Mm-hmm…" I hummed and broke eye contact.

"Should we go over the backstory again?" Zavier cleared his throat.

"Yes, okay. So, we met at a party, took an interest in each other, and not long after dating on the downlow, I got pregnant," I continued, memorizing the whole story we came up with.

"To protect you and the baby from being dragged into the media, we kept things a secret and even lived somewhat apart," Zavier added, and I nodded to confirm he was correct.

"Now that the secret is out, we live together, but we're trying to keep my identity safe for as long as we can. We are not married or engaged yet. We just love each other and our son and are taking baby steps towards the next point in our life," I added the last part. It was a lie, but man, we'd sell this to them so good.

"Sounds pretty solid to me." Zavier grinned.

"Should we go to bed, then? I have a lot of preparing to do tomorrow," I asked, letting out a yawn.

"Yes, I will run to the office in the morning for a meeting

before coming home, okay?" Zavier informed me, getting up and rearranging the pillows on the couch before he sat back down.

"Of course. Good night, Zavier." I smiled and hugged him without thinking.

"Good night, Amara," he replied and kissed my cheek. I just nodded and went to refill my glass of water before heading up to my room.

Chapter 19

Amara

I woke up to the sound of Sebastian's giggles next to me. I shut my eyes tighter for a moment before the realization hit me that it was already morning. Did he wake up before me? Whenever he did wake up before me, he'd sneak into my room and cuddle with me, or he'd wake me up and pout, saying he was hungry.

"Come on, bud, leave your mommy alone. She's still asleep," I heard Zavier's voice say and could feel someone reaching over my body. Was he here too?

"Okay," Sebastian mumbled in his disappointed voice.

"No, no, I'm up," I was quick to say, yawning and bringing my hand in front of my mouth.

I turned around onto my back and stretched out my arms. Sebastian saw that as his invitation to cuddle with me. It was moments like these that I valued the most: my baby and me cuddling. I wrapped my arms around him and kissed his face.

"Are you leaving for work?" I asked, remembering that Zavier told me he'd be going to work. I pulled Sebastian a little closer so that he could cuddle me comfortably.

"Not yet. I'll go in a little later; I'm going on a jog. Could you have breakfast done after? Or not, if you have a lot going on for tonight's dinner," he asked, rambling a little as he sometimes did. It happened whenever he tried putting in a request.

"I'll just make us something simple." I shrugged. I still needed to feed myself and Sebastian, but I knew I couldn't make a grand breakfast today. There was so much left to do still! I knew the maids came to clean on Thursday, but I wanted to tidy up the place a little more.

"Okay, can I do anything to help out?" Zavier asked, standing by the side of my bed, making silly faces for Sebastian.

"Uh...yes, actually. Could you get him ready before you go to work?" I asked, pointing to Sebastian, who stuck his tongue out at his father.

"Of course. I'll go now." Zavier smiled and ruffled Sebastian's hair before going on his run.

Sebastian and I continued to cuddle a little longer before we went into the bathroom. I set him on the counter, handed him his toothbrush, and applied a tiny amount of toddler's toothpaste on it, letting him brush his teeth while I brushed mine. Then, I set Sebastian back down and let him play on my bed while I started showering.

I put away the jasmine-scented body wash, rinsed all the bubbles from my skin, and took a good minute just letting the water wash down my body before turning the water off. I stepped out onto the mat and wrapped the towel around my body. I looked around the bathroom I'd come to love. It was so spacious. I could walk around freely and actually get ready in here. I quickly dried my skin and opened the door to check on Sebastian. He waved at me, smiled, and went back to the cartoons he was watching.

I quickly started putting on my clothes for the day, keeping them light and breezy: just a shirt and a pair of shorts. Once we were done, we headed downstairs. One of us went to play while the other started preparing smoothies and breakfast.

I picked up my phone and started texting Amelia.

"Hey, Am," I sent her.

"Good morning!" she responded.

"Are we still on for today?" I texted her, confirming whether she'd be able to babysit for me. Even though we confirmed it yesterday, I still wanted to make sure nothing had come up in her schedule.

"Of course, around 2 p.m. works for you?" she replied.

"Yes, afterward, will Ivan pick you up?" I responded, looking up from my phone and seeing Sebastian looking through his toys.

"No, I'll drive myself, then we'll get to hang out with Bash till after the dinner thingy, right?"

"Yes, yes," I replied and was given a stuffed animal by Sebastian.

"Good, we have the perfect movie night planned for him," she replied. I smiled and looked over at Sebastian. I knew for sure he'd love a good movie night.

"Okay, bye now! XOX," I texted, remembering I still had a few things to do for the morning.

"See you at 2, XOX."

When I put the phone down, I went to play with Sebastian while Zavier finished getting ready for work. Once he was done, we heard him coming down, so we all went into the kitchen to have breakfast. Like always, the two were goofing around. It was quite something to see how these two interacted with each other.

"Come on, bud, let's help out Mommy. Then, we can hang for at least five minutes," Zavier said, wiping Sebastian's hands and helping him down. Zavier collected most of the dishes and gave Sebastian the cups to carry to the sink while Zavier brought me the rest. He then took the countertop cleaner and a paper towel, walked back to the table, and helped Sebastian up so that they could wipe the counter clean.

As I washed the dishes, I heard Zavier mention getting ready to Sebastian. So, he hadn't forgotten about it, I thought to myself. I wiped the sink and went to sit on the couch. After a few minutes, I heard footsteps coming down the stairs and looked over to see the two rushing down, Zavier holding onto Sebastian so he wouldn't fall.

"Well, sweetie, I have to go to work now." He bent down to Sebastian's level and ran his fingers through his hair.

"Aww." Sebastian pouted, looked into his father's eyes for a moment, and hugged him without letting go. Zavier held onto him as he stood up straight and walked over to me, gently passing Sebastian to me before kissing the back of his head.

"See you later, okay?" he said before leaving.

"What do you say we go read some books about animals, hmm?" I asked, tickling him lightly on the stomach.

"Hmm, okay." He shrugged and held onto me, resting his little head on my shoulder as we headed to the couch to cuddle and do some reading. After the book, we started playing with some Play-Doh. I started testing him on his colors; he could finally identify the color blue.

Once we were done with learning, I cuddled with Sebastian for a bit. He then requested to watch some weird cartoon about two dogs and a parrot. I didn't understand what the cartoon was even about; it was so different from what I watched growing up, but Sebastian seemed to like it. While it was on, I could prepare some lunch for when Amelia arrived.

I texted Zavier to let him know I wouldn't be able to make

him lunch today. I prepared some pasta marinara for Sebastian and Amelia. While I cooked their lunch, I just ate the leftovers from breakfast. I heard my phone buzzing and went to check it. It was Amelia asking me to open the gates. I pressed the button, waited till her little red car got in, then pressed the button again so it could close. I walked to the front door and opened it for Amelia.

"Holy smokes, I felt so broke driving down here," Amelia said, looking around in disbelief. Neither of us had truly seen something like this in person before, and I remembered being in her shoes not so long ago.

"Imagine fake living here." I laughed, half-joking, half-serious.

"Why is the driveway so long?" Amelia asked, looking at the long path that led up to the house. Just walking to the front was a workout.

"I honestly have no idea why this place is so big," I mumbled, looking at the house. Zavier had said this was a "small family home." What did a normal-sized one look like to him? The mansion his mother owned?

"Wow," she mumbled, mouth hanging open as she looked up.

"Exactly…come on in." I chuckled, calling her over and walking into the house, holding the door open for her.

"Of course," she mumbled and kicked off her shoes, putting them to the side.

"I could give you a quick tour," I told her. If she planned on spending time with Sebastian, she'd have to know her way around.

"Yes, please. First, let me go hug my nephew and give him kisses."

We walked into the house, and Sebastian ran to his auntie,

hugging her and getting picked up by her. I started showing her around. There were four rooms upstairs, one of which was pretty much a storage room. Downstairs, there were more rooms, one that looked like a guest room, an office, a mini library, and, of course, Sebastian's play corner.

"This place is so amazing," Amelia said, looking around at Sebastian's corner.

"Yes, I love it!" Sebastian giggled and looked up.

"You do? Why don't you show me your favorite place?" Amelia set him down and lowered herself to his level.

"Hey, I made some pasta marinara for you two, okay? I'll go ahead and start with the preparations," I informed them, but they were both too busy and just gave me a nod.

I watched as the two went to play. Then, I walked to the kitchen and pulled out the ingredients. I started to prepare the appetizers and put them in the lower part of the oven for now. After that, I started making the dough for the pie and let it cool in the fridge.

Two hours later, most of the preparations were done, and I moved on to the dining room. It was so huge. I looked up at the crystal chandelier and sighed. I heard footsteps coming my way and saw Amelia coming back inside from the backyard with a sleeping Sebastian in her arms.

"Can I take a shower before leaving? I didn't plan on getting mud on me," Amelia asked quietly. I looked at her. She sure did look like she needed one. This was the aftermath of playing outside with Sebastian.

"Of course. Let's get him to nap first." I put down what I was busy with, wiped my hands, and took Sebastian from her to lay him down on the couch.

I led Amelia to my bathroom and gave her a towel and a new outfit to wear once she was finished. She looked around.

"This bathroom alone is bigger than my whole room," she said, looking around, clearly just as impressed as I was when I entered this room for the first time.

"I know! I was thinking the same thing." I laughed, putting down an extra towel in case she planned on doing her hair too. "Enjoy the shower."

I left the room to pack Sebastian's bag but then rushed back downstairs as I remembered I had put in a pie for Amelia to take back. She never accepted money for babysitting, but I still felt bad about it, so I paid her in different ways. I checked the pie, and I was right on time. I sprinkled the cinnamon sugar on top then wrapped it up nicely.

I heard Zavier coming in and walked over to him at the front door. "Hey."

"Hey. Wow, the house smells so good," he said, loosening his tie and walking over to me.

"That would be the apple pie I made for Amelia," I replied, taking off the oven gloves.

"Is she still here?" he asked, leaning against the counter as he watched me move around.

"Yes, she's showering quickly before leaving," I replied, putting the spices I used back on the rack in the order I preferred them.

"Oh, how is it all coming together? Need any help?" he asked, removing his suit jacket and resting it on the chair.

"Well, I could use your help with the main course," I requested, knowing he'd be a bit more familiar with this than I was.

"Of course. Is that all that needs to be prepared?" Zavier asked, already rolling up his sleeves.

"Yes, everything else just needs to be heated before being served, and I will bake the pie once we finish the main dish, so it can be fresh," I mumbled, turning back around and wiping the counter.

"Sounds good."

Amelia came down the stairs with Sebastian still sleeping on her chest.

"Hello, Amelia," Zavier said, looking at my sister and then at the sleeping boy in her arms.

"Hello, Zavier," she replied with a slight smile on her lips.

"How have you been?" he then asked, standing up straight.

"Work's been a little busy. I'm glad I'm able to spend some time with this little guy," she said softly, looking at Sebastian and then back at him. "You?"

"Oh, the same. Work's busy, but Bash knows just how to make someone's day." Zavier smiled as he spoke about his son and looked at him.

"Very true. Well, I should get going. Good luck with the dinner," she said, already walking to the front door.

"Thank you," Zavier said, leading the way to the door.

"Here, I baked you and Ivan a pie. Enjoy." I remembered the dessert and brought it for her.

"Oh, thank you so much." She smiled, holding the pie and Sebastian's bag in her free hand.

"Take care," I said, pressing a soft kiss against Sebastian's cheek after Zavier did the same.

I watched as she got Sebastian into the car seat and then securely settled the pie and his bag in the trunk. She finally got in herself and drove off. Once the gates were closed again, I walked back inside and went in search of Zavier.

"Shall we prepare the beef enchiladas, then?" I asked, looking over at him and leaning against the doorway.

"Of course. Let's do it." He got up.

We went into the kitchen and started preparations. Zavier

offered to cut up the vegetables and such, which was probably all he knew how to do, but I had never questioned whether he could cook or not before. We started chatting, mostly about random things while we prepared the food.

"So, do you know how to cook?" I asked as I moved the meat around in the pan.

"Somewhat. It's just not my taste? I don't know. I don't like my cooking that much; I preferred the cook's food—and yours, now," he replied, shrugging as he focused on cutting the tomatoes.

"Ah, I see. So, nothing at all?" I raised a brow at him, curious to know.

"I suppose pancakes and waffles. I do like when I make them myself, but the savory foods—not so much," Zavier answered, looking up at me.

"Understandable." I shrugged and turned to lower the heat.

"Shit!" I heard Zavier curse. I turned around to see his finger bleeding. I cursed quietly, rushed to get a towel, and moved to him.

"Is it bad?" I asked, patting the towel over the finger and holding it under the water.

"It's not too deep, but I was cutting the peppers before, and now it burns," he whined, letting me handle it. I gently moved my fingers over his, waiting till the cut stopped bleeding under the water before pulling his finger out from under the water stream. I turned off the water and took a clean towel to dry his finger before examining the cut. He was right—it wasn't too deep.

"Hold on. I'll go get a band-aid," I told him and went to a drawer to get one. I searched through the options and picked one of suitable length before coming back to him. "Let me see," I said, already taking his large hand in mine and opening his hand.

"Amara, it's not that big of a deal," he mumbled, watching as I carefully applied the band-aid for him. I stroked my fingertips over his to make sure it was all okay before I realized what I was doing and blushed a little.

"Thank you," he said, looking down at me. I looked up and was greeted by his gorgeous green eyes. My breath hitched as I looked at him, and I took a deep breath before taking a step back.

"I think I can handle the rest. Before you get any more cuts, you should go ahead and get ready," I told him. He wanted to protest at first, but I narrowed my eyes at him. I didn't want him to get any more hurt.

"Fine, fine. Just go get ready too, okay?" Zavier said before taking his leave. Once he was gone, I finished cutting the tomatoes, added them all in, and mixed the beef.

Once I was finished with the dish, I put it in the oven and checked the time. I had exactly an hour and a half to get ready. I went upstairs, straight to the bathroom. I stripped naked to take a shower and hopefully scrub the food smell from my skin.

After showering, I wrapped a towel around my body, got out, and pulled out the blow dryer. I applied some heat protection to my hair and then started drying it. Next, I picked out a black strapless bra and adjusted it to be the right fit, pairing it with some black bikini-cut bottoms. I'd most definitely end up wearing a dress, so I wanted to wear the correct underwear that would look flattering with it.

I stared at the options in my closet and couldn't decide. I put on a wool robe, walked to the vanity, and sat down. I looked around for my curling wand and plugged it in. I applied some more heat protection products and then lightly applied some makeup, leaving my lips for last. Finally, I went for a wine-red shade of lipstick with a layer of lip gloss on top.

I took out a jeweled hair clip and clipped back the newly curled strands of hair. I removed the wand's plug from the outlet and got up. I heard a knock on the door. "Amara? Are you done?"

I sighed and walked to the door. I tightened my robe first before opening up the door. I saw Zavier had picked out a black and red three-piece suit. I saw him in suits every day, but he looked absolutely handsome. It was the right fit for his body. Even his dark hair was combed back perfectly. He was wearing a gold chain under the dress shirt that matched his watch.

"Good?" he asked, spinning a full 360 degrees for me, making me smile a little.

"You look perfect, and I don't even know what to wear!" I sighed.

"Need help?" he asked curiously. I frowned at first, but then I remembered who the man in front of me was. Plus, he proved he was perfectly capable of choosing his own outfits.

"Sure." I stepped to the side and let him in. I watched as he walked to the closet and looked through the dresses that were hanging. I crossed my arms as I looked at him, watching him closely as he pulled out a bodycon red dress with small white stone detailing that would match the clip in my hair.

"This?" he asked, holding it up to my body and tilting his head.

"You tell me, Mr. Fuentes." I looked between him and the dress.

"Wear this. You will look even more stunning." He handed me the dress. "I'll wait outside for you," Zavier said and left the room, shutting the door behind him. I sighed and put the dress on.

It was the perfect fit, as always. I ran my hands down my sides, turning to look at myself from the side. A smile curled onto my lips. I loved it; I loved how it fit me perfectly. It wasn't the most comfortable dress as it fit me like a second skin, but I loved it.

"You can come in," I said, facing the door as I rested a hand on my hip.

"Amara...wow...come here," Zavier said, mouth hanging open a little. I sauntered my way to him. He took my hand in his and twirled me around, making me giggle a little as this was unexpected. He then rested his hand on my hip.

"My pretend girlfriend sure is beautiful." He chuckled and walked us to his room. Weird, but I went with it.

"Well, my pretend boyfriend isn't all that bad either," I teased.

"Wait here," Zavier told me, disappearing into his room. Not long after, he came out and motioned for me to twirl around. "I think this will be fitting," he whispered in my ear as I felt a cold pendant rest on my bare skin. I looked down and saw he was putting a diamond necklace on me. Was it real? How was this even a question with Zavier freaking Fuentes?

"Wow, Zavier...isn't this too much?" I turned around and looked up into his green eyes.

"Not for you." He smiled and booped my nose. Then, it happened: we did that staring thing again where I just got lost in his eyes, and it was as if the universe stopped moving as I admired his beauty.

We leaned closer to each other, his hands on my hips as mine rested on his shoulders. That was when Zavier's phone rang.

Chapter 20

Amara

"Hello? Oh, yes, hold on. I'll open it for you." By the way Zavier was talking, I could tell it was Mr. and Mrs. Fischer. He pressed the button to open the gates while we walked down the stairs.

I quickly went to the dining room, lit a few candles for the aesthetic, and walked quickly to the front door to greet our guests together. Zavier looked down at me and fixed my hair before giving me a nod and opening the door.

"Mr. and Mrs. Fischer, welcome to our house," Zavier said, looking between the two with a friendly smile on his face.

"Thank you for having us over," Mrs. Fischer replied with the warmest smile on her lips.

"Come in, please," I said, stepping aside a little so that they could both come in.

"You must be the lovely Amara I spoke with on the phone," Mr. Fischer said, extending his hand out to me.

"The one and only. It's nice to meet you two." I smiled, shaking his hand. His grip was so firm.

"The pleasure's all ours. We just can't believe how lucky

Zavier over here has gotten," Mrs. Fischer said, looking at the two of us.

"I think I'm the lucky one." I smiled, looking up at Zavier, making him smile too, which put his dimples on display.

"No. Trust me, darling. I'm the lucky one." Zavier kissed the top of my head, his hand on my lower back.

"You two have a lovely place," the woman said, looking around, though she was mostly looking at the big family picture we had hanging on the wall.

"Thank you. Follow me to the dining room," Zavier said as we led Fischer to the dining room.

"Where's your son?" Mr. Fischer asked as he pulled the chair out for his wife.

"Sebastian's with Amara's sister. Maybe you'll get to see him when she brings him back home," Zavier answered, doing the same for me. I thanked him quietly and watched as he took a seat too.

"Sebastian Fuentes? What a lovely name," Mrs. Fischer commented, her red lips curling up in a smile again.

"All her idea." Zavier looked at me, holding my hand. I knew we had to keep up our appearances, but this wasn't exactly spoken about. Not that I hated it—I was just taken by surprise. "Actually, it's Sebastian Silas Reid," Zavier corrected them.

"Oh, right. You two aren't married yet," Mrs. Fischer mumbled, looking between the two of us and making Zavier chuckle awkwardly.

"No, we're taking our time with things, Mrs. Fischer," I said, squeezing Zavier's hand.

"Oh, you can just call me Mei Zhen," she responded.

"And you can call me Dan," Mr. Fisher added.

"I'll go get the food," I said, remembering that they came

over for dinner.

"Need help, sweetheart?" Zavier looked at me as I got up.

"No, I've got it." I smiled and tapped his shoulder before walking away.

"Oh, is there no staff tonight?" I could hear Mr. Fischer asking as I walked away.

"Since she and I started, I had to let go of my staff. We wanted privacy, given the situation," Zavier replied, getting up and pouring wine into the glasses.

I got the appetizers and walked back, putting them in the middle for us all to enjoy. I sat back down next to Zavier.

"So, how did you meet?" Dan asked as he took one of the shrimp tartlets, put it on Mei Zheng's plate, and took a few for himself.

"We met at a party and immediately hit it off," Zavier started, looking at me with adoring eyes.

"Given we both love our privacy, we kept things a secret," I added on, smiling. This lie would be sold so well to them.

"As much as I wanted to make it clear to the public I'm not an eligible bachelor, I couldn't anymore because we then found out she was pregnant," Zavier continued, finally looking away from me. "It happened too soon, and, of course, the media would paint her as a gold digger or cheater, and we didn't want that."

"Oh, it's understandable. We chose for our lives to be in the spotlight, but, sometimes, it's a little too much." Dan sighed, taking a napkin and wiping the side of his mouth.

"What about Mei Zhen? How did you meet?" I asked curiously. These two seemed so in love. I loved hearing stories from couples about how they fell in love.

"Oh, I was on a business trip to Turkey, but it then got canceled. So, I was stuck in Turkey and had to stay there three days," Dan started, a smile on his lips—one that his wife had too.

"I happened to be on vacation there, and when I came across him, he asked for directions—not that I knew how to give them. We started chatting and found out we were from the same state," Mei Zheng added to the story.

"When I got to America, I asked her out officially. The rest is history. We got married five years later and now have two lovely kids." Fischer smiled.

"That sounds lovely," I replied, biting into the cheese-stuffed mushrooms. I had to hand it to myself—this tasted amazing.

"Yeah. So, Amara, what is that you do?" Mei asked curiously. Unlike Zavier, it wasn't like I was known for my work.

"Oh, I have a degree in culinary arts and spent some time working for a restaurant. After the place was closed down, I decided to just stay home," I told her, thinking back to how I actually landed this job and how it led me here: a five-course dinner on which a special deal depended.

"Oh..." Mei Zheng mumbled, trailing off. I could tell there was slight confusion in her eyes.

"She does have dreams of opening her own restaurant one day. I'm rooting for her—her food is delicious. These dishes right here are proof," Zavier was quick to add, surprising them. His words seemed more to their liking, so I assumed they liked ambitious people.

"You cooked this yourself?" Mei asked, still surprised.

"Of course. I love to do it anyway, so I figured why not." I shrugged, smiling. I always loved the way people reacted to my food.

"Wow, that's amazing," she complimented.

"I'll go get the second dish, dear." Zavier winked at me and got up.

"Okay," I mumbled, watching as he walked away.

"So, do you have any siblings besides your sister?" Dan asked, and man, I'd never been asked this many questions before in my life.

"No, it's just us two. We have a small family. It's really just her, my brother-in-law, and our friend, who we also consider a sister," I answered, playing with my bracelet.

Zavier came back with the French onion soup. He sat back down and looked over at me. I gave him a slight nod.

"Oh, wow. What was it like coming into his big family? I remember meeting Mei's family for the first time." Dan chuckled, looking at his wife.

"I was beyond surprised, but even more with Bash being the first of the grandchildren," I answered truthfully. "Well, shall we enjoy our meal, then?" I raised a brow at them, looking at the steaming soup. The room smelled so amazing, and the pie wasn't even in yet.

We chatted a bit more as we ate the soup. Next came the salad, the main dish, and, of course, dessert. Dan was a huge fan of the dessert.

"Wow, I've never felt so full before." Dan laughed, leaning back into his seat as his wife rested her head on his shoulder.

"You outdid yourself, sweetheart." Zavier rested his hand over mine and squeezed it.

"Oh no, you're making my head big." I smiled, holding onto his hand for a moment.

"He is right—this was absolutely delicious. Especially the pie," Mei replied, sitting up straight.

"Should I get some for you to take home to the kids?" I offered. There was still so much left.

"Only if you want," they replied.

"Of course," I replied. How could I not give them more food?

"Can we go talk in private?" Dan looked over at Zavier, and I could see his face lighting up.

"Of course, Mr. Fischer," he replied. Zavier got up and led the way to the backyard with Dan to talk business, I assumed. I'd say things went truly well. They were good people.

"Come on, let's go pack up that pie," I told Mei after we watched our "lovers" walk away from the table.

I got up. Mei Zheng got up too and followed me to the kitchen but stopped in front of one of the walls of pictures we had, so I walked back to her and looked up at them too. We looked so normal.

"This is such a lovely photo." She pointed to the one where I had on hair extensions.

"Oh, that one was taken shortly after we found out I was pregnant. We don't have that many pictures together, sadly, but there are tons of Sebastian," I replied, looking at the picture. It wasn't even taken that long ago.

"Oh, could you show me?" she asked, making me laugh nervously.

"Only if you show the ones of your boys." I winked and walked into the kitchen with her behind me.

"Of course."

I took out two pie slices, put that to the side for Zavier, and then packed up the rest for the Fischers, handing it over to Mei Zhen. "Sadly, I can't give you the ice cream, as it'll melt."

"Trust me; this is all my husband cares about." Mei laughed, holding onto the pie.

"Understandable." I laughed. It was safe to say they loved my food.

"Your dress is lovely, by the way, and the necklace is also stunning," Mei Zheng said, her brown eyes going up and down my body.

"Oh, thank you. This is a very special Fuentes piece, and this was a gift from Zavier." I twirled around and then touched the necklace I had forgotten about for the moment.

"I'll let Dan know I need some more Fuentes dresses in my closet," she joked, laughing softly.

"That sounds like a good idea." I smiled, almost laughing at supporting my "boyfriend's" business.

"Oh, the pictures. Here." She remembered and pulled out her phone, already heading into the gallery. "This is our oldest, Jian, and our youngest, Oskar." She showed me a picture of the two sitting on a couch in matching suits.

"Oh, they're handsome little ones. Oskar looks a lot like you," I replied, looking at them. They looked a little older than Sebastian. Oskar sure had his mother's lips, nose, and face shape.

"Yeah, but he sure has his father's attitude and is most definitely a daddy's boy. They both are." She looked up at me, shaking her head and letting out a sigh.

"Little Sebastian clings more to me, but when it comes to playtime, Daddy's the one he runs to," I told her. Of course, he clung more to me than his father—he just got to know the man.

"Oh, this is Jian at his game. He loves playing tennis and is quite good at it. Oh, this is when we took them to an aquarium. Oskar loved that place a lot. He sure loves the water kingdom." She started to go through more pictures and telling me about them.

"That's adorable." I sighed, wishing I could do these things with Sebastian. At first, I never had much free time, and now, it was for his privacy. "This is Sebastian at the park. We mostly take him to a specific private one. Now, with the news out, we might take him to some amusement parks, so I'll keep that aquarium in mind," I added.

"It's a little sad he didn't get to enjoy his privacy for long." Mei put away her phone in her purse and then looked back up at me.

"Do you have any bad experiences with these things?" I asked. She'd be the perfect person to ask. Tiffany and I didn't exactly have a bond, and things weren't so digital during her time.

"Many occasions. We got judged for where we took them out to eat, the clothes we let them wear, and so on. The worst was getting called bad parents because our son was throwing a tantrum as normal kids do. Obviously, we can't control their emotions, but the media seems to think they should be perfect," Mei started to tell me. Each part of the story worried me more and more. By the tone she was speaking with, I could tell this bothered her.

"Wow, now I'm actually scared," I mumbled, accidentally saying it out loud.

"It's a bit stressful at first, but what's important is that you and Zavier know where you stand in your relationship and are both doing what's best for your child and what makes him comfortable," she advised, rubbing my shoulder.

"Thank you for such great advice." I smiled, getting lost in my thoughts.

"Of course, dear. Oh, look in this one—you can tell he has Zavier's eyes," she said about the picture I had of Sebastian as my lock screen.

"There's no denying that." I laughed.

***

Zavier

Mr. Fischer and I sat outside and discussed some things, mostly business-related, but he hadn't mentioned anything about us going into business so far. I knew for sure the dinner went well, and Fuentes business had never been involved in any scandals.

"Well, Zavier, it's getting late, and we should get going," Dan spoke up, turning to face me. I was sure we'd get an answer about a business deal, but maybe not yet? "I think working with you might be a wise idea, so I look forward to meeting again and coming up with a deal and plan," he added.

"That's amazing, and thank you. We're just as excited to work with you and your wife," I replied, smiling. We did it—we'd closed a deal.

"Maybe in the future, we could even get into the shoe line. But, for now, we'll focus on the clothes," Dan added, shrugging. That was exactly what I was hoping for.

"Of course, Mr. Fischer." I nodded.

I led him back inside and saw Amara and Mei Zheng coming out of the kitchen, Mei holding her purse and pie in her hand as she linked her free arm with Dan's and followed us to the front door. When those two weren't looking, I took a peek at Amara and showed her two thumbs up, making her smile.

"It was lovely having you two over," Amara said, her hand on my waist as she was glued to my side.

"You two were great hosts, and again, the food was delicious," Mr. Fischer responded, holding Mei Zheng's hand in his.

"Thank you so much," I replied, looking down at Amara

for a moment.

"Maybe next time, it will be at our place," Mei said, stepping into the car after Dan opened the door for her.

"Looking forward to it. Drive safely," Amara responded, waving at them with her free hand.

"Definitely. Take care," I replied, waving too. I watched as they drove away. The moment they were out of sight, she removed her arm from around me while mine stayed till I saw a small red car coming in. It was Amelia. She parked the car, and Ivan stepped out and got Sebastian from the back.

"Good night," Ivan said, holding onto Sebastian.

"Hello, Ivan," I greeted him, trying to be kind, but the look he gave me made it clear he didn't feel the same way towards me. I took Sebastian when he handed me my son and held onto him.

"How did it go?" Amelia asked, looking at Amara then me.

I looked over at Amara and then at her older sister. "It went great."

"I'm happy to hear that," she replied, smiling. "I'm so sorry. We're both tired and want to go home, so have a good night," Amelia then said with an apologetic look. Given everything she had done for us, it was understandable.

"Thank you for everything," Amara replied, holding onto the dino bag.

"We really appreciate it," I said as I watched them go to the car.

Chapter 21

Zavier

When Amelia and Ivan left, Amara and I went back inside. I made sure the gates were closed, and when we got into the house, Amara locked up immediately. She walked over to me and looked at our sleeping son in my arms. Sebastian tucked himself into my neck, holding onto the fabric of my suit tightly.

"He's knocked out," Amara said, tilting her head a little as she looked at our son.

"He must've had a great day," I said quietly and gently rubbed his back. His rhythmic breathing calmed me as well.

"He most certainly did, and they probably spoiled him with food too." Amara giggled softly and looked up at me. My eyes stayed on her taupe ones, smiling a little.

"Shall we put him to bed?" I finally asked, noticing he was in his shark PJs, so he must be ready for bed already.

"Yes, let's go." Amara cleared her throat.

We walked upstairs to Sebastian's room. I turned on the nightlight and gently placed him on his bed, pulling the blanket over his body. I smiled, looking at the blanket and remembering when he told me just how much he loved it. Of course, he did. It was covered in animated vintage cars. I looked over and saw Amara putting down his dino bag. Then, she walked over to my side, resting her hand on my shoulder as we both looked at our son.

"He's so precious," she said randomly.

"I'm really lucky I got to meet him and be in his life," I mumbled, looking over at her.

"With the way you're treating him, you deserve to be in it." Amara tapped my shoulder, looking at me with her usual smile on her lips.

"Thank you. That means a lot to me. Come on; we should leave him before he wakes up." I smiled proudly, looked down at Sebastian again, and saw him moving in his sleep, which was our cue to leave.

We exited Sebastian's room, making sure to close the door quietly. I looked over at Amara, remembering she didn't know how much of a success tonight was. I extended my hand out to her. She looked at it for a moment, and I gave her a nod. She placed her small, soft hand on top of mine and followed me as I walked farther away from Sebastian's room and stopped in front of hers.

"I want to thank you for everything tonight. It went so well," I said, absentmindedly running my thumb over the back of her hand.

"You're welcome. It's what we agreed on, no?" Amara smiled, looking up at me a little. Without any shoes on, the height difference was seen clearly.

"Yes, but still. You outdid yourself with everything. I know we didn't talk about physical touches, so I'm sorry if I made you feel awkward at any point," I replied, both of our eyes falling on our hands that were still connected, but neither of us pulled away.

"You didn't. I'm glad they believed us," she was quick to

say.

"So good, they're even considering going into business with us," I informed her, remembering we didn't get a chance to talk privately until now.

"Wow, really?" Her eyes widened.

"Yes, sweetheart, and all because of you." I twirled her around without even thinking about it. When she came spinning back, she crashed into my chest and held onto me as she looked up at me, smiling. "Not to mention how beautiful you looked tonight."

"Oh, yeah." She smiled, blushing a little, and looked down at her dress. "Um, I definitely got complimented on the dress and necklace."

"Well, they do suit you well." I traced the diamonds of the necklace. I bought it for more than it was worth, but it was auctioned for a cancer fundraiser for kids.

"Mm-hmm, can you take off the necklace?" she asked, turning around and pulling her curls to the side.

"Of course." I took it off for her and placed it in her hand. Amara turned around and put it back in my hands.

"Oh, I want you to keep this." I handed it back to her, smiling.

"Why?" Her brows furrowed a little.

"For everything you've done for me. You didn't have to," I replied honestly. Even after everything, she still pulled through and helped me with my lie. I wasn't sure I'd ever lie for someone like this.

"Zavier, this is a bit much. Are you sure?" she asked, looking down at the gems of the necklace.

"Yes, there's no one more deserving of it. But, keep it safe; those are real diamonds." I grinned and winked at her.

"Oh, wow...thank you?" she mumbled, looking up at me

again.

"You're welcome. Good night, Amy." I kissed her cheek.

"Night, Zavier." She patted my shoulder, her brown eyes focused on me for a moment.

I walked into my room and sat down at the end of my bed, staring at the wall. There was no denying how I felt for Amara. I knew I liked her—I never stopped liking her. But last time, I messed it up when I doubted her. She said we'd never happen again, but I was starting to wonder if she truly meant it or not.

***

Amara

Three weeks had passed now, and in those three weeks, we all grew closer to one another. We almost seemed like your typical family. Sebastian loved us both so much, and of course, we spent much more time together. As for Zavier and me, we were becoming good friends. We sometimes went to public places just for the media and made sure they knew we were still together. Only, we kept things private. I still hadn't found my photo on the Internet. Of the ones I could find, I was always covered up, or the quality was too low to see me fully.

We were currently at a pool party. It was something small organized by Tiffany. Sebastian was quite excited. What child wouldn't be? First, he'd get spoiled by his grandmother, and he'd also get to swim!

I checked the time and saw he had to have his lunch now. He always forgot about lunchtime whenever he was busy playing. Sebastian was currently in the water with Zavier, giggling loudly as the two splashed around.

I got up, adjusted the sheer covering I wore over my blue

bikini, walked over to them, and leaned down. "Don't you boys know it's lunchtime?" I asked.

"No." Sebastian giggled and whispered something into Zavier's ear, making me frown. What were they talking about? They called me closer, and when I leaned in, I got pulled into the pool by them, Sebastian's giggles filling my ears. I gasped, the cold water surrounding my body as I was dragged in.

Zavier held onto both me and our son, a wicked smirk on his face. He looked over at me. "Can you swim?"

"Yes, I can. Meanie." I poked him as he let go of me and just held Sebastian.

"It was all his idea." Zavier laughed, pointing to Sebastian, who just smiled at me.

"Five more minutes and then we'll all be having lunch, okay?" I ruffled Sebastian's hair. I swam around with these two a little longer, playing around. Sebastian sure thought he was faster than he actually was, but we let him have his moment until it was time for lunch.

I wrapped the towel around Sebastian, watched as he ran off to his grandmother for food, and then turned to Zavier.

"I don't have an extra pair of clothes, you know." I narrowed my eyes at him as I wrapped my towel around myself.

"Who comes to a pool party without extra clothes?" He frowned, drying off his skin. My eyes slipped down to his abdomen for a moment, then back up at his green eyes.

"I didn't plan on swimming." I shrugged and pouted.

"Oh, I'm so sorry. I'll get you some clothes—no need to worry." Zavier patted my back and led me to the outdoor seating area, where everyone had their lunch.

By everyone, I meant the whole Fuentes family plus Tessa. For lunch, Tiffany ordered sandwiches, mini burgers, drinks, snacks, and much more. After lunch, Arlo, Sebastian, Zavier,

Tiffany, and Carolyn all went into the pool while Tessa and Charlotte both sat with me, and we just enjoyed each other's company in silence before we exchanged small talk. Nothing too big. I had to admit that out of everyone here, I felt the most comfortable with these two. I never felt judged or anything like that.

A little later, we all got ready to go back home. I immediately got Sebastian ready for bed. On the way home, we'd be stopping to buy food, and I knew after all the swimming, he'd pass out the moment he lay on the bed. After we got the food, we ate in the parking lot, and the moment the car started to head home, Sebastian was knocked out.

"How was your day off from work?" I asked curiously. From what I heard and saw, he didn't take much time off.

"I won't lie—today's been great. I got to spend time with my family, have great food, and relax," Zavier answered, his eyes focused on the road, but he quickly looked over at me. "Yours?"

"Well, I got pulled into the pool by two annoying people, but other than that? Perfectly okay," I sassed, rolling my eyes playfully. I was currently in a shirt of his because I didn't have anything else to wear, and I wasn't about to walk around in a sheer piece of clothing under which my bikini could be seen clear as day.

"We're not even sorry about it." He laughed, making me gasp.

"That's cruel, Zavier." I gently punched his shoulder.

"Life's cruel," Zavier smirked, making me sigh. "Also, the Fischers came to the office, and honestly, the deal is better than I thought it would be," he informed me, taking me by surprise at how quickly this was going.

"That's great, right?" I asked, noticing that he hesitated.

"Yep, they only have one request. They want a full collection based on the dress you wore," Zavier said, stopping as we got held up by a red light.

"That's a bad thing?" I asked, confused. Wouldn't that be good for business?

"Not really. It's just that I designed that piece, and it was a private piece. Recreating a whole collection based on that aesthetic will be challenging for us, but I think we'll manage," he answered. I then remembered some pieces weren't exactly part of a collection or released to the public.

"Yeah, you will," I assured him, tapping his shoulder as our eyes connected. We stared at each other till we heard a honk and saw the light was green.

"I want to take you out tomorrow to make an appearance. Are you free for dinner?" he said randomly. Yet another date? Sooner or later, they'd find out who I was...

"Let me check with my assistant," I teased, remembering what he told me the first time I started working for him.

"Ha-ha, funny," he said sarcastically, rolling his eyes.

"I'm down, but what about Sebastian?" I looked over at him. This was a little too soon. Of course, many people were willing to babysit him, but I didn't know if they were available.

"Charlotte asked me for a sleeer, but I told her she'd have to talk with you first, so she might call tomorrow about that." He shrugged. Charlotte was good. Sebastian said he loved going to her house and hanging out with her.

"If he has a babysitter, then I'm available." I shrugged, leaning back into my chair.

When we got home, we put Sebastian to bed and went to our own rooms. I took a shower and got ready for the night. Even after everything today, I still wasn't too tired. I figured I'd write a little. My novel was slowly getting somewhere.

When I decided I wanted a little break, I went downstairs and saw Zavier had fallen asleep on the couch watching TV. He had one in his room, yet he always watched TV down here. It might be because this one was a lot bigger. I walked over, gently pulled the blanket over his body, and put a pillow under his head so that he wouldn't wake up with a strained neck. I made myself some hot cocoa then went back to my room. I wrote a little longer before finally brushing my teeth and going to bed.

**

Charlotte had already come by to pick up her nephew. I had baked her a carrot cake as she had mentioned loving it once. Zavier was already home. Work seemed to have gone well.

We were both getting ready and had less than 10 minutes left before we had to be out of the house. I didn't know about him, but I had already showered and done my hair in a simple high ponytail with some curls hanging loosely. But, I was struggling with my eyeliner. One wing came out better than the other. After three more attempts, I let it be. They looked identical enough. I applied some mascara, picked a light red shade of lipstick, added some lip gloss over it, and finally got up to find an outfit.

I opened the closet doors and immediately saw a leopard print silk tank. I took that without thinking twice. I'd have to switch bras because the straps were thin, but I didn't mind it too much. I loved the shirt and planned on pairing it with a nude skirt. Once I put on the outfit, I took the necklace I was gifted and put it on.

Just as I left the room, I saw Zavier coming out of his room dressed in a pair of black jeans and a grey sweater that was just the right size. He wore his thin silver necklace that matched the watch on his wrist.

"Do I look good enough to be seen with you in public?" he asked teasingly, making me roll my eyes.

"Could've been worse," I teased back, walking to him and fixing a single strand of hair that went the opposite direction.

"Come on, missy, we'll be late if we don't go now." He took my hand in his and led the way.

Tonight was so special. He first took me out for dinner then for dessert at a place I loved because they made the best cheesecake. I thought that would be all for tonight, but it wasn't. He took us to this place where they had hot air balloons. It was then that he decided to ask me whether I was scared of heights—which, lucky for him, I was not.

"Have you ever done this before?" I asked as we stepped inside.

"First time for everything, dearest." Zavier shrugged and went over the instructions with the man again. Soon enough, the temperature started rising, and we slowly went up. Once we were up, we both looked around. It was funny how on one side, there were mostly skyscrapers and many buildings close to each other. However, on the other side, there were more trees. The houses were farther apart from each other, and there were not too many tall buildings.

"This might be the best decision I've made," Zavier commented, turning to look at me, and my god, did he look pretty under the light of the stars. There was a speck of yellow on his face from the light.

"It might just be...it's incredible," I replied and turned to look at the view. We remained quiet but close to each other. I rested my head on his shoulder. The night breeze would have been freezing if it weren't for the fire that kept us up in the air. I felt him placing a kiss on my head before he rested his over mine and placed his hand on mine too. Neither of us moved or said anything. Once the time was up, he lowered the temperature of the fire, and we slowly went down.

Zavier helped me step out and walked me to the car. On the way home, we decided to pick up Sebastian and then went straight home, and everyone headed to their beds. It was a good day for us all.

***

I'd just dropped Sebastian off at Amelia's, along with some lunch for her and Ivan. I had to go to Zavier's office and give him his lunch. I figured I already had to buy some groceries, so I'd make it a trip. The cleaning ladies came, and I didn't want to be in their space. I gave them their privacy to clean up.

"Hey, here you go," I said, giving him his lunch. Of course, on the way up here, there were still some looks, but I'd gotten used to them, and some actually got used to me and waved. I didn't blame the others who weren't as friendly because I never truly introduced myself. I just kept a kind smile on my face.

"Thank you. Would you like to sit down with me?" Zavier asked, peeking into the bag to see what I had made.

"I have to go do some grocery shopping, but if you want me to stay, I could stay," I replied, looking around the office and noticing a picture of him and Sebastian.

"Oh, I thought you had nothing to do, and with the cleaning ladies, I knew you'd want to be out of the house." He chuckled, walking to the water dispenser and getting himself some water.

"That's sweet, but sadly, I do have things to do. I'll see you later?" I smiled, getting up and holding my purse.

"Of course. Think Sebastian forgot I promised we'd play outside, by any chance?" he said in a joking tone, walking me to the door of his office.

"Hmm, no, I don't think so." I laughed.

"Yeah...drive safely, okay?" He watched as I walked away. I was so lost in thought I entered the storage room instead. The moment I opened the door, I saw Arlo pinned to the wall by Tessa. Their hands were all over each other, and their lips were sealed together. My eyes widened as I realized what was happening. They both looked over at me, shocked.

"I promise I saw nothing." I closed my eyes and turned around, shutting the door behind me as I sped off straight to the elevator.

Chapter 22

Amara

By now, two weeks had passed since the incident—the violation of two people's privacy. It felt so wrong, but like I promised, I kept it to myself, though I had many questions. I noticed that whenever Arlo and Tessa were in the same room, there would be weird glances between the two, but every time, I just avoided them at all costs. In front of Zavier and the others, I only spoke to them when they asked or told me something.

Today was Saturday, meaning there was a family lunch party at Tiffany's mansion. Sebastian was excited to go because Tiffany mentioned having a surprise for him. Usually, it was a toy or dessert specially made for him. When we arrived, I stepped out of the car, adjusted the blue floral maxi dress I wore, and then closed the door. Zavier had already helped Sebastian out of the car seat and put him on his own feet. Sebastian immediately ran to the gate, knowing we'd be in the backyard.

"Hey, buddy!" Charlotte said, surprised when she opened up the gate for him.

He ran into her and hugged her feet. "Auntie Charlie!"

"Missed me, buddy?" She hugged him, kissed the top of his head, and set him down.

"I did." He smiled and ran off to greet his uncle, Aunt Tessa, and, finally, his grandmother.

"How are you two?" Charlotte asked us as we came closer to her.

"I'm good. We're a little tired because a little someone had lots of sugar and didn't want to go to sleep last night," Zavier said, waiting till I got inside before closing the gates.

"Well, be ready for that to happen tonight again. Mom's surprise is a sundae bar." Charlotte laughed, leading the way to the others. I greeted them politely before taking a seat. I saw Tessa staring at me, making me a little uncomfortable.

"Hey, Ames, do you mind helping me with the French toast kabobs?" Tessa asked, catching me by surprise.

"Oh, uh, no," I stuttered and got up. Zavier's eyes were on me for a moment, but once we both disappeared inside the house, there was no one around to hear or see us, giving us some privacy—if that was what she wanted.

"Listen, we need to talk." Tessa stopped in the kitchen, leaning her hand on the counter and facing me.

"I already told you; I saw nothing," I replied, turning to face the cabinet as if it were interesting.

"Please...then why is everything awkward between us?" she said, stepping closer to me and forcing me to look at her. She was right. Things weren't exactly normal between us.

"Fine, let's talk about it." I sighed.

"Arlo and I just want to take things slow—" she started, making me chuckle. She raised a brow at me.

"His hands were on your boobs, and yours were down his pants. Is that taking it slow?" I mumbled. I wasn't judging her, but I was pointing out what I saw, which seemed a bit different from what she was saying.

"I thought you didn't see anything."

"Well, I still got scared," I pointed out, laughing.

"Touché." She chuckled too. "Okay, truth is: Zavier's the reason we didn't make this official." She gave in.

"How so? Won't he be happy for you two?" I frowned. Why would he not be happy?

"Arlo's his brother. I'm his best friend. Not to mention, Arlo has been told to never pursue a romantic relationship with me by Zavier," she started to explain, occasionally looking over her shoulder to make sure we were alone in the room.

"Why would he do that?" I wondered. Obviously, there was so much more to the story.

"Sweetheart, if you were to Google Arlo, you won't find the good work he has done. You'll find the media dragging him for sleeping with so many people." Tessa sat down on one of the chairs and pulled the one across from her out for me.

"So, Zavier just wants to protect you from his brother, who's a player?" I frowned. It made some sense, but surely people changed, right? At least some of them.

"Basically, but Arlo and I really do like each other, and it seems serious," she said a lot more softly as she leaned closer to me.

"How long have you known?" I asked curiously, knowing these two grew up together.

"I've honestly had a crush on him since I was, like, 15 or something," she admitted, avoiding eye contact with me now.

"Oh, wow—" I said, surprised. I didn't expect that.

"Exactly, and when I turned 18, he did confess he liked me. The only problem was that he's five years older, and after trying to date in secret for two months, he ended things because he didn't want to be accused of being a pedo or groomer," she started explaining. Everything made much more sense now, though the age difference confused me a little.

"Five years? There's a whole eight years between Zavier and me," I pointed out to her. Of course, I didn't know his age at the time we got together. We were both consenting adults.

"That's different. You were already 21 when you met him. For Arlo, it would've been different," she mumbled and let out a sigh.

"I see, and I understand. I just don't want to be involved in any drama." I nodded, making it clear what I wanted from this.

"I wouldn't want to drag you into any either. I just wanted to clear the air between us. I promise once we're ready, we'll tell Zavier." Tessa rested her hand on my shoulder, squeezing it. She seemed sure about this, which was all I wanted.

"I think you should. He's your best friend, after all," I pointed out, resting my hand over hers and squeezing it before letting go.

"Thank you." She sighed, a small smile on her lips as if she had been waiting to get this off of her chest.

"Of course. Now, let's go bring out those French toast kabobs." I smiled, getting up and grabbing the dishes.

We went back outside with the dishes and set them down on the big table. I somehow got dragged into a game of catch, and everything went well. Tiffany and I still barely talked, but it was better than her usual judgmental remarks on what I did or said. Everyone ate the delicious lunch she ordered, and, of course, we then had the sundaes we got to decorate ourselves. Tiffany banned us from bringing our own food—not even a cake. She said this was her thing, where she got to spoil her kids and grandchildren. Zavier explained this was the one time she got to make food and snacks like her own mother would make for her.

I looked over at Arlo. His eyes were mostly focused on Tessa. I did plan on keeping their secret; in fact, I'd pretend I didn't know anything at all. All I was wondering was how would this work? From what I heard, he seemed to be a ladies man, so wouldn't they wonder why he didn't have one on his arm?

"Mommy, Mommy, look!" Sebastian called me, standing between my legs and showing me his car toy. It was a vintage blue one.

"Wow, that's cool, buddy. Where did you get this?" I asked, looking at the car he showed me as he put it on my leg and let it ride on my skin.

"Auntie Charlie." He pointed to her and waved at her.

"That's so sweet of her. Did you thank her?" I ruffled his hair, placing the strands behind his ears. He hummed and ran off to show Zavier what he had gotten.

I knew this life we were living was fake. At least, some parts of it were, yet I found myself enjoying this a little too much. I tried reminding myself none of this was permanent, but I failed to remember that.

After staying for two more hours, Sebastian was finally ready to go home. The rest of our Saturday went as usual: bathing Sebastian together, having dinner together, and cuddling on the couch to watch a movie together.

I had to admit I was excited for tomorrow. Zavier said we'd be going out again. For us, this was just two friends hanging out, but for the public, we were a couple going out. Little by little, I started believing the latter more rather than the former.

When tomorrow came, I got Sebastian ready. Amelia and Ivan would have Ivan's brother over at their place. He and his family were visiting town for the week, and they had a son around Sebastian's age, so he loved spending time with them. I was assuming today's date would be a movie. I mean, he did ask what my favorite movie was.

I decided to switch shampoo and conditioner today. This time, I'd be using a coconut and aloe vera one. Nicole recommended it to me. It smelled good and added volume and a shine to her hair, so I was hoping it would do the same for mine. When I stepped out, I immediately started getting ready. For once, I already knew what I'd wear. After putting in some heat protection product, I blow-dried my hair and finally added the hair moisturizer from the same brand. I applied some light make-up and went to the closet. I put on my peacock-colored satin tank top and tucked half of it into some dark-wash jeans. Next, I put on a golden-buckled belt that would match my earrings and bracelet. I knew I'd get cold if we were going to the movies, so I took a knitted beige sweater with me in case.

Just as I stepped out the door, I saw Zavier coming out too, once again dressed so handsomely, and all he wore were some jeans and a hoodie. How could someone look so good when he was dressed in just his casual wear?

"Are you ready, dearest?" Zavier asked, pulling me out of my thoughts. I just smiled for a moment.

"Where are we going tonight?" I asked, following him down the stairs. By now, I was used to our arms linking as we walked.

"I rented out a movie theater for us. We'll be watching your favorite movie, and there will be blankets, your favorite snacks, and drinks," he told me, smiling. I could tell he was proud of himself, like it was his mission to make sure I would have a good time.

"Wow, that sounds so amazing," I said, surprised and

already getting excited.

"I'm glad you like the idea." Zavier grinned, looking at me. The grin on his face made him look so adorable.

"You always make sure I'm having a good time, but what about you?" I asked curiously, looking up at him. It would feel wrong to be the only one to enjoy this. He was a busy man, yet he made time for all this. I turned to face him when we got to the car.

"I'm great as long as you're happy. That's my main priority right now—and Sebastian, of course," Zavier responded, gently brushing a strand of my hair over my shoulder and smiling at me.

"That's really sweet." I could practically melt at his words. The more time we spent together, the sweeter he had become.

"Of course, I am. Come on." He winked at me, opening the door for me to get in.

When we got to the theater, we were led to our room. There were lots of people looking, and somehow, for the first time, I truly didn't care. This was inevitable, so it was best to get used to it. When we got to the room he rented out, I noticed it was guarded much better than the other rooms.

When we walked through the doors, a man stood there and led us to some carts full of different snacks. There were so many options to choose from, but I kept it simple and only took salted popcorn, gummies, and a bar of chocolate. Zavier took some snacks for himself and then led me to our seats. The seats in the middle had thick, comfy blankets for us. This would truly be a nice experience.

We got comfortable, and once we were ready, the man started the movie and left us alone. At some point during the movie, without thinking, I rested my head on his shoulder and looked at the screen in front of us. Because of how close we were, my hand rested right between us, and his arm went around me, pulling me closer to him.

"Did you use a different hair product?" he asked, making me look up at him. How did he know?

"Oh yeah. How'd you know?" I frowned, wondering what gave it away.

"Your hair smells different—in a good way," he replied, shrugging. I never realized he'd remember something like that. I didn't know if it was creepy or just sweet. He always seemed to remember the tiniest things.

"The other one was good, but this one is supposed to add some volume and shine," I explained, focusing on him rather than the movie. Of course, he'd have my fullest attention when I needed to watch a movie.

"Oh, okay," Zavier mumbled, his other hand stroking my cheek and pushing a strand of my hair behind my ear. "God, you're so beautiful," he murmured.

I stared into his deep green eyes, opening my mouth to say something, then closing it again. I just rested my hand over his, still gazing into his eyes before I leaned closer to him. Our lips brushed together, then locked together, and I kissed him. He never pulled back. Instead, he moved his hand to the back of my neck and pulled me closer as I stroked his cheek.

Once I came back to my senses, I realized what I was doing and pulled away, my heart racing faster than it should. "I'm sorry."

Zavier stared at me, surprised, and opened his mouth to say something. But then, he just nodded and turned back to watch the movie.

***

Zavier

A week had passed since we shared that kiss at the theater. Honestly, I was surprised at first, but I'd be lying if I said I wasn't enjoying it. The more time we spent together, the more I realized that I liked Amara a lot. I should've said something when she kissed me; I should've kissed her back better. That might've been my only chance.

Ever since I had accused her of lying, she never gave me a chance to start something romantic. Everything we did was as friends besides when it was for the media. Then, we were pretend boyfriend and girlfriend, but I wanted it to be more than just a lie—I wanted it to be true. I'd tell her tonight. It was her birthday, and of course, there was something planned.

And tonight was the night I'd be telling her about my feelings. Besides a dress, heels, and earrings, Sebastian and I got her a very special gift. We also got her the pots and pans she had been wanting. I didn't get what was so special about them, but she was talking about them on the phone with her sister, and I happened to hear, so I made sure I got her the correct ones by asking Amelia first. What was important was that she loved the collection. The dress was my personal design, so it needed to be made. Luckily, it was completed on time.

I decided to shower at work and get ready. I still had some work to do, but I took half the day off. After the shower, I looked through the clothing options I had. There weren't that many. I picked out a dark pair of pants and planned on wearing the forest green dress shirt. I tucked it in perfectly, then put on my belt, rolled up the sleeves, and put on my watch. I figured we'd be taking pictures, so I'd be matching with Amara. She asked me my opinion on clothing. I picked one of the emerald dresses. The silk material fit her so perfectly, not to mention that it seemed tighter in some areas, and, of course, there was the slit on one side. The last time she was dressed in a dress like that, she looked stunning, which she'd be this time, no doubt.

Once I got to the house, I noticed many cars here already, and I could see Charlotte and Nicole coming behind me from the rearview mirror. I stepped out of the car, waited for them, and greeted them before leading the way to the back, where the party would be held. When I got through the door, I saw Sebastian sitting on his grandmother's lap, and they were chatting about something. Tessa and Caro sat together and seemed to be talking about something. Ivan, Amelia, and Arlo sat at one table and seemed to be getting along. I let Nicole and Charlotte say happy birthday to Amara first and hand her a gift. Once the two left her side, I walked up to her and kissed her cheek.

"As expected, you look stunning," I said, smiling as I looked at Amara from head to toe. She was wearing the necklace I had gifted her. It suited her perfectly.

"Well, it's from this brand, Fuentes. I don't know if you've heard of it," she replied in a joking tone, smiling too.

"Oh, wow, whoever the designer is is quite incredible." I winked and cocked my head to the side. By my body language, I asked for her to follow me, which she did.

"Yeah, he's not too bad," she mumbled, following me to the living room.

"Stay right here. I'll go get your gifts," I told her, getting excited to give them to her.

"I thought it was the cooking collection, wasn't it?" Amara asked, a little confused. She had assumed that was all she'd be getting.

"That was Sebastian's gift to you." I shrugged and smiled. "Ohhhh, riiight." She nodded, then rolled her eyes playfully.

**

Amara

This day had been so wonderful so far. Every meal served was made by me. Amelia and Tessa surprised me with the cake, cupcakes, cookies, and even donuts! The treat table sure was looking good! As for Zavier, I kept getting these mixed signals. He disappointed me initially, but with all this fake dating, I was lowkey looking forward to it being real. I'd confront him, perhaps, but not right now. I watched as he walked in with three gifts wrapped up in iridescent paper with purple ties. Now, I didn't want to open them because they looked so adorable.

"Happy birthday, girlfriend," he said in a joking tone, handing me one of the gifts.

"Thank you, boyfriend." I blew him a kiss as I took the first gift.

I opened up the first present to see a red box with "Fuentes" written in cursive letters. I opened the box and saw a pair of block high heels. They were the kind that laced up.

"I love these! I own a similar pair but in black," I said in awe as I admired them. I was not sure when I'd find the perfect occasion to wear them, but I'd make sure there was one, so I could put them on.

"I'm glad you love them. Open this one next." Zavier smiled, handing me another gift.

"Okay." I nodded, put the shoes aside, and opened the one he pointed to. I gently tore the paper open and took out the lilac dress. It was a satin slip dress with thin straps that crisscrossed down the back.

"Zavier—" I muttered, running my fingers over the soft material.

"Do you like it? It was a rushed drawing, but I can make a new one if you don't like it," he rambled on, a little unsure. My reaction wasn't readable to him.

"Like it? Zavier, this is a masterpiece," I exclaimed, holding the dress up.

"Oh, you had me thinking you didn't like it for a moment." He let out a long sigh as if he had been holding in his breath.

"No! I love it," I assured him.

"I know you won't accept this one, but I think you still deserve it," Zavier said as I put the dress to the side and took the last gift, removing the wrapping paper.

I frowned and looked at the smaller square box. What could this be? I opened it and saw it was a blue velvet box. Dammit, did he get me jewelry? I loved jewelry, but this man bought expensive stuff and made me feel bad for accepting it all. I opened the box and saw a pair of diamond earrings; they'd go perfectly with my necklace, but I couldn't accept this.

"Zavier, this is too much." My brows furrowed as I looked up at him and held them up to him.

"Nonsense. You can't just walk around with an incomplete set," he responded, pushing them back to me gently.

"When will I ever wear these things?" I looked down at the earrings. They were so beautiful.

"If there's no occasion, I'll make sure there will be one, so you can still dress up," he assured me, closing the box and setting it aside. He pulled me closer to him and cupped my cheek. I looked up at him, my eyes moving from his green ones and down to his lips, watching as they parted. Just as I was about to lean closer, I heard Sebastian calling me.

"Yes, dear?" I turned around and leaned down to pick him up.

"Auntie Melia is calling you," he informed me, and I nodded and walked away, only looking over once at Zavier to see him just nod and smile.

* * *

Almost everyone had left, but Tiffany was still around. She just wanted to put Sebastian to bed before leaving. I walked to my room, took off the necklace, and set it down on my vanity. I heard some voices outside. The balcony door was left open, and right underneath it was the patio. I walked a little closer and could hear Tiffany and Zavier talking. I normally wouldn't eavesdrop, but I heard a mention of my name, so it caught my interest.

"When will you leave Amara?" I heard Tiffany ask, taking me a little by surprise.

"What do you mean, Ma?" Zavier asked. I stood still by the door and listened further. I knew it was wrong, but for some reason, I felt this pain in my chest.

"Well, the deal's pretty much sealed, right?" she then asked, clearly determined to have something her way.

"Not officially. Plus, we decided on some extra time so that things would seem normal," I heard Zavier answer. I bit down on my lip as I tried to follow along.

"And afterward, you'll be leaving her, right?" I let out a quiet sigh at Tiffany's question. What about me made her hate me so much?

"Why are you so keen on me leaving her? You do know she's still Sebastian's mother?" Zavier replied, his voice slightly louder, and I could tell by his tone that he was growing annoyed with his mother.

"Is that what you're worried about? We can get you the best lawyers, and you'll get full custody," Tiffany said in a reassuring tone. My blood was boiling at this point. How dare she think she could take Sebastian from me like this!

"What is your problem?" he then asked.

"Grace. I miss her. She was a much better girlfriend for you. Don't tell me you are actually over her," Tiffany pointed out. Of course...I did some reading online, and Grace was his ex-fiancée. He broke things off with her a few months before we hooked up at that party.

I truly believed something was happening between Zavier and me, but it appeared I had mistaken his acts of kindness for something else. It explained why he wasn't so responsive when I kissed him that night, and afterward, he didn't once mention it. Maybe he really wasn't over his ex, and I was just standing in his way. I decided I had heard enough and left the balcony and went straight to the bathroom.

Chapter 23

Zavier

"Are you serious right now?" I asked. Did she drink today?

"Yes. Did I say something wrong?" Mom shrugged, leaning back into her seat.

"Grace cheated on me and had the audacity to try and change the narrative as if I were in the wrong—" I stated.

"Well, you're always so busy, so—" Mom started to say. My blood was boiling. Didn't she understand when to let something go?

"Amara's not even in a true relationship with me, yet she's remained loyal to me. When I go out with her, she gets attention, yet she brushes it off and focuses on me and solely me," I told her, my voice rising a little, but I had to keep in mind that Amara was somewhere inside.

"But—"

"Papa was always busy too. Did you ever cheat on him?" I asked, raising a brow at her, clearly overstepping the line a little, but enough was enough.

"Don't you dare go so far, Zavi." She stood up, pointing her index finger at me.

"I've tolerated enough from you, Mama. You come into

our house, and you disrespect her like that? She's better than Grace or any other girl you prefer for me because, unlike the others, she has a personality I like. But to you, you see that she's not wealthy, so she doesn't deserve your respect." I got up too, glaring at her, this time keeping my voice down a little.

"How dare you speak that way to me!" Mom huffed, glaring back up at me too.

"I think you should get going before it becomes any darker." I picked up her bag and handed it to her.

"Yes, I'll be going." She grabbed it from my hand and walked out. I followed behind her to open and close the gate once the driver picked her up.

I stood outside and looked up at the sky for a moment as I took deep breaths, trying to calm down before heading in. Perhaps tonight wasn't the right day to tell Amara about my feelings...

***

Carolyn

I paced around the room, biting the gel polish of my acrylic nails as I stewed in my thoughts. I felt conflicted about whether to do this or not. I walked to the desk and picked up my phone. Upon unlocking the phone, I scrolled through my contacts and made a call.

"Hello." Luckily, they answered. It had been years since I had contacted them. "Yes, of course. It's me," I replied, a little annoyed, rolling my eyes. "I think it's time for you to come back." I smirked as I could already hear them get excited on the other end of the line. I wasn't too sure if my plan would work, but it was worth a try. "Next week. I'll text you the time and place." I looked out the window and waved at my mother. "I can't wait. I missed you," I said before ending the call. I looked over at the door when I heard it open and saw Charlotte entering the room.

"Who was that?" Charlotte asked me as she stepped into the room, staying by the door.

"No one important," I brushed her off quickly, putting away the phone.

"'I missed you' sure seems like someone important. Make sure this one knows you have a twin, so they don't accidentally kiss me," Charlotte replied, wiggling her eyebrows playfully at me, making me roll my eyes.

We definitely didn't agree on everything, but despite our differences, we were still as close as two people could be. We had been womb mates, for God's sake.

"Don't worry. I won't make the same mistake twice." I chuckled, shaking my head as I picked up my water bottle and sipped the lemon, strawberry, and mint water.

"Let's go work out?" Charlotte asked. Usually, we worked out together whenever we lived together.

"Mm-hmm. Why did you move out? I miss you here." I pouted, following Charlotte to the gym room.

"I'm your personal motivator?" she teased.

"Yes, but since you decided to be Ms. Independent, I'm all alone," I replied, rolling my eyes after letting out a loud sigh. I was the only one in the mansion with Mom. Arlo used to stay over four to five days a week here, but lately, he had been staying at his place more often.

"I really wanted this. I asked you to join me." Charlotte pouted, holding the door open for me to go in first before following me into the room.

"I guess I didn't want to leave Mama all alone." I shrugged, setting down my towel and water bottle on the table and then looking at Charlotte as she did the same thing.

"Understandable. Come on, then. Cardio first." Charlotte sighed and walked to the treadmills.

***

Zavier

By now, a week had passed since my mother and I had our little disagreement. I honestly didn't understand why she was keen on me taking Grace back. Amara was so much better. I actually felt like I had chemistry with her. This wasn't set up by Mom or someone else. Since that night, Mom hadn't called or texted me. She was clearly avoiding me in the group chat, and when the others asked questions, I didn't fill them in. As for Amara, she did wonder why we didn't go over for the Saturday lunch, but I just lied and said I had plans for her and Sebastian.

Things between Amara and I went back to normal—worse, even. It was like the first day we moved in together again. We only spoke when needed, and she only talked to me when I asked her something. I had no idea what had happened. It was like one moment, she did like me, and I missed that opportunity by not telling her that night, and ever since then, things went back to just being two strangers who only had a child in common and were sharing a house. She even canceled date night, but that might be because her face had been seen since the day we went to the theaters. Maybe the media pressure was too much for her? I wanted to talk to her about it.

Breakfast was over, and Sebastian went to play. I picked up my cup with the remainder of my smoothie. I slowly walked up the stairs as I sipped it and found myself lost in thought. I picked out a white dress shirt and put it on, tucking it in.

Then, I put on the other pieces of clothes belonging to this red suit. After putting on my tie, I picked up the empty cup and walked downstairs. On the way to the kitchen, I winked at Sebastian, making him giggle.

I looked over at Amara. She stood by the sink and washed the dishes as she stared out the window. See, this—I loved this. Something about just seeing her made me feel so happy, and I could only imagine how much better it would be once things were official.

"Amara, I think we've got to talk," I said, walking closer to her.

"About?" she asked, drying her hands and turning to face me.

"Us," I answered, looking down into her honey eyes.

"Is it time for the breakup already?" Amara asked, breaking eye contact.

"No, not that," I was quick to answer her. That was the last thing that I wanted.

"Then, what is it, Zavier?" Amara asked.

"I—" She waited for me to say something, but I couldn't say anything. I opened my mouth, but nothing came out. My mind went blank. By the look on her face, it was as if she were searching for something in me, but she gave up.

"You're running late for work." She sighed. Sebastian came running up to me, pulling me out of the failed conversation. I looked down at him and picked him up.

"Bye-bye, Daddy!" He kissed my cheek.

"Uh, goodbye, buddy." I kissed his cheek, set him down, and then leaned down to give him a high five.

"Have a good day, Amara," I told her, watching as she nodded and replied with a soft, "Be safe."

I walked to the car, disappointed in myself. I should've

done better. I would take her out on a date, and I would finally confess how I felt—no more chickening out. I just had to brainstorm the perfect date. What would she want?

For now, I had enough on my plate. The collection Mr. Fischer wanted was delivered, and today would be the photoshoot. Then, if he approved, we could start producing some more besides the exclusive collection. I walked into the office, past security, and went straight for the elevator. The first stop was my office, after that, the floor to where the shoots would be held.

I got off on my floor, walked through the lobby, and looked around. Where was Tessa? She was never late, especially when we had photoshoots. She was in charge of making sure those went well.

I pulled out my phone and called her.

"Hey, Tess, is everything okay?" I asked, walking to my office and taking a seat.

"Y-yes. Why do you ask?"

"Because you're never late? Is that a man I hear in the background?" I replied.

"Um, yes. My car broke down, and Arlo was the only person I could call at the moment, so I'm coming to work with him," she replied, making me sigh. I knew she was responsible, but for a moment, I did think differently.

"That explains why you're late. Okay, tell him to drive safely," I mumbled and ended the call. I continued to work while I waited for her.

Once Tessa arrived, she took the files from my desk and rushed down a floor to organize the shoot. I had some paperwork and my emails to go through.

"Hey, will you be dropping by for lunch?" I texted Amara, biting down on my lip. Maybe I could tell her during lunch?

"Do you want me to?" she responded.

"Yes, I'd like us to have lunch together," I typed and sent the text, watching as she was typing only to respond with a "Got it."

I set aside the phone and finished checking my emails. I got up and saw Amara walking into the office. Had the time gone by that quickly? I really had to check downstairs.

"Hey, you." I smiled, looking up at her.

"Hey. Here you go." Amara smiled back, placing the bag on my table.

"Thank you. Do you want to check downstairs with me first? We have the shoots going on for the Fischer collab," I said, looking through the bag and smelling the delicious lunch she made.

"The one inspired by the red dress?" Amara asked in a slightly curious tone, finally showing some interest.

"Yes, that one." I smirked, looking up at her.

"Of course, I'd like to see it!" she said excitedly.

"Okay, let's go then." I smiled and got up, walking and leading the way to the elevator. I pressed the button to go a floor down and looked over at Amara, seeing her looking back at me with a slight smile on her lips.

"Zavi, we've got a problem," Tessa said the moment the doors slid open.

"What do you mean we've got a problem?" I asked as we got out of the elevator.

"Remember the Thakurs?" she asked, holding the clipboard by her side.

"Sorry, I'm bad with names," I mumbled awkwardly, waiting for Tessa to respond. This shoot could not be canceled. Whatever issue she said there was must be fixed.

"Two sisters who model for us who are also allergic to

shrimp," she replied, raising a brow at me to see if I knew who she was talking about.

"Yes? I think so." I shrugged. Amara still stayed by our side, quiet as this didn't really involve her.

"There's a small problem." Tessa scratched the back of her head and started to walk, making us follow her.

"What problem?" I asked, looking around. Everything seemed normal right now.

"They went to a party and something they ate must've contained shrimp because they're in the hospital. They're okay, but the allergic reaction left some rashes and marks," she started to ramble, and as glad as I was that they were doing well, I had other worries too.

"Please tell me only one of them was scheduled for today's shoot," I whined, knowing by the tone she used that both of them had become unavailable.

"I'd say that, but then I'd be lying to you," Tessa said, resting the clipboard on a random table.

"Let me guess—there's no one else on standby?" I sighed, resting my hands on my hips. I needed all six dresses to be displayed, not just four.

"Yes..." she mumbled and pressed her lips together.

I clenched my jaw and looked over at the models who were getting ready for the shoot. I was missing two. I walked over to where the dressed mannequin was. The emerald dress and baby blue dress were the only ones left, and I wasn't planning on skipping over these two. They belonged to the collection. However, I couldn't reschedule.

"Tessa, can you please come here?" I called her over, running my fingers through my hair. I'd have to put on the cutest face—the one that always made her sigh and say, "Fine."

"What's up?" she asked as she walked to me and stood

right in front of me now.

I lifted my hand, almost touching her, but of course, I had to ask first. "May I?" I asked.

"Sure." Tessa frowned and stood still. I brushed her hair over her shoulder and lifted her chin, taking in the details of her face. She definitely radiated friendliness and confidence.

"No, no, no. I know that look." She stepped back, eyes widened. So, she knew where this conversation was headed.

"Come on, Tess, there's nothing else we can do," I said sweetly, trying to convince her. "Arlo, what do you think?" I called him into the conversation as I caught him staring at us. He walked closer to us, resting a hand on her shoulder.

"Come on, Tessa, you'd be helping us out," Arlo said.

"Fine..." She sighed. One down, one more to go...

"Where's Caro or Charlie?" I asked. The two would make suitable candidates.

"I already called them, but they weren't scheduled to be in. They're stuck in traffic," Tessa said, leaning against the wall and letting out a sigh.

There went my solution. I looked over and saw Amara standing by the window. She stared into the distance and seemed to be daydreaming. I bit my lip, watching her closely. It was no secret how gorgeous she was, and she had great posture, so this might come naturally to her.

"Amara," I called as I walked over to her.

"Yes?" She jumped as I pulled her out of her thoughts.

"Remember when I told you you could model for us?" I asked, watching as she first frowned. Then, a moment of realization hit her.

"No, no, don't—" she started to say, walking away from me.

"Amara, please, I really have no one else here," I pleaded.

She was our last option right now unless I planned on walking the streets to find someone.

"I'm not a model, Zavier," she reasoned, but that wasn't true. At least for me.

"That's because you won't let me put you in a dress and in front of the cameras," I replied, watching as she opened her mouth then shut it again and pouted. "I'll owe you one."

"Dammit, fine." Amara finally gave in.

I thanked her and watched as she and Tessa went to get ready. I sat down and scrolled through my social media feed. I looked up for a moment and saw both Tessa and Amara walking through the curtains, their hair blowing over their shoulders due to the fans. Both were made up beautifully.

"Damn," I mumbled, watching both of them as they sauntered towards us.

"You can say that again," I heard Arlo mumble, making me frown.

"What do you think?" Amara asked, raising a brow at me, a slightly smug look on her face.

"That you both look stunning," I replied, still in awe.

"I thought so," Tessa smirked, flipping her hair.

"Can I talk to you for a moment?" I asked, looking over at Amara.

"After the shoot. We're kinda busy now," Tessa told me, taking Amara's hand. One photoshoot and they were full-blown divas.

"Wow..." I was left surprised and watched as the two walked away.

Tessa showed Amara the ropes, and soon enough, she was posing and smiling in front of the camera. It was all coming together again. I watched as all models had their photos taken. Each of them was breathtaking, but I might be biased as I was the one who designed these dresses.

**

Amara

This felt different, being in front of so many cameras. I felt a little nervous, but Tessa gave me quite a good pep talk before we came out. Tessa looked so different dressed like this, and I could tell Arlo, too, found her just as beautiful. His eyes were glued on her, just like how Zavier's were on me. Was I not doing something well? Surely, he'd speak up if there was something wrong.

Once it was all over, Zavier called me over, but I told him to hold on. I walked back into the other room and stripped out of the dress gently, making sure it remained just as perfect as it was before I put it on. I walked back out to him, pulling out the pins in my hair. They were definitely irritating me.

"Yes, Zavi?" I asked, walking closer to him.

"Listen, I really need to talk to you about something. I've needed to tell you this for a while now," he said in a serious tone. I noticed he had been wanting to tell me something, but each time, something came up.

"W-what is it?" I asked nervously, running my fingers through my hair.

"Zavier!" I heard a woman say out of happiness as he was about to speak. We both frowned and looked over to see a ginger-haired woman running up to him, his sisters and mother right behind him.

"Grace?" He frowned as he was pulled in for a tight hug. My mouth hung open for a moment. I felt this deep anger rising, but I couldn't explain why.

"Who's this?" I asked, turning to Zavier with an eyebrow

raised at him.

"I'm Grace, his ex-fiancée and also the mother of his firstborn daughter," she introduced herself. I looked at her. It was her. I now recognized her from the pictures I'd seen online.

"Excuse me?" I narrowed my eyes at her.

"What the fuck?" both Arlo and Zavier said.

"What did she say?" Tessa stepped forward, frowning.

"Shortly after you left me, I found out I was pregnant and left town," Grace started to explain. "I-I was scared of what you'd say, so I never told you."

"Whoever your daughter is, I'm not her father," Zavier replied in a harsh tone.

"Oh, but you are. I have a birth certificate to prove the date," Grace said, obviously wanting to be believed. "Look." She pulled out a piece of paper and showed it to us. I checked the date that Andrea Tiffany Smith was born. She was born three months before Sebastian. I didn't know why, but I felt so angry, as if he had betrayed me.

"I have to go. Goodbye, Zavier," I mumbled, a hurt expression on my face as I walked off.

Chapter 24

Zavier

"Amara—" I called out, rushing behind her. Luckily, I managed to catch up to her before she went into the elevator.

"Zavier. Not now." She glared at me then turned to abuse the button for the elevator to come, as if that would speed up the process.

"Please, let me explain," I pleaded, wanting to clear the air. I hadn't seen her this angry since the night I accused her of lying.

"Explain what, exactly? You know, for a moment, I believed you and even started liking you. I was willing to give you another chance, and then I found this out. Were you ever planning on telling me?" Amara said nonstop, never giving me a chance to prove my innocence. When she finally stopped speaking, the elevator opened, and she went in.

"Amara—" I called out, but she had pressed the button already.

"I have to go pick up Bash," she replied, unamused as the doors slid closed. I let out a groan and ran my fingers through my hair, looking through the glass door and seeing that the others were still there and discussing the situation. I took a deep breath and walked back inside.

"Zavi—" Grace called out, touching my arm.

"Don't ever touch me again," I hissed at her as I removed her hand from my bicep.

"Don't speak to her that way." Carolyn glared at me as she gently patted Grace's back, offering her comfort, but for what?

"You'll ruin my chances of meeting my granddaughter," Mother scolded me, causing me to let out a chuckle.

"Trust me when I say that child isn't mine," I concluded, watching as my mother's facial expression turned worse.

"Zavier, do the math. I got pregnant while we were still dating," Grace insisted, the smallest smile on her lips. Did she enjoy doing this?

"So? Don't pretend like you weren't fucking around with two other men during that time too," I retorted, making Arlo chuckle, but he stopped when Mom glared at him.

"Zavier Alejandro Fuentes! Don't you dare disrespect her like that." My mother pointed her finger in my face again.

"Why? Tell me why I shouldn't? In fact, go ahead and tell me why I can't have her kicked out by security," I mocked, taking a step closer to Mom.

"This building is not yours. It's ours, and secondly, she's the mother of your child," she yelled back, pointing to Grace, who stood there with an angelic look on her face.

"Did you treat Amara any differently?" I queried, watching her as she couldn't answer me. "Why didn't you ever show up? Hm? Why now?" I turned back to Grace, looking at her, which only served to remind me of what a snake she was and how I believed the lies that rolled from her silver tongue.

"You put her up to this, didn't you?" I looked over at Carolyn. Out of everyone here, Carolyn was the closest with Grace.

"Zavier, calm down." Tessa gripped my arm, pulling me back a little.

"B-because I was scared of rejection, Zavi," Grace said in a broken tone, one I was familiar with.

"There's only one thing you love more than life itself, and that's money," I hissed.

"This is your child, and I expect you to step up to your duty, as you did for your son," she yelled at me, poking my chest until I slapped away the hand.

"We'll do a DNA test." I shrugged, knowing that would prove she was lying.

"No, I don't consent to that. How dare you!" she yelled again, her sharp voice giving me a headache.

"We're done talking for today, then." I waved my hand around and walked away. I could hear my mother and Carolyn ordering me to come back.

"Zavier?" Tessa said quietly as she walked with me to the elevator. "Zavi, how sure are you that that girl isn't yours?" she asked in a whisper, looking around.

"If she got pregnant a year before, there would be a chance, but the last six months of our relationship, she was trying out different types of birth control pills because the old ones gave her issues. I remember that vividly because she asked me to wear condoms again, which I did every time," I replied, taking a deeper breath and finally starting to calm down a little.

"Oh. A little TMI, but wow. You think she'd lie about something like that?" Tessa frowned a little.

"Grace can be manipulative, and my mother surely must've gotten tricked. I need that child tested," I replied, biting down on my lip. I had to find some way.

"But she didn't consent." Tessa's brows furrowed as she looked at me.

"We have to find a way around it then." I sighed.

"I-I actually think I can do it," she replied quietly. I raised a brow at her.

"Don't even worry about it. You go talk to Amara, and I'll fix this, okay?" She patted my shoulder. Usually, I'd ask what the plan was, but this was Tessa, so I trusted her enough to leave it in her hands.

***

Grace

After a lot of discussion, I finally left. I knew I had Carolyn's and Tiffany's support. Usually, it was easy for me to get Zavier to do what I wanted, but this time, it didn't work, and I didn't understand how that was possible. It was probably because of Amara and their son Sebastian. When I first read that Zavier had fathered a child, I assumed it wasn't true or that the child wasn't his, but when Tiffany called me months ago, I was told a DNA test proved differently.

Even after everything I had done to Zavier, I noticed Tiffany and Carolyn still wanted me back in their lives, so I devised a devious plan. After I left him, I found out I was pregnant. I had no clue who the father was, but the child's eyes were blue, and her hair was pitch black. Andrea looked a lot like the businessman I had slept with, but I refused to admit that, convinced that Zavier was the father. Since I had left him, my funds were running low after I made some wrong investments. Getting back into the Fuentes' lives would secure me something, which I could do through my little girl.

***

Tessa

I took a deep breath as I stood in front of Grace's address. It took everything in me to do this, but it was necessary. I had to do this, and it wasn't just for Zavier but also for Amara. I saw the hurt look on her face. I had been Zavier's friend for long enough, and he only thought he impregnated a woman once, and that woman was Amara. I knew Grace always searched for my approval after she failed to remove me from Zavier's life. Once she figured out I would forever be in Zavier's life and that he trusted me a lot, Grace knew she had to win me over somehow, but she never managed to do so.

I knocked on the door and waited till Grace came and opened the door.

"Tessa?" she asked, surprised, never expecting me to come by her place.

"Hey, Grace, I just came by to check on you," I replied, a small smile on my face as I looked at Grace faking her kindness.

"Oh. Come on in," she mumbled, taking a step back and holding the door wider for me.

"Of course...how are you?" I stepped in, looking over at Grace as she followed me to go sit down.

"Honestly, I feel terrible. I should've come years ago when I first found out. Now, it seems difficult to make him bond with Andrea...how did that other woman do it?" Grace started to talk, trying her best to seem kind in front of me, knowing my influence on Zavier.

"Amara never came to him. He found out himself." I shrugged.

"Oh..." Grace mumbled and went silent.

"Wow, a little girl. I never would've thought Zavier would

have two children." I changed the subject and laughed softly.

"It was a surprise to me too." Grace laughed too.

I continued to chat with her a little longer, showing some empathy, even if it was fake. I still tried to make Grace feel like she could trust me.

"Hey, can I use the bathroom?" I asked, looking around.

"Of course. It's over there." Grace smiled and pointed to the door.

"Thank you." I smiled and got up, walking to where Grace pointed and locking the door behind me. I looked around and found a hairbrush with black strands of hair. I put them in a Ziplock bag, tucked it into the pocket of my blazer, and then flushed the toilet and washed my hands. I hoped this DNA would suffice.

After drinking some tea with Grace, I finally left and went straight to the doctor's office, leaving Grace to her thoughts.

***

Grace

After Tessa left, I figured it out! I finally knew how to get back at Zavier: through the media, of course. What better way was there to hurt the man who hated his name being used in gossip magazines? I made several tweets in which I called him many disgusting names and called him out for being Andrea's father and refusing to step up to his fatherly duties. It didn't take long before they blew up and began to trend online.

***

Amara

When I called Amelia to check if I could come pick up Sebastian, I was told she was at the park with him and Ivan and that he was playing with his friends. They'd only just got there, so I couldn't get him unless I planned on ruining his get-together with his friends, which was the last thing I wanted. Maybe this was good. I got to have a small moment to myself to think things through. I started the car and started driving to a cafe nearby. I could use a caramel macchiato.

I parked the car once I found a parking spot, stepped out, and went to the cafe. I placed my order immediately then sat down, sipping my coffee as I scrolled through my phone.

"Angel? Is that you?" I heard a woman with a familiar voice say. I looked up to see it was my mother.

"Mylah?" I raised a brow at her. What was she doing here? And how did she even find me?

"Is that how you greet your mother?" she asked in a stern tone, almost as if that would work. I chuckled and rolled my eyes.

"She means nothing to me." I shrugged and looked back down at my phone.

"Oh, you have no idea how long I've been looking for you," she mumbled, taking a seat in front of me and resting her hand over mine.

"It shouldn't have been difficult, but you blocked my number, remember?" I glared at her, pulling my hand away from hers.

"Listen, sweetie. I'm only here because of your little boy. I'd like to meet my grandson someday," Mylah replied. I could hear how fake she was being. She was here for something—what for, I didn't know yet.

"No," I concluded and sipped my coffee.

"What do you mean no?" She frowned, anger rising in her tone of voice.

"We want nothing to do with you. Our lives are going

perfectly fine without you, and we'd like to keep it that way," I explained, giving her the fake smile I learned from her.

"You have no right to keep us from meeting!" she exclaimed, her fists slamming on the table but not loud enough to cause a scene.

"The day you kicked me out while I was pregnant was the day you lost your right to be in our lives," I whispered-yelled as I glared at her.

Looking back at how she treated Amelia and me just brought a wave of sadness over me. Knowing your mother, the woman who went through the effort of bringing you into existence, never truly loved you was painful. To her, it was all just a task that ended the moment we turned 18.

"What do you really want, Mylah?" I asked, clearing my throat. I watched as she huffed then gave in.

"I need Amelia's number. The house will be taken by the bank, and I expect you two to pay off the debts, as well as take care of me. I deserve it," she requested, crossing her arms as she glared back at me.

I stared at the woman in disbelief before bursting into laughter. The entitlement!

"No. None of that will ever happen. From the moment we learned to cook, we needed to do that ourselves. Not to mention when we turned 19, we had to contribute to paying off the bills, so you have no right coming here and demanding money," I told her. I was correct: she was here for something. I got up and grabbed my cup. I suddenly didn't want the coffee anymore, so I started to walk away from her.

"You walk away now, and I will never accept you back into my life." I heard the chair move under her as she stood up hastily.

"Good, that's just what I want." I rolled my eyes, walking

to the car. I decided to take the long way back to the park.

***

Tessa

I looked down at my phone and saw it was Mr. Giovanni calling. I quickly picked up the phone and was told I could come by to get the results. I had to admit I was nervous about getting them. I signed the last papers I was required to sign and got up, grabbing my bag and water bottle and making my way to the car. Now, I was on my way to the doctor's office.

"Thank you," I said to the man after he handed me the results.

"You're welcome, and have a good day." He waved at me and was called back by one of the men working for him. I waved too and went back to my car. I looked into the envelope and took a deep breath before opening the letter.

I dragged my index finger over the words as I read the results. No, it couldn't be. This wasn't what I was expecting...

Chapter 25

Tessa

No, no, this couldn't be right. I closed my eyes and rested my head against the steering wheel. I looked back down at the piece of paper that said I was pregnant. It was obvious who the dad was, and that was exactly the problem. Arlo and I had been keeping our relationship a secret for weeks now. Things were going well, and now that I was pregnant, what would he say? We never spoke about kids, or marriage, or anything other than planning when we'd tell our families. Was I even ready to have a child?

I heard the phone ring, looked down, and saw it was Zavier calling. I pushed the paper away as I picked up and opened the DNA results.

"So? Have you picked it up already?" he asked. I could tell by his voice that he was a little nervous about the results. I took a deep breath and tried focusing on the paper in my hand. I read through the results till I got to the end.

"Y-yeah, hold on," I mumbled, rereading it to be sure. "Oh my God, Zavi. You're not the father!" I yelled into the phone, smiling.

"I knew it!" Zavier cheered and then chuckled.

"What are you going to do next?" I asked curiously. What would happen now that she had dragged him publicly and lied?

"Meet me at the mansion. I heard she has been staying there, and, well, I'll clear up things," he replied in a severe tone.

"Wow, I'm so happy for you," I mumbled.

"Thank you. For everything," Zavier replied before ending the call. I started the car and turned up the AC. I looked over my results and bit down on my lip. What to do about that?

I pushed aside the thought and pulled out of the parking lot, driving to the mansion. Part of me felt bad for how this DNA sample was obtained, but it had to be done.

***

Zavier

I sat on the edge of my bed and put the phone next to me. Finally, I had proof that Andrea wasn't mine. It was safe to say that yesterday, when I got back from work, things didn't go well between Amara and me.

***

Yesterday...

After I left, I went to pick up some coffee and waited for thirty minutes to pass before heading back to the office. In those thirty minutes, I tried calling Amara, but she kept letting the phone go to voicemail. When I got to the office, Arlo was the only family member there, and he didn't bother me at all. We both just did our jobs then went home.

"Amara? Sebastian?" I called out when I came through the door and saw Sebastian walking over to me. He was rubbing his eyes, dressed in a dino onesie, and his hair was washed. It was clear that Sebastian was ready for bed.

"Daddy." He hugged me, and I lowered down to his level and picked him up.

"How are you, buddy?" I asked, running my fingers through his hair.

"Sleepy." He pouted. I looked over at Amara. She leaned against the doorway, not even bothering to greet me as she would have before.

"Did you have dinner?" I asked, looking at Sebastian again and watching as he played with my tie.

"Mm-hmm, me and Mommy." He nodded, then yawned, and rested his head on my shoulder.

"I see...should I tuck you in?" I asked, noting just how tired he was. He must've stayed up waiting for me. I was a little disappointed they didn't wait for me to start dinner. Usually, they waited. Perhaps he was hungry.

"Please, yes," he hummed, wrapping his free hand around me and closing his eyes.

"Okay, come on, then." I kissed his cheek and walked upstairs. I turned on the lights and put him on his bed, making sure to tuck him in and kiss him on his forehead. I looked through his book collection, trying to pick a book to read him. Once I found one, I turned around and saw he had already drifted off.

I looked at him. He looked so calm and relaxed. I smiled softly and put away the book, dimming the lights and walking out without making any noise. I went downstairs, saw Amara sitting on the couch, and walked over to her.

"So, you won't talk to me?" I asked, standing by her, arms crossed as I looked down at her.

"What is there to talk about?" Amara replied, taupe eyes

focused on the screen like she wouldn't even acknowledge my presence.

"The situation with Grace?" I replied, raising a brow at her. Surely, this was why she was acting like this and why she stormed away at work.

"No. I totally understand. That's what you wanted to tell me, right?" she replied, turning to look at me.

"I—" I frowned, looking at her, unsure what she meant by this.

"Your mother loves Grace, and you're also not over her. I knew this was all fake, but I expected you to be real with me," Amara replied, looking down at the pillow she played with. By her tone, I could tell she was a little saddened.

"Amara, what are you talking about?" I asked, unsure where she got that information from.

"I overheard the conversation between you and your mother on your birthday. Like I said, I knew this was all just fake, but you shouldn't have kept your other child a secret from me, as well as how you felt about Grace all this time. When I kissed you, I had no idea you had someone else. Had I known, I wouldn't have acted on my feelings," she started to say, pressing her lips together and avoiding looking at me after talking.

"Amara, please let me explain the situation," I pleaded. This was all a misunderstanding. Surely, she didn't hear the entire conversation.

"You don't have to do that. Good night, Mr. Fuentes," she said, getting up and making her way to the stairs without looking over at me once.

"Amara, good night," I called out, but she didn't turn around. It only made her go faster, so I gave up for now. The moment I had the DNA results, I'd hopefully be given a chance to explain the situation without her jumping to conclusions or storming away.

***

Present...

I was pulled out of my thoughts when I saw Mr. Fischer calling. He had been calling since Grace posted the things online, but I had been ignoring his calls just like how Amara had been ignoring me. Finally, I could pick up and tell him the child wasn't mine with confidence.

"Hello, Mr. Fischer," I answered, lying back on the bed and staring up at the ceiling.

"Zavier...we have some things to discuss, as well as you ignoring my calls," he said. I let out a soft sigh, knowing where this was headed.

"My apologies, Mr. Fischer. As you can see, things have been a little busy. I know what you read in the magazines, but I can tell you that my ex is just back to ruin my image, as well as my relationship with Amara," I replied reassuringly.

"The timeline of the child—don't you find that suspicious?" I heard him asking. I could also hear children's voices in the background and assumed those were his boys.

"When we broke up, it was because she had been cheating on me, but I never made that public. I had this daughter of hers tested, and it's not a match. I'm only a father to Sebastian," I replied, putting the phone on loudspeaker for a moment and resting it on a table as I started putting on my belt.

"Oh...it's quite malicious of her to ruin things for you like this. As for our contract, I just received the photos, but with you trending like this now, I'm not sure whether we can release the selection so early," Mr. Fischer replied. I could sense a dash of uncertainty in his voice. I didn't blame him, though. I'd hate to be in business with someone whose public image wasn't ideal.

"Don't worry about it. I will clear my name. I have to go now. Have a good day," I reassured him, knowing today it would all be taken care of.

"You too," he responded, ending the call as I heard the giggles of the boys becoming louder.

I walked out of the bedroom and went down to see Sebastian running to me. "Morning, Daddy!"

"Morning, baby." I smiled, bending down to pick him up.

"Sleep well?" he asked, holding my face in his hands and forcing me to look at him.

"Hmm, yes. You?" I answered and looked at the stairs as I walked down them.

"Good!" Sebastian smiled, running a finger down my stubble.

"Can I put some cartoons on for you? I want to go talk to Mommy for a moment," I asked, putting him down on the couch.

"Okay." He grinned and leaned back, resting his hands behind his head. I smiled, looking at him, then turned to put on the cartoons.

I put on some cartoons for Sebastian and helped him get comfortable on the couch before walking to the kitchen to talk to Amara. I saw her standing by the sink.

"Amara, good morning," I said and waited for a good minute but didn't get a response. "Seriously? We have to talk now."

"What do you want?" She set down the dishes and turned to face me.

"Andrea isn't mine. Tessa did a DNA test for me in secret," I informed her, hoping this would change things around.

"I see..." Amara replied, frowning a little and leaving me confused. Why was she still acting this way?

"That's all you have to say?" I asked, slightly annoyed. I thought maybe now we'd have a normal conversation.

"I'm tired. Sorry," she mumbled. She was lying. I knew she went to bed around nine.

"I understand. Don't worry about breakfast. I'm in a hurry, and I'll just buy something," I replied coldly. I saw she was still busy preparing it.

"I'm almost fin—"

I interrupted her. It hurt her that I wouldn't have breakfast, but I couldn't deal with her right now. "As I said, I'm in a hurry." I walked away to my room and continued putting on my clothes. Dealing with her was slowly becoming harder and harder as she kept confusing me. What did she want me to do, exactly?

Before leaving the house, I made sure to kiss Sebastian goodbye. I drove over to my mother's house, knowing everyone would be there, and I was right. Grace would be gone for good this time. Once I got to the house, the butler opened the door for me and took my coat. I spoke to him for a short moment. It'd been a while since I'd seen him. I remembered growing up with him and his children, one of whom had even become a model for the company.

"Zavier, you came," my mother said happily, interrupting the conversation, but it was coming to an end already.

"Have a good day," I told the butler, then saw Tessa coming through the door. "Have you got the papers?"

"Here," she said, handing me an envelope and then taking off her shoes and walking in farther with me.

"Thank you. A lot," I mumbled to her, reading the paper then walking to the living room where I saw everyone.

"You came." Grace got up, smiling.

"I don't know what spell she has you two under, but this shit ends today." I cut straight to chase, glaring at Grace.

"What do you mean?" She frowned. My mother and sisters were obviously confused too.

"I did a DNA test with the help of Tessa, and it turns out that your daughter isn't my child," I responded, looking over at Grace then at my mother as she walked up to me.

"What do you mean, Zavier?" Carolyn asked, getting up and looking at the paper I held in my hand.

"Here." I handed her the results, watching as she read through them and gave them to Mom. Grace looked over at the paper and looked mortified, unable to form words. "You couldn't accept that I dumped you, which was your fault since you cheated on me with not one but two men, so you decided to come back into my life after almost four years just to ruin the one good relationship I had with the woman I love." I unloaded on her, making sure to keep my hands to myself and keep myself as calm as possible as I lectured on. Every time she opened her mouth, she closed it again, unable to muster up some other lie to tell. I did blame her for ruining things between Amara and me.

"Me mentiste! You told me she was my granddaughter." My mother glared at Grace, fuming with anger.

"How am I supposed to know who the father is?" she broke down, shouting.

"Pack your things up and leave now!" Mom shouted and pointed to the door.

"How could you?" Grace glared at Tessa, walking up to her and raising her hand, but Arlo stopped her from moving even an inch closer.

"You were planning on getting away with ruining a good

man's reputation. Adios, Grace." Tessa waved at her. Grace looked over at Carolyn, seeking some defense, but she wasn't given any, so she ran to get her things, I assumed.

"I need to talk to you in private," I told my mother and led the way to the next room.

"I owe you an apology, huh?" she said awkwardly, looking up at me.

"More than that, even. You owe Amara an apology too. That conversation on her birthday—she heard it. It was beyond disrespectful, but I figured she hadn't heard, but it turns out she did," I responded, crossing my arms, watching as she rolled her eyes.

"Why are you so keen on that?" Mom asked, crossing her arms too and raising a brow at me.

"Why? Because I love her, but she won't give me a chance with my mother talking nonsense and having her think I care about Grace, and, on top of that, nothing you said that night was kind towards her. She has been nothing but sweet. If I were her, I'd cut you out of Sebastian's life," I responded, clearly hurting her with the last sentence. She might not like Amara, but it was clear she loved her grandson.

"You speak so highly of her, but don't you ever wonder why her own mother won't speak with her?" she then asked, still avoiding admitting that she was wrong. I knew how older people were, and usually, I'd let it go, but not this time. This was important to not just me but also to my family.

"I know exactly why. She told me, and it's not really your concern as it's private." I shrugged. "Listen, Mama, I love you, but at some point, I'll have to choose my own family. So, if you don't apologize to her as well as treat her kindly, don't expect us to come here or invite you over."

"I see…" Mom mumbled.

"Ya voy," I said lastly before leaving.

***

Tessa

I saw Arlo and walked closer to him. "Can we talk somewhere in private?"

"Of course," he mumbled and looked around. Everyone was busy right now, so we could easily sneak away. He turned around, led the way to the garden out back, and sat down on the bench.

"What's wrong? Do you want to tell them already?" he asked, turning to face me and leaning closer as he looked at me, a slight smile on his blush lips.

"I think that should wait..." I mumbled, holding my hands together on my lap as I looked down at them.

"What? Why? Did I do something wrong?" Arlo questioned, his dark brows furrowed in a frown.

"Arlo. I...I'm pregnant..." I blurted out, taking a deep breath as I looked into his forest-colored eyes. "Say something," I mumbled after he hadn't said a word. Instead, he just stared at me.

"Carajo," he mumbled, making me frown, and then my anger rose.

"¿En serio?" I scoffed, moving away from him a little.

"No, wait, I'm just surprised," Arlo replied, pulling me back down and holding onto my hand.

"Do you even want children, Arlo?" I asked. I thought we'd be having this question a little later in our relationship, but it appeared not.

"I wasn't too sure, but when I met Bash—he changed my mind a little. Then, Amara spoke about her difficulties during pregnancy with Char, and now I'm not sure. I don't want my partner to get hurt," he rambled on as Zavier would do.

"Dammit. Yes or no?" I groaned, wanting him to cut straight to it and not lead me on.

"Yes. If you're the mother, of course. There's no one more caring than you," Arlo replied nervously. His hands were sweaty, but then again, mine were too.

"I see..." I mumbled.

"You? Do you want kids?" he then asked, looking back to make sure no one was around.

"Yeah, but I thought I'd be in an established relationship before this would happen." I sighed, pulling away from his hands and wiping mine off on my pants.

"Well, what do you want to do? I'll support you no matter what," he asked, retrieving his hands. "I can tell them that we're dating and that you're pregnant," Arlo offered.

"No! I think I want to wait a little longer," I was quick to say. I didn't know how to tell Zavier and, on top of that, my parents. Sure, I was an adult, but they still had some views on things.

"Till you start showing?" he replied, a little annoyed. I could tell he was excited to tell our parents and be with me without having to hide it.

"You said you'd support me no matter what." I glared at him. I didn't need his sass right now.

"You're right. I'm sorry. We'll figure this out, okay?" he promised, and I gave him a slight nod.

* * *

Zavier

I once again took the day off from work, but after leaving

my mother's, I still planned on going in until I saw that Amara had messaged me and asked if I could come home. I dropped everything and rushed home. I asked her what the problem was, but she didn't respond till I was already at the gate. When I opened the notification for the text she sent me, I saw the video of my conversation with Grace posted online. The only person who could've recorded it was Charlotte. Judging by the comments, it was clear the people didn't like who she truly was. I wasn't sure how I felt about this—her being dragged publicly. It was the same thing she did to me, but in the middle was her innocent daughter, who didn't deserve this at all.

***

Amara

When I saw the video, part of me was relieved things were cleared up, but then, I realized he mentioned loving someone… the relationship she ruined for him: it was me. I overreacted, and now, I was not sure if I had driven him away. He tried apologizing this morning, but I never gave him a chance.

"Hey, is everything okay?" he asked as he walked through the door.

"Be honest with me right now. Do you love me?" I asked, not bothering to beat around the bush. I wanted an answer, and I wanted it now.

"Amara—" he started, making me sigh. I didn't want a story; I wanted a yes or no. I knew how I felt, but I kept getting mixed signals from him.

"It's simple. Yes or no?"

"Yes, I do. How could I not? With all the time we've spent together, I only keep falling more and more for you. You're one of the sweetest and strongest women I've ever met," he replied, his green eyes focused on me as he took a step closer to me and took my hands in his.

"Zavier—" I mumbled, but he continued to speak.

"I never got the chance to tell you. Grace is in the past. She cheated on me, which is why things are over. You don't ever have to worry about me having feelings for another woman because you're the one I have feelings for. Also, no other person will come forth with a child of mine," Zavier said, the last part of his sentence making me chuckle a little.

"I'm sorry for the way I acted," I mumbled, realizing how mean I had been to him before by never even giving him a chance to apologize.

"It's okay. I only have one question: is the feeling mutual?" Zavier asked, making me frown. Wasn't the answer obvious to him?

"Of course, it is, idiot." I shook my head and got tugged into his chest. He cupped my face and leaned down for a kiss. His soft lips moved against mine, his stubble under my touch as I held the side of his face.

"Ew!" we heard Sebastian say, and we pulled away, laughing at him.

"Let me take you out on a true date," he said, letting go of me and walking over to pick up Sebastian.

"When?" I asked, watching as Sebastian hugged his father.

"Well, this whole weekend." Zavier shrugged as if things were that simple.

"But Sebastian—" I pointed out.

"I'll arrange it all. I'll just need you to pack your bags, okay?" he asked of me. I opened my mouth to protest, but what was the point. We deserved this date. We deserved to have another shot.

"I...okay." I nodded.

***

It was now Friday morning. We'd all gotten ready for the day and were currently on the road. Till now, Zavier still refused to tell me where we'd be going. The days leading up to today had been hectic for him, and honestly, I felt a little bad. I told him he didn't have to go over the top, but he refused and said I deserved nothing less. So, between him being in the office and planning, it was busy, but he still had more than enough time for Sebastian and me. As for babysitting, Sebastian would spend the first night at Charlotte's and the second night at Amelia's. Both were more than okay with this.

We stopped at Charlotte's place. This was the first time I'd come here, and her place looked good. It was a small house, perfect for just her, and a decent-sized yard with a sandpit Sebastian kept talking about. We stepped out of the car and helped Sebastian with his bag as he ran straight for the door.

"Hiya, buddy." Charlotte picked him up and hugged him as he squealed with excitement. "Hey, you two," Charlotte then said as we walked up to her.

"Hey, Charlie, thank you for looking after him," Zavier said, hugging her and then handing her his bag.

"Hello. Yes, thanks a lot," I added, smiling at her and Sebastian.

"Of course! You two enjoy your time, okay?" She smiled and looked over at Sebastian, who played with her necklace.

"We will." I smiled. "Goodbye, baby." Zavier kissed Sebastian's forehead, and he waved at him.

"Be good to Aunty Charlie. Goodbye, Charlotte." I kissed his forehead too and was given a kiss on my cheek, and Sebastian then waved at us.

"Goodbye, you two." Charlotte smiled at us and waved, waiting till we got in the car before going inside.

***

"You have your own jet?" I asked, looking at the jet before taking Zavier's hand and walking up the stairs with him. The inside left me shocked. It was so luxurious.

"Of course, I do. I sometimes have emergency meetings, so this comes in handy. I also tend to rent it out from time to time as I don't want it to sit and collect dust," Zavier explained as he walked to the pilot to go speak with him and left me there.

"Wow, I'm surprised," I mumbled, wandering about the place.

"Come on." Zavier returned and pulled me down to sit next to him.

"Will you finally tell me where we're going?" I asked, turning to face him and admire his green eyes, as well as putting on the sweetest look I had in hopes it would convince him to tell me.

"Somewhere in Europe." He gave in but didn't exactly tell me where.

"Oh." I frowned and made my thinking face as I thought of where it might be.

"That's all you're getting from me, missy." He booped my nose then pulled me into him.

"Zavier, what do you want from all this?" I asked randomly, looking up at him.

"All what?" He frowned, looking at me with his brows furrowed.

"Us dating, you know?" I added awkwardly. I didn't want to ruin the moment, but I felt I had to know this.

"Every day, I want to come home to you and our adorable son. We spend so much time as a family together, which I don't want to ever stop. When we went on those dates for the media, I always wished it could be real. That we could hold each other, kiss each other, and be there for each other as more than just friends," he explained, playing with a strand of my hair.

"Good. I'd like the same thing." I smiled and kissed his cheek. Zavier smirked and put on a movie to watch. A flight attendant offered us some snacks and champagne. After the movie, we both dozed off until there was an announcement that we were arriving.

We had arrived in Rome! I'd always wanted to come here. I still had no idea who the informant was who told him all these things, but my bet was on Nicole. After we got off the plane, the first stop was a market to pick up some groceries, and as such, I learned that Zavier spoke Italian, which came in handy when I was searching for specific items. When we finished buying groceries, we saw a pastry shop across the street. I bought some cannoli, along with other little pastries they had. When I stepped out, I was handed a bouquet.

"Too much, or do you love them?" he asked, looking down at the flowers he bought me and pressing his lips together.

"I love them. Thank you." I smiled and brought the bouquet to my nose, smelling it.

"You're welcome. Are you ready to go to our place?" Zavier smiled, taking my hand in his and leading the way through the market stalls and shops.

"Yes. Here," I answered and handed him the pastry bags.

"Did you buy me any cannoli?" Zavier asked, raising a brow at me.

"Yes, yes. I made sure to get the cannoli." I chuckled, stepping into the car after he opened the door for me.

"Thank you." He smiled and sat next to me. We were then driven to a beige-colored villa, the ones you'd see in movies that had big bushes with flowers growing on the walls. When we got inside, the first thing we did was unpack.

"Thank you so much for taking me here. I'm excited to see the place!" I said, looking around before sitting down and letting out a sigh. The place was lovely.

"I know you are. In fact, I think we should go out for dinner. Your food is good, but, babe, we're in Italy!" Zavier said, turning to face me after opening up one of the curtains.

"You don't have to tell me twice." I laughed. I loved cooking, but I didn't plan on doing much of it while in Rome.

"Shall we get ready then?" he asked, taking my hand to help me sit up.

"Sounds good to me." I nodded.

I walked to my room and closed the door. I picked out my outfit before heading into the bathroom with my bag of toiletries. I looked around. The bathroom was so spacious, with so many windows on the beige stone walls. I unpacked my stuff in the bathroom and went into the shower. I spent some time just letting the water wash down my body before turning the shower off.

I picked out the breezy sage dress that came to my knees and had some buttons down the middle. I liked how it looked, and it would go perfectly with the layered necklace and straw crossbody bag. Once I was ready, I stepped out and saw Zavier had just finished getting ready as well.

"You look lovely," he complimented me, taking my hand in his and placing a kiss on top.

"Thank you. You don't look too bad yourself," I replied, following him to the garage.

We ended up going to dinner at a busy restaurant. However, it wasn't fancy or anything. Just cozy and perfect. We had dinner by the fireplace. We talked as if it were any normal conversation, but there was occasionally flirting here and there. Zavier was quite charming. I guess I didn't see that before, given we had just been friends.

After dinner, he took me out to get gelato. We walked down the street together, holding each other's hands as we passed the lights, and we would occasionally look at each other with a smile on our lips.

When we made it back to the place where we were staying, we decided to check out the pool and make use of it. I looked at my green bikini. I knew I had packed it and everything, but I wasn't sure about wearing it. I walked out to the pool and saw Zavier had turned the pool lights on and was already in the water.

"I was starting to think you were joking about going in the pool," Zavier joked, swimming closer to the edge where I walked to.

"Oh no. I just had to search for something to wear," I replied, setting my towel down on one of the lounge chairs.

"You sure are wearing something," he mumbled, his green eyes going up my body before meeting my eyes.

I sat down by the edge and dipped my feet in, the temperature making me want to pull away, but Zavier placed himself between me, looking up into my eyes. His hair looked even darker now that it was wet. He ran his fingers through it, pushing it to stay back, but some strands still hung over his forehead.

"Won't you join me?" he asked, causing me to snap out of the trance I was in.

"It's a little cold," I mumbled, swinging my feet in the water.

"See, you brought this upon yourself." Zavier sighed dramatically, his cold hands resting on my thighs.

"Brought wh—Zavier!" I was about to ask when he pulled

me into the water, his arms wrapped around my waist as he looked at me, smirking. I wrapped my legs around his waist, my arms around his neck. The look on my face displayed annoyance.

"Come on; you had that coming." He smiled, still holding onto me. I rolled my eyes, and his hands moved down my sides, trying to hold me closer to him, as if it was possible to be any closer. Zavier leaned in to kiss my cheek, but instead, I let our lips meet. Zavier's lips were slow at first, as if he were testing the waters, but soon enough, he got the message and moved one hand to the back of my head, pulling me closer into the kiss while my hands tugged on his hair.

"Zavier, I want you..."

This was day one of the two and a half we'd be spending together, and just tonight was more than enough. Zavier made sure we'd have a great time, and we did. I truly couldn't have had a better date. He sure deserved another chance. I was excited to see what the future held for us.

***

Tessa

Three months later...

I invited Zavier and Amara over. Today was the day that Arlo and I broke the news to them. So far, we'd told my parents, as well as Arlo's family. It was only Zavier who we still needed to tell. The families weren't too angry, but they did wish we had come forward about this earlier instead of now when I was four months along. I'd be lying if I said I wasn't scared.

The little bump would be a surprise, but honestly, I didn't show too much even after four months. However, according to the doctor, both the baby and I were fine.

"They're here," Arlo said, walking to open the door.

"You're here too?" Zavier asked, looking at his older brother.

"Come on in. How are you, Amara?" Arlo stepped aside and waited till they both got in before closing the door.

"I'm good. You?" she replied, smiling. The two really were happier since they started dating officially.

"Good, but then again, I haven't gone on any whirlwind trips to Rome, so maybe just fine?" Arlo teased, leading the way to the living room.

"Well, you should go soon," she advised him.

"It's next on the list," Arlo replied, smiling.

"Hey, buddy," I said, getting up and pulling down my oversized shirt as I hugged Zavier. When our stomachs pressed together, he frowned a little.

"Hey, how have you been? Thank you for running things while I was gone," he said and let go of me, going to sit down next to Amara.

"Of course." I smiled. I could feel Amara's eyes on us. She definitely knew what would happen today.

"So?" Zavier asked, looking at Arlo and me as he sat down next to me.

"Arlo and I have something to tell you," I started, biting down on my lip.

"Okay..." he trailed off and looked between the two of us.

"We're in love," I blurted out.

"¿Qué?" Zavier frowned.

Amara smiled and said, "Saw that coming."

"What do you mean you love him? That Arlo?" Zavier said in disbelief, clearly trying to wrap his head around it.

"I swear I'm good to her, Zavi," Arlo sighed.

"We're also engaged. He proposed last week." I got that out of the way, showing my ring finger that had a ring on it with a big stone. This all was happening so fast, yet it felt right.

"What's next? You're pregnant too?" Zavier scoffed and looked at us when he realized neither of us really laughed or reacted with a "no." "Oh my god, you are, aren't you?" His mouth hung open.

"Zavier, please understand—" I leaned over to him.

"No. Him? Out of all the men?" He pointed to Arlo as if he were the worst guy in the world when he wasn't. Not the Arlo I got to know.

"Dammit, I can't control who I fall in love with!" I huffed, crossing my arms.

"Zavier, let her explain and give him a chance, will you?" Amara said, looking at her boyfriend.

"Listen, we've liked each other since high school, but because of obvious reasons, we couldn't be together. I love her more than everything, and I promise I'll make sure to take care of her and our baby," Arlo promised. Usually, he was a playful guy, but the way he spoke in this conversation was all serious.

"You hurt her—" Zavier started to say but got cut off.

"You won't ever have to worry about that," Arlo assured him.

"Even my dad took this better than you," I mumbled, rolling my eyes.

"Congratulations, you two. I'm sure Sebastian would love to have a cousin." Amara smiled, looking at the two of us.

"Thank you so much. Now, dinner?" I replied, grinning. Her support meant a lot because I knew, in the end, Zavier would follow her lead.

"Yes, please!"

Chapter 26

Amara

Two years had passed by now, and things went perfectly fine—but not for everyone.

Tessa sadly lost the baby. Their daughter wasn't planned, but everyone was excited to meet her. Arlo stayed by her side and tried his best to be there for her in every way he could. Zavier gave her three months off from work and gave her the option to take more if needed, even though she refused at first until he showed her the rules for maternity leave. Tessa decided to get some therapy to help with the loss of their child, and it did help. She hadn't returned to the old her, but instead, she turned into an even better and stronger woman. Just last year, she and Arlo got married.

There were small fights between Zavier and me, but we both agreed that communication was important, so we always resolved our issues—maybe not on the same day, but it would get done in the end.

Zavier was someone who did want a family, but he told me that at some point, he lost sight of that dream until Sebastian and I came into his life. Now, we were his everything. The very same man who always prioritized work had no issue taking a free day now.

Tonight was a special night. He took me out on a date just like the first one we ever had as a fake couple. Zavier seemed slightly nervous. His hand was sweaty, and he kept getting distracted.

He suddenly stopped walking when we reached a well-decorated vacant building and turned me around to face him.

"Everything okay?" I asked him, crossing my arms over my chest as I looked up at him.

"More than okay," Zavier answered, smiling and moving to take my hands in his. "I love you."

"I love you too, silly," I replied, slightly frowning. Why was he stopping in the middle of nowhere to do this?

"More than those special pans of yours?" he asked, narrowing his eyes at me.

"Hmm, tough question...you're close enough," I teased, squeezing his hands before he let go of mine.

"Guess I'll have to accept that." He sighed.

Zavier pulled his pants up a little before sinking to one knee, pulling out a red velvet box from his pocket, and opening it up. The box contained a ring with a rose-cut fire opal stone in the middle. It was exactly the ring I wanted. Though he bought me a lot of jewelry, rings were the one type he never got me.

"Amara Reid, will you do me the honor of marrying me?" Zavier asked, sweat forming on his forehead. His hands were shaking a little.

"Zavier—" I gasped, hands over my mouth as I looked at him and the ring. "I-I don't know what to say."

"A yes or no, perhaps?" Zavier chuckled awkwardly as he still waited to be answered.

"Yes! Oh my god," I finally answered. Zavier inhaled

sharply, and he quickly slid the ring onto my finger and got up immediately to pull me in for a kiss.

"I have a surprise for you," Zavier told me, holding me in his embrace.

"There's more?" I asked, frowning.

"Of course, there is. See this as your gift."

"But I didn't get you one." I sighed. He always got me gifts randomly, and although he kept saying he didn't need one back, I still felt a little guilty.

"That's fine..." He shrugged. "So, remember how we kept talking about your own restaurant, but you somehow put off searching for a place?"

"Yes? What did you do?" I raised a brow at him, wondering what he was up to this time.

"I sure hope you like this place because the papers are already signed." Zavier handed me a set of keys and turned me to face the building we were in front of.

"Zavier. I'm—wow. I'm speechless...I—" I looked at the place with my mouth hanging open. "Is this really mine?" I had always wanted this but was too scared of taking such a huge step.

"It sure is." Zavier smiled and pulled me by his side. "If you're not too sure, I can always help with the money. That way, if things go south, you still have yours," he explained. He sounded unsure, as if he were scared of how I would feel about everything.

"No, no, that won't be necessary at all," I replied, turning to face him and pulling him closer to kiss his cheek. "Thank you. For everything."

"Come on, let's go inside..." Zavier smiled and laced his fingers with mine.

***

Four months later...

Today was the day of my wedding. Both Zavi and I were excited and nervous at the same time. I paced around, taking deep breaths as I kept overthinking everything. At this point, the only difference this made for our relationship was that by law, we'd be bound to each other till death do us part or until a divorce.

I eyed myself in the mirror, loving how the blush-colored mermaid dress fit me perfectly. It was a special Fuentes piece. The V-cut wasn't too deep, but it managed to show off the necklace Zavier had gifted me years ago. I adjusted the fallen off-the-shoulder straps then turned around to see if everything else fit perfectly, and it did. I looked incredible; it wasn't just Zavier who'd love the dress.

I heard the door opening and turned around to see who it was. Nicole, Amelia, and Tessa stepped in. I looked down at Tessa's stomach that poked through her dress. This time, she was pregnant with twins! Everyone was excited to meet her and Arlo's children. No doubt, they'd be mischievous. I was pregnant too, just not as far along as Tessa, and no one knew yet. I'd tell Zavier today.

"Are you ready?" Amelia asked, walking to me and helping adjust the necklace.

"I-I think so," I replied, looking at her in the reflection of the mirror.

"Go get your billionaire, girl," Nicole joked, making us all laugh.

"You look amazing. Zavier couldn't have gotten luckier," Tessa said, resting her hands on my shoulders as she looked at me. I could understand why she was so happy: Tessa never got to grow up with any siblings, so Zavier was the closest person she had to one. For Tessa, this wedding was like seeing her brother getting married.

"Thank you. It means a lot coming from you." I smiled and took a deep breath.

"Of course. We should get going; the wedding will start soon," Tessa replied and looked at the others, waiting to follow them out.

I walked over to the window and peeked out; the garden was set up perfectly. Tiffany's flowers were all blooming, and the fountains were all shiny. The arch was made of blush and white-colored roses, just as I wanted. Everyone was already seated, and Zavier stood at the altar, waiting for his bride and looking dashing as always.

***

Grace

I was late. I knew I had already missed my opportunity, but that didn't stop me. I managed to sneak my way into the wedding. I deserved everything Zavier and Amara had—especially Amara. Today should've been my special day!

When Charlotte posted that video proving Andrea wasn't Zavier's daughter, Andrea's real father found out he had a daughter and did a DNA test to confirm his suspicions. Once the results proved she was his daughter, he filed for and won full custody. My parents cut me off after they found out what happened. I lost everything—my daughter, my Zavier, my money.

Today was the day I'd get revenge.

I saw Amara dancing with her husband, the two smiling like crazy as they gazed into each other's eyes. It infuriated me. I pulled out the gun from my purse and aimed at the bride.

Without thinking twice, I pulled the trigger, only for others to get up at that exact moment and get on the dance floor. As a result, the bullet intended for Amara pierced through Tessa's shoulder blade.

Everyone started panicking, and security caught up to me, forcing me down on the ground. "No!" I screamed. My plan had failed, and I'd only had one chance. "Let go of me! Let me kill the bitch!" I yelled as I tried breaking free from the guard's hold. "You took everything from me!"

***

Arlo

It hadn't taken long for paramedics and the police to show up. There was so much going on, and no one knew what to focus on. I helped my wife to the ambulance and went with her to the hospital while the others were forced to stay at the scene a little longer and give their statements. When I was in the waiting room, Zavier called me with details. No one saw a single thing. The only thing that helped was the security footage. The only reason Grace knew how to get in without being spotted was that she had lived there before and knew exactly where the blind spots were located in the mansion garden.

A few hours passed, and the whole family got to the hospital, waiting for the doctor to return with hopefully good news.

"Arlo, please sit down," Mom said. I had been pacing ever since Tessa entered the operating room. I let out a sigh and sat down, my leg bouncing.

"What if something bad happens? They're taking too long, right? Maybe I should go ask," I said, getting up again, but

Zavier pulled me down.

"Please, don't do that. They're busy right now. Let them do their job," Zavier said, rubbing my back. I opened up my mouth to say something, but just at that moment, the doctor stepped out.

"Who's the husband?" the doctor asked, removing his gloves.

"I am. How are they? Are they okay?" I asked, jumping up.

"Your wife's wound has been taken care of. She got lucky. The bullet didn't do much damage. As for the babies, there have been some complications since she fell, so we had to do an emergency C-section. Congratulations, Mr. Fuentes," the doctor explained. Everyone was quiet as they took in the information they were given.

"So, they're all fine?" I raised a brow at the doctor and looked into the room.

"Your wife will need a lot of time to recover, and your children have been placed in an incubator," he explained. "Would you like to meet your son and daughter?" he asked me, but I couldn't even answer. I went straight into the room to check on my wife and meet our children for the first time.

Epilogue

Amara

Five years later…

I looked through the options of dresses I could wear. It was Zavier's birthday, and of course, there would be a party. I even had the best surprise for him. I settled for an elegant purple dress. I didn't have much time to do my makeup, so it was just mascara, eyeliner, and lipstick. I had to be quick because I refused to have a nanny, so of course, I had to get the boys ready as Zavier was still in the shower.

I walked out of the room and saw Sebastian stepping out of his room dressed in a maroon suit, looking just as dashing as his father.

"Wow, you look so handsome, buddy," I complimented him, running my fingers through his hair and adjusting his tie.

"Thanks, Mom. You look beautiful." He smiled, looking up at me. It was Mom now…I guess when children turn eight, mommy gets shortened to mom. Good thing the twins still called me Mommy.

Five years ago, we had two boys, Matias Reid Fuentes and Marcos Ivan Fuentes. Sebastian loved his brothers a lot. Even though it was different in the beginning, he got used to it. Sebastian's last name was now changed to Fuentes too. Having these three boys in the house sure made me go crazy sometimes, but there was no one I loved as much as I loved these boys.

I got the twins ready, and soon enough, the guests started arriving. Around an hour later, I looked through the window. I watched as the twins played with Arlo and Tessa's twins, Izaan Lucas Fuentes and Farzeen Ximen Fuentes. The boy's middle name was from Tessa's father, and Farzeen had both her grandmothers' names. Arlo and Tessa sure made cute children. Sadly, after the twins, she was told she couldn't have kids anymore, but they were happy and lucky as a family of four. I was thankful things worked perfectly for them. They deserved nothing but happiness.

I looked over and saw the twins and Amelia's son, James, running after Izaan. Yup, Amelia and Ivan finally took the big step and adopted a boy. Just as predicted, they are amazing parents, and James was an absolute angel.

Charlotte got married three years ago, and one year after that came her beautiful daughter, Isabella. She was only two and was currently on her grandmother's lap. I saw Carolyn sitting next to her and playing with Isabella too. Sadly, Carolyn had no children of her own, though she wanted some. Her marriage had come to an end. However, I did hear her ask Ivan and Amelia about the adoption agency they used.

It was safe to say that play dates these days were a lot more hectic than when it was just Sebastian.

I saw Nicole sitting down next to her husband. Her career as an architect had taken off. She always had projects, big ones, and I was happy about it. She deserved this. She was always career-driven, so it was good to see everything pay off in the end.

I felt a pair of strong arms wrap around me, and Zavier's familiar scent filled my nose as he nuzzled himself in my neck. "Whatcha looking at, cariño?" He kissed the side of my neck.

"Just the people. I'm being a total creep." I chuckled and turned around to face him, caressing his face as I looked up into his green eyes and smiled.

"I love you." He kissed my forehead then pulled me into a hug.

"I love you tons," I replied and kissed his jaw. I remained in his embrace a little longer before pulling away. "Come on, let's go tell the others the good news," I said, watching as his face twisted into a confused expression. He assumed I was talking about the third restaurant I had been looking into opening. "We have an announcement to make," I said, waiting till I got everyone's attention, or at least all the adults' attention. When we did, I turned to Zavier.

"Here you go, babe." I handed him the envelope. Once again, I could tell he thought it was about the restaurant. He opened it up and saw a sonogram. Yes! I was pregnant again! Hopefully, for the last time.

"Wait...are you really?" he asked, mouth hanging open as he looked at me.

"Yes, Zavier." I smiled and got pulled into a tight hug.

"What is it?" Tessa asked, wanting to know too.

"We're having another baby!" Zavier grinned as everyone began telling us sweet and kind words. I had a feeling this one would be a little girl. I always worried Sebastian would have just Amelia, Ivan, Nicole, and me, but now, he had a big family. Neither of us was alone. I couldn't have asked for a better life than the one I'd been given.

Other books on Readict by Deliza Lokhai:

BOUND BY THE MOON GODDESS
SERENDIPITY

ALSO ON READICT

Craving more stories like this?
Download the Readict app, where you can read the
following page-turners for FREE!

MORE THAN A BILLIONAIRE
BY CHRISTINA TETREAULT

Everyone thinks Grayson Sherbrooke is just another carefree billionaire living a life of luxury. However, Gray is much more than that. And now he must choose between the woman he loves and the secret he's kept from the world.

THE SHERBROOKES OF NEWPORT - BOOK 6

MORE
THAN A
Billionaire

CHRISTINA
TETREAULT

USA TODAY BESTSELLING AUTHOR

BAD NIGHT STAND
BY ELISE FABER

The man seemed so innocent in the bar—okay, not innocent, per se. He'd been hot, hard, and practically irresistible. But Abigail never expected him to skip out of town faster than a villain in a B movie.
It wouldn't have been the worst thing in the world, just another one-night stand, except her stupid IUD had to fail.

Bad Night
STAND

USA TODAY BESTSELLING AUTHOR

ELISE FABER

FALLING FOR THE TYCOON
BY AURORA RUSSELL

Deserted by her fiancé only three months before their wedding, a devastated Annelise decides to go on her Caribbean honeymoon alone. One wild and passionate night leaves her with amazing memories— until her vacation fling reappears as a VIP client.

AURORA
RUSSELL

Anywhere and Always

Falling for the
TYCOON

*What happens when your mysterious
vacation lover shows up in your boardroom?
She's about to find out...*

RANDOM ACTS OF CRAZY
BY JULIA KENT

Darla never intended to pick up a naked hitchhiker wearing nothing but a guitar. But when a gorgeous man needs a lift, you give him a ride. Right?

RANDOM
acts of crazy

JULIA KENT

TRYING TO SCORE
BY KENDALL RYAN

Teddy King excels at many things. Playing hockey.
Check. Scoring on and off the ice. Check. Being
stupidly attractive. Double check. But an amateur
video from his college days is about to cause a major
scandal. That is, unless he and an old friend can
work together to stop it.

Secrets were meant
to be revealed.

HOT JOCKS 3

TRYING
TO SCORE

New York Times & USA Today Bestselling Author

KENDALL
RYAN

ABOUT READICT

True to our name (a portmanteau of "reading" and "addict"), Readict publishes totally addicting fiction that keeps our readers turning pages.

Having started as a reading app, we are uniquely positioned to harness a combination of data and editorial expertise to ensure we are publishing what our readers are most excited about: stories full of drama, romance, and epic adventures.

Read. Write. Enjoy!

CONNECT WITH US!

Website | www.readictnovel.com

Facebook | www.facebook.com/groups/readict

Instagram | www.instagram.com/readictnovels

Made in United States
North Haven, CT
25 March 2022

17512752R00171